apothecary shop at the fron
years.

'Now. Come ladies, back
be fit for anything if you c
her arms in the general direction of the hens enclosure
still on her knees in the border. As she sat back on her heels, her face clouded over at the thought that there was still no sign of anyone coming forward to take over the apothecary shop in the market town of Tupingham.

Lucie slowly rose to her feet, letting out a breath as her ageing joints creaked in protest. The dandelion snuggled in her wicker basket beside the red seeded nettles she'd picked for Goodman Bussell's sciatica. He'd not thank her for prescribing him this, but it was the best remedy and all else they'd tried had failed. Despite herself, Lucie felt a smile twitch on her lips as she imagined Bussell's wife's reaction when told she would be expected to whip her husband's sore back with the herb. Placing her hands on her own aching lower back, Lucie stretched her spine. On straightening, she almost jumped out of her skin.

'How long have you been standing there, Dick?'

Dick Cobb shyly held out a folded note. He'd doubtless brought a message from the Boar Inn where he lived as a servant with his mother Joyce.

'Here Dick, you take my basket, and I'll take this note. I expect it is someone ordering some medication. Isn't it another hot day? I'd say we'll both benefit from a cooling draught inside, don't you think?'

Dick took the proffered basket and Lucie opened the folded paper. She knew not to expect a verbal response as the lad, who was small but sturdily built, had been born feeble-minded, and couldn't speak. Lucie had brought him into the world and never forgotten how fiercely his navel string had been caught around his neck, so tight it had all but strangled him. Despite his poor start, she'd seen him grow strong when early on many had said he wouldn't survive infancy. The outside of the note was a receipt for a delivery of strong waters, but the inside was in a different hand, one she could not place and simply read: 'Pray come to the Boar as soon as you read this. Your son awaits you.'

'Not again; it can't be!' Lucie staggered and grabbed at the wall to steady herself. She gulped for air, fighting back a sudden urge to yell at Dick to ask how long he had loitered in the ginnel before she noticed him. Of course, he couldn't say if he even had any notion. She closed her eyes a moment and took a deep, deliberate breath of the warm, still air then arranged her expression into as near a kindly smile as she could manage while her heart continued to thud in her chest.

'Thank you, Dick. The content of this missive took me by surprise,' she tried to hold her voice steady so as not to scare the lad. 'But you have done very well to bring me it safely. We must both take a cup of cordial first, but then will you be so kind as to walk me to The Boar? It seems my son Simon has come to visit us.'

Dick's face lit up at the mention of Simon, and she felt her own face soften in reply as she ushered the lad through the scullery and into the cool, dark kitchen.

'Of course, you remember Simon, don't you Dick? He drew silly pictures and read his stories to you last summer, didn't he?' Lucie prattled on, supplying the conversation for both of them. Anything to stop her thinking about what news was awaiting her. She pulled the cork from a bottle of cordial, and the summery scent of strawberries filled the kitchen as she poured their drinks.

'He'll be tired I expect, for he lives in London. That's a very big city, a good two-days' ride from here.'

Having finished their drinks, Lucie absentmindedly rubbed her twisting belly with one hand as she looped her other arm through Dick's and set out for the inn, pulling the scullery door firmly shut behind her.

The Midwife's Truth

Sara Read

Wild Pressed Books

First Edition.
This book is a work of fiction.
The publisher has no control over, and is not responsible for, any third party websites or their contents.

Contact the author via twitter: @saralread

Editor: Tracey Scott-Townsend
Cover Design by Tracey Scott-Townsend.

ISBN: 978-1-9163774-5-5
Published by Wild Pressed Books: 2023
http://www.wildpressedbooks.com

For Becky and Sarah

The Midwife's Truth

Late Summer, 1666

Chapter One

Lucie Smith adjusted her position on her cushion to attack a particularly large dandelion that was growing in her small physick garden. Jabbing at the dry soil over and over, she was determined to dig it up, roots and all. The season had been exceptionally hot and dry, the ground hard and almost unworkable.

'You might be looking bright and gay when most of my plants are fatigued, but still you must go,' she told it. The riot of colour and heady scents of early summer which had given Lucie so much pleasure had now faded, and the garden herbs were running to seed. 'Victory!' Lucie's hens turned their heads towards her, only to lose interest when they saw the midwife waving a large green plant with yellow flowers, rather than a juicy worm for them. 'Piss-a-bed, that's what folk called this herb.'

They were thought good for helping those who could not sleep, but too effective at helping folk make their water. The two attributes combined made for an unhappy outcome for the laundress. And, if Lucie let them grow where they pleased, she'd soon have nought but a dandelion patch to show for her years of labour.

Her eyes scanned her plot, crinkling into a smile of pleasure at the sight. Pride might be a sin, but God help her, this was a herb garden that any apothecary would be proud to inherit. It had supplied the makings of many of the cures sold in the

Dan Bickle, the innkeeper, was a kindly looking man of middle years, with a stout body and ruddy face. He leaned on the wall by the open front door, frowning. His leather jerkin flapped open over his shirt.

'What's ado, Mister Bickle?' Lucie tried to keep her voice steady. 'Is he well? Simon?'

'Oh, my dear woman, he arrived exhausted and filthy, but well enough, I'd say.' Bickle pushed himself up from the wall until he was standing straight. Lucie felt her pinched face relaxing slightly.

'Thank the Lord. It is not the return of the pestilence then?'

'Nay, it's the fire. You've not heard? Most unlike him to be so dishevelled, with a week's growth of beard. His hair is full of ash and his clothes filthy. I think, though, that he is not harmed bodily.' Bickle mopped his sweaty brow with a dirty clout.

'Fire? Smoke? I must go to him.' Lucie's heart began pounding once again and she tried to push past the innkeeper, but he stood his ground.

'There's no hurry, Widow Smith,' he said, easily restraining Lucie by placing two heavy arms on her shoulders. 'Your lad's fast asleep on the same guest bed he used all last summer. One of my good rooms.'

If Simon was here and resting the news couldn't be so bad, could it?

'Come on inside, I'll tell you the reports from London,' Bickle guided the midwife gently indoors with his arm around her shoulder. 'A fire has destroyed large parts of the city. Flattened it. The King himself and his brother the Duke toiled with the common folk to quench the flames, so they say,' Bickle's eyes widened in admiration as he spoke. He gestured to the serving girl who immediately brought a jug of beer and two tankards over to the table.

'Who says this?' Lucie replied in a small voice.

'Eh?' Bickle looked at Lucie quizzically as he was pouring the beer.

'You said, "they say". I desire to learn who you mean.'

'Oh I'm with you now, my apologies,' he slid a tankard towards the midwife. 'Mister Smith arrived in the Calstone coach, and it was the two green liveried servants who helped him. We gave them a cup of ale each of course. They both guzzled greedily in this heat, then left for the Manor. They said they were in haste to reach there.'

Lucie raised her cup to her lips, taking a long, slow swig of her small beer as her brows furrowed. The Calstones were bound up with her Simon yet again, she thought, as her sigh blew over the rim of her cup. Her late husband had long said no good would come from the likes of them keeping company with aristocratic types.

'The Calstone coach?'

'Aye, no sign of his Lordship, just your lad and the two coachmen.'

Lucie nodded slowly. She was glad that Lord Calstone was not with Simon. He was a rakehell, a puffed-up man who could not be tolerated. Lucie shuddered, remembering how she'd had to treat his wife for the terrible disease he'd inflicted on her last year.

'Her Ladyship is not at the Manor as far as I know,' Lucie said.

'If you'll excuse me being indiscreet, Widow Smith, I've heard there's not much love lost between those two.'

'That's often the way with the marriages of their sort. Family and money matter more than affection.' Lucie felt sad for Lady Calstone who was the only one of that family she had much time for. She and her ladyship had enjoyed several pleasant conversations the previous summer, and Lucie would never forget her unwavering support through the tribulations at the end of the year.

Snapping out of her reverie, Lucie made to get up, 'I will go and wait for my son to rouse, so I can hear from him what has occurred. I pray to the Lord no further tragedy has been visited on my family; although it is a comfort knowing Simon is sleeping under this very roof.'

'I think you should count him lucky. He lays in a clean, comfortable bed when masses of poor London citizens are camping under canvas outside its walls. A sea of displaced folk as far as the eye can see, the men told me,' Bickle took Lucie's hand, giving it a gentle squeeze.

Lucie looked at the floor.

'Nay, nay Widow Smith. I meant no reproach. Joyce here made some fresh lemonade today and will have some brought to your son's chamber. The weather is absurdly hot yet, even though the afternoon is late.'

Once alone with her son, her nursing instincts took over and she gently unbuckled and eased off his dirty boots. Dust motes jumped in the air as she tugged at the leather. Strong sunlight streamed in through the leaded window. Looking up the bed to her son's peaceful face, Lucie saw Bickle was right about the growth of beard which she had never seen on him before. She stood transfixed for a moment, her hands resting on her son's grimy stockinged feet, uncertain she would have recognised him if he had passed her in the street looking like this. A gentle snuffle as he slept gave Lucie a sudden memory of Simon as a boy on his pallet at the side of her bed. She found herself biting her lip to push down the rush of emotion the memory brought.

Lucie winced as she noticed her son's hands were scratched and blistered with burns. She longed to kiss them better as she had when he was a child. But a mother's kiss would not be sufficient here; how she wished she'd had the sense to pick up her midwifery bag on her way out of the Three Doves. Burns were so common that she always kept a jar of soothing ointment in there.

I'll see if I can arrange to have it brought to me, she thought as she completed her examination. There was not much else to note as Simon was still fully clothed, but there were no signs of serious injury to his person. A tap on the door not five minutes later was from Joyce Cobb, Dick's mother, bringing in the lemonade.

'Thank you, Joyce. That looks delicious. Do you think Dick might be free to run to the Three Doves to fetch my midwifery bag? The scullery door is not locked,' Lucie said.

'I'll go presently, Widow Smith,' Joyce replied. 'It would take too long to make Dick understand this.' She smiled apologetically.

'That's very good of you, thank you,' said Lucie, reaching under her apron into her pocket for a halfpenny. With nothing to do but wait, Lucie pulled a chair over to the bedside and sat watching Simon sleeping while she sipped on the cooling lemonade.

Joyce was back speedily, and Lucie quickly found the jar she knew would be in her bag. Scooping out a large measure of a thick mixture of frankincense and bacon grease, Lucie gently applied it to her son's injured hands. With luck, they would feel a little less sore when he awoke. The day grew into evening and the light began to fade. Although only just the second week of September the nights were drawing in at pace. Before long Lucie needed to make use of the chamber pot, and the chair scraped on the wooden boards as she rose. Simon jerked awake.

'Watch out below! Have a care!' he yelled, jumping to his feet. Caught up in a tangle of sheets, he almost hit his head on the bed post.

'Hush Simon, you are safe in Tupingham. Mother's here. Just sit back down a minute and settle yourself before you get up properly.'

Falling back on the bed with a thump, Simon apologised huskily.

'I fancied I was back in the midst of the fire,' he explained. 'The canopy over the bed seemed to be falling on you in my daze. So much falling timber came down. I'm sorry to have frighted you, Mother. You'll have heard what happened?'

'Only the bare details. You must tell me all. Are you well? Uninjured? Apart from your hands, I mean?'

Before Simon could answer, Joyce Cobb knocked on the chamber door again and poking her head around the door, asked if she should bring up some supper.

'That would be very welcome. Could we have some warm water and a linen towel for Simon to wash himself too please?'

'Dick's bringing that up just now,' Joyce replied, with a concerned look in Simon's direction. 'We heard the sounds of stirring and I said to our Dick the first thing Mister Smith will be wanting to do is clean himself a little.'

Lucie smiled and nodded, and her son said, 'You know me very well Goodwife Cobb, my thanks to you and the lad.'

Dick came along the landing minutes later carrying an overfull pail, water lapping the edge. Lucie took it from him on the threshold and carried it across the room without losing a drop, her deftness acquired from long years of being handed containers of warm water from anxious expectant fathers and worried maids.

'Oh Mother, I should like to have greeted my young friend.'

Lucie's eyebrow shot up as she gave Simon a knowing look.

'We've got to get you back to yourself again before you receive company,' she said, twisting the soggy clout with both hands before going to the bed to wipe her son's face and neck.

'I don't want you washing off my healing ointment,' she explained, her blue eyes crinkling into a warm smile. Brushing off his protests, she reminded him that it was hardly the first time she had tended to him, and she would brook no argument.

'You know how costly frankincense is; I'll not have it wasted.' She walked back to the pail to rinse the cloth again. As Simon's familiar features emerged from under the grime, Lucie found herself having to bite her lower lip once again to keep back tears. The realisation of what might have been, threatened to overwhelm her. *My precious son.* She turned from Simon and dropped the cloth in the bucket of grimy water.

Over a supper of cold meats, salad leaves drenched in olive oil, and fresh bread and butter, Lucie coaxed the story of the fire from her son. She was amazed to hear it hadn't seemed remarkable when it broke out at the beginning of the previous week.

'Sir Thomas Bloodworth is a fool of a Lord Mayor,' Simon said, jabbing his bread in the oil before taking a big bite. Lucie had to fight an urge to take the bread from him, it pained her watching him move his blistered, lacerated hands.

'You don't need to look so concerned; my hands are as nothing compared to some. I was saying, bloody Bloodworth considered it so little threat he'd refused to allow fire-hooks to be used to tear down houses in the flaming path to starve it. More feared of being sued by the property owners, than of the fire.' Simon sprayed out particles of bread as he told his mother how the mayor was overheard saying the fire was so slight a woman might piss it out. Lucie shook her head; Simon's right to be angry, she thought.

'No, I would believe it not if I were hearing this for the first time too. London is unrecognisable,' he went on, pausing to pick up his mug awkwardly in both hands. In a low voice, as if he couldn't comprehend what he was saying, he continued. 'Tens of thousands of citizens are made homeless. Myself too, I regret to say.'

'Your print house?' Lucie gasped, putting back down the knife that was halfway to her mouth.

'Gone. All gone. At first me and the other booksellers around St Paul's thought we might be able to save our stocks. The men at Paul's gave us leave to place all our goods in the crypt. They thought it impossible it would go up in flames because of its thick stone walls, you see. Well, you'd think so too, wouldn't you? We worked night and day to cram everything in there.' He paused to take a sip of wine and gazed past Lucie into the distance as if seeing it all before his eyes.

'But it was a doomed scheme, Mother. They hadn't reckoned on the scaffolding surrounding the Cathedral. The building was wrapped in tinder! Mother, it was awful. Like a sight from Hell when it went up. The heat. The stench. The air. Not a clean breath to be had. The paper we'd put inside only added fuel for the flames. All the unsold books, boxes of 'em, page proofs, our store of unused paper, boxes of ink powder, gone. Trays filled with type that'd cost a fortune to build. We thought we'd acted to save the business, John and I, if not the building. Ashes and sparks flew. When the lead on the roof melted, the stones went up like grenados.' His speech fractured as he was forced to relive the terrible events, and tears streamed down his face.

Lucie reached across the small table and gently dabbed her son's face with her handkerchief. 'Oh son. What could have started such a terrible blaze?' She pushed her plate away, her appetite vanished.

'No one knows yet. There are some saying it was just a fire in a bakery – the baker who supplied the King himself, they say. He had a house on Pudding Lane.'

'Makes sense,' Lucie answered. 'They do leave their ovens burning overnight after all.'

Simon nodded, fiddling with his knife distractedly. Lucie wanted to take it off him, worried about his sore hands, but stayed herself.

'Others say it is the Dutch, in revenge, for just last month the Navy burned over a hundred of their ships in an attack in a place called the Vile estuary. Foreigners are being most terribly abused on the streets, Mother. Yet more blame the Catholics. I don't know what to think, I'm sure,' he dropped his knife and took up his cup, taking a sip while Lucie sat on in silence, waiting until he was ready to continue telling his story.

'One of the courtiers told me the fire had been foretold by a witch at York, one Mother Shipton, I think he said.' Simon's eyes rolled at the notion.

'War, plague, and now hellfire,' Lucie whispered, her eyes misted with tears. 'God's displeasure seems clear.'

'It was just like I imagine Hell, Mother. The heat, the terrible dry heat. The screams and shrieks of women and children trying to outrun the fire with their worldly goods. The smoke. I can still taste the smoke.'

The pair sat in silence in the dusk for a few moments.

'Son, tell me again. Your shop, it is completely lost?' She shuddered at the thought.

'Gone. Burned to the ground. But Mother, John Miller and his wife and young family are safe, God be praised.'

'Amen,' said Lucie quietly. Simon stood up from the table and began pacing the small room.

'Kate, dear Kate, was not so lucky,' he said with a catch in his throat. 'Sorry Mother, she is not someone you would have heard of before. The Millers' servant, you see. Was, I mean. She perished. And the world is poorer without her.'

Simon turned his back to his mother, and she could tell he was struggling to keep his composure.

'Shall we pray for her soul together, Simon?'

He didn't hear, lost in his grief. Some moments passed before he spoke.

'There is nothing of our print house left standing. Nothing but a pile of rubble and ash. I have but the clothes I am wearing.'

'And your hands?' Lucie rose from her chair to comfort her son.

''Tis nothing. Not compared to some anyway,' Simon's answer was sharper than was perhaps fitting.

Lucie instinctively tensed. Simon didn't have much in common with his late father, but that flash of anger brought Jasper to the front of her mind. How quickly his choler rose too, but it too subsided just as speedily.

'Well, it was good of the Calstones to send their coach to bring you home. You have done the right thing returning to

Tupingham to recuperate.' She hoped her soft tone would mollify her son as she rubbed his back.

'I'm afraid I have not yet told you all the story, but that can wait till the morrow.'

Lucie's head shot up to meet her tall son's eyes.

'Please don't worry. You know all my news; I have kept nothing of that back, the rest can wait until the morning.' He bent down and gave his mother a kiss on the cheek. 'God bless you, Mother. I think I'd better go back to bed now, by your leave.'

Lucie's hand instinctively reached under her apron to stroke her belly. Simon's words had set off another gripe.

'Very well. God bless you too, son. I will pray for the Millers' servant. Kate, I think you said? The jar of burn ointment is on the mantle shelf. Make sure you apply it plentifully, some now, and again upon rising. I will leave you to sleep and see you on the morrow.' She picked up her midwifery bag and turned to leave. 'Son, I will thank God every day for the rest of my life, be it long or short, for sparing you to come home to me.'

Chapter Two

The window had been left open and unshuttered against yesterday's stifling heat and the bed curtains left undrawn. Sunlight was already beaming brightly into Lucie's bed chamber. Lucie had a few brief seconds thinking about the day ahead as if it were a normal weekday, before turning her head and sensing a faint scent of smoke on her pillow. This brought memories of the previous day's events flooding back. She was amazed she'd slept at all, but the full cup of Spanish wine she had taken with Mary Thorne before bed must have helped. She could tell by the height of the sun that it was well past six of the clock, but despite the brightness the air felt somewhat cooler than on preceding mornings.

As she dressed, she told her housemaid, Deb Healey, about the fire, Simon's poor hands, and the displaced souls living in tents outside the city walls.

'Don't pull so hard, Deb, please. I cannot tolerate tight laces at my time of life.' Lucie clasped her hand to her mouth. 'Deb, Simon said he had only the clothes he was wearing. They are filthy and he lacks a change of shirt.'

'He'll not like that, Mistress Smith. Your son is always so smartly dressed,' Deb replied.

'Indeed he will not. Pray go look in the chest and see what we have remaining of my husband's linen.'

Lucie had been working through Jasper's shirts and shifts, cutting them up for clouts or making baby clothes but with her hands being stiff she was much slower than she used to be, and several items remained to be reused. Deb carried an armful of linen and dropped it on Lucie's bed.

'Look here,' said Lucie, shaking out a set of clothes and spotting a pair of stockings. She couldn't do anything by way of breeches, but this was better than nothing. 'Let's make up a parcel ready for when Simon awakens. He was sore tired last night and so I'd expect him to sleep late.'

Into the clothing she placed a slice of soap cut from her block and added Jasper's tortoiseshell comb and his razor. She wished she had thought of this last night. Simon was such a fastidious man, normally so well groomed. She gave the bundle to Deb to convey to the Boar.

Knowing she could not bear to sit around waiting for Simon to return and reveal his news, Lucie resolved to open the apothecary shop as usual. After being widowed so suddenly last Christmastide when Jasper succumbed to the plague, the council had implored Lucie to keep the drug store open so the citizens of Tupingham could buy remedies until a new chemist could be found. Being unsure what else she might do in her changed condition, Lucie agreed to the request, initially glad of the chance to stay in the home she had lived in for over thirty years.

A steady trickle of customers shopped for medicaments from Lucie's counter during the morning. Goodman Russell called by, requiring some treatment for corns on his feet.

'I've been paring them down myself, Widow Smith, but they come back proper sore each time,' he explained.

'I expect your wife has persuaded you to come to the Three Doves,' Lucie said with a smile. 'It is always the same with you men.'

She went to the shelves and found the pot containing a mixture of black soap and snails, advising the goodman to spread it on leather and bind it to his feet.

'You'll need to renew it every fourth day for a fortnight,' she instructed. 'But it will cure them.'

Many of her customers had heard that Simon was home

and quizzed Lucie for intelligence of him and of the London fire. The midwife had known most of these people for decades; delivered some of them with her own hands even. But after everything that had happened in the last year, Lucie knew she'd lost something of her easy manner with the townspeople of Tupingham, and she chose to keep her answers polite but brief.

Deb popped her head around the door between the kitchen and the shop to see if Lucie had any further instructions for her. 'Not long until we can close,' she said cheerily. Lucie smiled warmly at her young housemaid.

'You must be reading my mind, my dear. I confess to being more than usually grateful that we only open in the mornings.'

Part of the bargain she had reached with the council was to open the shop for just a few hours each day since she could not provide the full range of services of an apothecary. She offered mainly some simples and her kitchen physick, made from the produce in her beloved garden. She also ordered in a few readymade remedies from Grantby.

'I will reckon the takings and then I'll join you in the kitchen for a drink, but I won't take my meal until I have been to see my son.'

Lucie turned the key on the cash chest. She had walked over to lock the shop door when it burst open.

'Ah well met, Mother,' Simon said cheerily.

Lucie's knees almost buckled at the flood of relief she felt at the sight of her son, who was looking much more like his old self.

'You've been in the river I'll warrant,' she replied, noticing the red healthy glow of his skin.

'A wash in the basin in my chamber would never be equal to the task of removing the grime that covered me,' he said with a chuckle. 'I awakened feeling much brighter, so took the soap you kindly sent me and scoured myself in the cool waters. Even my ears had been clogged with filth.' He twisted round to show his mother how clean they now were, just like he had as a boy, and they both laughed.

'That ointment has soothed your hands a little, I see, but you need to keep the regimen up, son.'

He looked so much better without the long periwig he normally wore. Now clean and wearing his father's clothes – albeit with the grimy breeches he had arrived in yesterday – and refreshed from a night in a good bed, Simon looked altogether healthier.

'Thank you for sending the clothes, they're most welcome. I think it must be over a week since I last had a clean shirt on my back. I left my shirt, shift, and stockings with Joyce at the Inn, instructing her to do as she will with them. Perhaps the shirt will make a few decent clouts, but I'd be surprised. You are finished here, now?' he enquired.

Lucie nodded, 'You can join us for some food, my dear.'

'No, I am afraid neither of us has time to eat. We have to leave for the Manor right away. Gather as many of your wares as you can and the Calstone coach will be outside presently to carry us. Ask Deb to pack you a change of clothes. No, I'll run up to your chamber and gather your clean linen. Is Mary home or will you leave her a note? I don't know how long we will remain at the Manor but it might be some time.'

Lucie couldn't make sense of his rambling. 'Whatever are you talking about, Simon?'

'Mother, you're needed at the Manor. I will explain on the way.' He took Lucie's arm and ushered her towards the shelves. Then a thought struck her.

'Oh, don't tell me you have got a wench with child? Is she at her time, son? Why did you not bring her here?'

Simon had the grace to look bashful, 'No mother, it is your healing skills I need. Come, what shall we take? We need medicaments for burns, wounds, exhaustion, infection, and so on.' As he spoke, he was throwing jars, boxes, and bags into his satchel without looking what was in each.

'Simon, stop that. Put these items down, you make no sense.' Lucie used the firmest tone she could muster, absentmindedly reaching under her apron to rub her belly. 'Even if I knew what you were about, I cannot just leave. What about Mary? She might need me. And Martha will think it most unlike me to go away and not take my leave of her and the children.'

'Mother there is no time for this,' Simon put both hands on his mother's shoulders and looked straight into her eyes. 'As I said, I will explain all. Please Mother, I need you. In truth, I'd have had us set off yesterday if it wasn't for the exhaustion which overcame me. You can leave a note for Mary, and she will speak to Martha. Mother, I will beg if I have to.'

Lucie's guts twisted; she was in a dilemma. Thoughts rushed one after the other. Was the plague back? Please God no. After a few moments' reflection, she realised Simon would not be so forceful without good reason.

'I see. Well, in truth I am not entirely sure I do see, but I will of course do as you bid. You will need to be honest with me and tell me the whole reason for this strange behaviour as we travel. Have we some food for the journey? For it is dinner time and you need to recover your strength.'

The Calstone coach was waiting on the cobbled street outside the Three Doves. A small crowd had gathered around to see what was happening. Alderman Robbins was talking to one of the coachmen. Trust him to be at the heart of things, thought Lucie. Since Jasper was no longer on the council as an experienced and steadying hand, there had been a change in Robbins. He threw his weight around the small town, and Lucie knew he rode out to the Manor when Lord Calstone was in residence. Simon went over and explained that he was taking his mother to Calstone Manor on personal business for a few days and the shop would necessarily be closed for the duration. The alderman's eyesbrows shot up.

'Widow Smith has obligations in Tupingham,' he said

imperiously. The Three Doves was leased from the town council, which Alderman Robbins appeared to think meant from him personally.

'With respect, Sir, I do not answer to you. I have need of my mother's skills and that is an end to it,' Simon replied. In tone and stance he did a fair imitation of his friend Sir Robert Calstone. Lucie looked at the floor, shuffling her feet and feeling uncomfortable at the confrontation. The two men squared up to one another, and Lucie realised she needed to step in.

'I'm sorry Alderman Robbins. I don't rightly know what this is all about, but it is clear my son needs me to accompany him. There is some injured soul at the Manor in need of my care, and I have to trust his judgement in the matter.' She spoke in a quiet tone, before accepting the green-liveried coachman's help to climb aboard. Inside the coach Lucie saw that the cook from the Manor had supplied a generous picnic in a wicker basket on the floor between the two seats.

Settled on the seat which was newly upholstered to match the green of the Calstone livery, Lucie was anything but comfortable as she felt the ball of tension in her stomach grow.

'I worry about Mary being left like this, son,' she said. 'She is most competent, of course, but her confidence is helped since she knows she can send for me if she gets into difficulties, or if there's more than one birthing at a time.'

The young woman was now the small town's midwife, fully discharged from her apprenticeship with Lucie. While it had been a joy to see her capable deputy rising to the role, Lucie knew it was yet early days for Mary in practice. The coach lurched into life, throwing Lucie's head back against the padded back rest, and she grabbed at the seat to steady herself.

'Come now Mother. Perhaps she needs to prove to herself she can manage without running to you. Your brief absence might be the making of her.' Simon's tone was jovial, but Lucie was unconvinced.

'May you be right.' The pair sat in silence a while, and Lucie ran her hand across the lush pile of the velvet seat. The last time she had been in this coach was at the behest of Lady Calstone, who had been quite unwell. Perhaps, thought Lucie, her ladyship would be at the Manor too, she would welcome the opportunity to discourse with her. That might be something good to come from Simon's mysterious behaviour. The correspondence the two had exchanged in the past months had been a comfort to Lucie as she became accustomed to widowhood. That thought sparked another.

'I suppose I might use this travelling time together to discuss commissioning the headstone for your father's grave at St Andrew's.'

A sudden jerk from the coach as it jolted on an uneven cobble masked Simon's reply.

'They should do something about the disrepair of High Street. That alderman might think to get the potholes repaired rather than interfering in people's private business,' Simon said crossly. He had been in the middle of pouring his mother a cup of small beer when the coach had jumped so, and he now had a wet lap.

'Indeed. A waggon broke its axle some weeks ago in this same place. Thank you,' Lucie took the cup and sipped from it. She was beginning to wonder if Simon was deliberately delaying responding to her enquiry about Jasper's headstone, when he spoke up.

'Andrew's is lost. Like St Paul's.'

'Oh no, no,' Lucie shook her head as if trying to shake off the news.

'I am so sorry, Mother,' Simon reached for Lucie's hand. 'The church will need to be rebuilt. There is nothing there to salvage.' Gently he explained that the fire had razed St Andrew's in the Wardrobe to the ground, and with the site under debris, it would be impossible to locate Jasper's grave and have a headstone installed. Lucie couldn't speak for a few moments. How could she have not asked about St Andrew's last evening? Her tummy churned and she thought she might vomit. Simon moved from his seat opposite her and shuffled to sit beside her, putting his arm around her shoulder.

'While travelling home it occurred to me that we might commission a marble plaque to place in All Hallows to commemorate Father's life and works. That way his blessed memory will be near to my brother and sisters, as they lay in the churchyard outside. It will be more expensive than a headstone but perhaps the council will contribute towards the cost. Then his memory will be assured in the town of his birth forever,' he said gently, while hugging his mother closely.

Lucie's breath caught in her throat at the mention of her dear children. Jasper would tell her it was not fitting to mourn them too much now they were safely gathered into the Lord's bosom. It was sinful, indulgent, he had instructed. But without him to lean on, and to support her when the melancholic humours got the better of her, she found herself thinking about what might have been had they lived. It was happening more and more regularly.

'I pray for them nightly, and visit their grave each Sunday,' she said in a quiet voice.

'I know you do. Father too when he was with us.'

'Simon, your father never stopped grieving for Peter, Sarah, and little Hannah,' Lucie allowed herself to sink against her son's chest. 'Only I knew the blow it was to his heart and his faith when they were taken,' she whispered into his shirt.

The coach swayed along, and after a few minutes Lucie sat back up, recovering herself.

'There is some sense to your scheme, Simon, let me think on't a while, please. Take some food from this basket; it is a shame to waste it and you are still convalescing.'

Lucie leaned back in her seat, pleased Simon stayed next to her, for there was a comfort from his proximity. They relaxed into the rhythm of the coach as it bounced on the mud track, the cobbles of Tupingham having been left behind some time ago. She closed her eyes. She hoped Simon would think her asleep, but that was out of the question as her thoughts whirred. Why hadn't she gone to London over the summer to commission the headstone as she had promised herself she would? She had not seen for herself the place where Jasper lay. Yes, it had been hot, too hot, all summer but that was a poor excuse. Lucie reproached herself and felt ashamed. Now it was too late. Tears spilt from her eyes. No visit to his grave, ever. Denied performing the last service too. Oh how carefully I would have laid his body out, she tormented herself, not for the first time. As a country midwife it was a service she had performed for dozens and dozens of others over her years. A wave of sleepiness suddenly washed over her, even as slow tears spilled onto her apron, and before they had gone much further, Lucie had drifted into a doze.

After they had trundled and bumped along the baked hard dirt roads for over an hour, Lucie was roused by Simon trying to get up and return to his seat opposite.

'Oh Mother, I am sorry. I tried so hard not to waken you. My sudden return yesterday and the worry has quite exhausted you.'

'I did not mean to sleep, son. Perhaps you are right. I feel better for it and think I will take a piece of that pie, if you wouldn't mind passing me some.' As she swallowed the last mouthful of what had been a very tasty pigeon pie, Lucie knew she must ask Simon to tell her the true reason for their journey, but first she really must ask him to make the coach stop so she could relieve herself. The two cups of small beer she'd taken since setting out and the bumpy coach made her need for the pot rather urgent.

'Thank you,' she said as the coachman helped her back inside. 'I feel much refreshed from the break and a chance to stretch my legs for a moment.' She caught the agitated look on her son's face.

'Right, it is time you told me what this escapade is all about. Leave nothing out,' she settled back into her seat.

Simon started talking, taking his mother back to the fire in London. It had begun on Saturday, and by Sunday the King and his brother James, Duke of York, had appeared amongst the throng. They had not made the same decision they had last year of abandoning the plague-ridden capital to its fate, Lucie mused.

'Mother, the Duke worked so hard. He didn't stop all day or night and had a way of inspiring the people. The people love him for what he did,' Simon enthused. 'No one man did more, I think, to quench the fire.'

'Son, what has this to do with our journey to the Manor this day? Please don't tell me it is connected with the Duke and the fire, pray not that.'

Simon had the grace to look ashamed. 'Sir Robert was one of the courtiers given a command post by the Duke. He was so impressive. He toiled long and hard, giving out instructions and using the fire hook to tear down a house practically single-handedly. I was amazed. I hadn't expected him to rise so well to this challenge. I knew he was strong but had not thought a man unaccustomed to toil would be able to work so long and hard without complaint.'

'"Arise, for it is your task, and we are with you; be strong and do it." The Lord made the man equal to the day,' Lucie replied. She cast her mind back to when she delivered Sir Robert's first child sixteen months ago. He'd seemed so young at that first meeting. So young and so flamboyantly dressed, she remembered. As if reading his mother's mind, Simon said, 'He speaks highly of you and your service to his young wife, Mother. He has a second child due in a matter of weeks.'

'Oh that poor girl,' said Lucie, thinking of the teenage mother who'd been in long travail giving birth to Sir Robert's son. The sound of tapping on the coach roof stopped further conversation. Simon put his head out of the window to speak to the coachmen, then sank back into his seat.

'We only have a quarter part hour more to go. I must tell you everything before we arrive at our destination.'

Lucie felt her stomach tense. Simon's tone had changed and become more urgent.

'It truly felt like the end of days. I'm not ashamed to admit to the terror I felt more than once. Much more than when I fled from the plague, and I thought that the worst thing I'd ever see. It's hard to put it into words.' Simon shifted uncomfortably, wincing as his sore hands brushed the velvet.

'There was no time to lament our shop and print house going up for we had work to do and everyone was in the same situation. But the next day when the wind dropped, we dared hope it would stay the fire's progress.'

Lucie nodded, encouraging Simon on. He looked down, 'Our optimism was misplaced, Mother. Yes, the fire was slowing but Stephens – one of my journeymen printers – came back from firefighting with that dreadful news about Kate, God rest her.'

'Amen,' Lucie answered.

With a catch in his voice Simon told his mother how Kate, who'd had wits as sharp as a whip, had been taking flagons of ale to the men to keep them refreshed, when she succumbed to a choking fit in the smoke and died where she fell.

'I shall truly miss her company. She was a good friend to me. When I sent word that I was returning to London last year after the plague abated, she slept in my bed for three nights to make sure it was properly aired for me.'

'She sounds like a good woman,' Lucie replied. 'I'll keep her in my prayers.'

She wondered for a moment if Kate was somehow connected with their journey but didn't want to waste time speculating when Simon should be finishing his story.

'It was the same day, Mother. The houses we'd pulled down and the low wind made it seem like the firebreak was working. It certainly felt much less intense.'

Lucie shuddered. She felt truly chilled. Her son, her only living child, had been in such great danger and she'd had no idea. She hadn't even been able to pray for him.

'The thing is, Mother, we were wrong. This whishing sound came down the alley we were in and the next we knew a gust blew a smouldering timber from one of the houses they'd partially pulled down. It lifted and flew through the air.'

'Oh thank God it didn't hit you, Simon,' Lucie was listening intently, staring directly at her son, for as much as Simon's account had chilled her, she felt compelled to know all.

'It didn't hit me, but Sir Robert took it straight on, knocking him onto his back,' Simon's eyes brimmed with tears at the memory. Lucie's eyes widened, and she felt a wave of guilt. She had been so relieved her boy was spared, she hadn't thought of anyone else.

'He has survived?' she asked in a quiet voice. Simon nodded.

'It is surely not he who is at the Manor in need of assistance though?' Lucie asked. 'He will be attended by the best physicians his father can summon in London.'

'The situation is this, Mother. Sir Robert is refusing to see anyone. For the first two days he was given laudanum to keep him drowsy and free from pain. There was a supply in the house, fortunately.'

'Their house was spared?'

'The Calstone's town house is in Covent Garden, and that area escaped the ravages of the fire.'

Lucie's hand shot to her mouth, her eyes wide. 'What about Ned? Ned. Oh Lord please let him have been spared.'

'Mother, very few lives are thought lost. You know what our Ned was like, if anyone was going to be well, then he will be.' Simon and Lucie exchanged hopeful smiles at the memory of Jasper's last apprentice, who was now working under John Battersby in London.

‘May you be right. Where is Sir Robert now?’ Lucie asked, still sure it could not be he who was awaiting her at the Manor.

‘He’s been in and out of delirium all the weekend, at Calstone House, and every time he roused, he refused to let his father’s physician in. Mother, I was desperate for him, you see. So on Monday I persuaded him to agree that if we took the coach to Tupingham and fetched you, he would admit you and accept some treatment.’

‘A journey like that could have killed him, Simon,’ Lucie frowned, shocked at the recklessness of what Simon had done.

‘I was quite out of my wits thinking how to help him, Mother. He is in agony in his body, but I fear for his mind most, he is most disordered.’ Simon spoke defiantly. ‘We could not take a room at an inn on the journey, he would not allow it. So the coachmen and I slept outdoors, leaving Sir Robert the comfort of this coach at least.’

‘Why would he agree to see a country midwife and not one of the many physicians in the ranks of courtiers? I am confused.’

‘As a kindness to me, Mother. I told him I could not bear to see him suffer, and you know how highly he and his family regard you after the services you provided to Lady Eleanor.’

The coach slowed right down and as it made the turn into the lane leading up to the manor house, Lucie caught her first glimpse in many months of the red brick building through the coach window.

‘I don’t know how we will find him. I pray for some improvement,’ Simon looked at his mother imploringly.

Chapter Three

The cool interior of Calstone Manor was a welcome relief from the stifling heat of the coach, though Lucie's eyes took a few moments to adjust to the gloom of the hall.

'Someone's busying themselves,' she commented to Simon, nodding towards the scaffolding timbers, sacks of sand piled along the walls. Nothing appeared to have altered since her last visit some months ago, but some changes were clearly being planned. The house was still. Only a few servants remained on the estate, since Lord Calstone was in London and his wife, daughter-in-law and their children were at their property in the North of England.

'Good day to you, Widow Smith, Mister Smith.' Friswell, Calstone's steward, greeted them formally. Despite being dressed in the same green satin doublet that all the male servants wore, Friswell never for a moment acted as a servant. At least not to those he considered beneath him. His face was haggard with drooping jowls, but his nose remained firmly in the air while he spoke to Lucie.

'You are come to attend to Sir Robert, Widow Smith? His man said to expect you. I fear he is gravely ill and, if you pardon my frankness, is in need of the full care of a physician not a country midwife.'

Lucie raised an eyebrow as she glanced at Simon but shook her head discreetly as if to advise her son not to argue with the steward. For all his complaining, the steward led the pair up the sweeping staircase. The musky scent of recently applied beeswax, warmed in the late summer heat, filled the air. They ascended the broad oak steps, and then went along a panelled corridor to Sir Robert's suite of rooms. A servant carrying Lucie's bag of medications followed behind the party.

The light was better there than downstairs, with sun pouring in through the tall leaded windows. Lucie couldn't help noticing the large portrait of a man with a clear likeness to Sir Robert hanging above the fireplace.

'That's the wine merchant who founded the dynasty,' Simon explained. 'Sir Robert's great-grandsire.'

They did not linger in the outer chamber for Sir Robert's man had already opened the bedroom door and was ushering them through. Lucie tutted as she marched toward the bed, quickly taking in the dark scene before her.

'Please open the shutters,' she said as she walked.

Sir Robert was sleeping as a result of the laudanum he had apparently been dosed with every time he'd seemed like he was rousing. Lucie pulled back the sheet, shuddering as a charcoal-like smell filled her nose.

'You poor boy,' she muttered. Sir Robert's face was deathly pale and his lips were cracked. Lucie took a pace back and bowed her head in silent prayer just as she had before every delivery she'd ever attended. That done, she felt her resolve grow strong, and asked for some freshly drawn water and a sponge so that she could get some fluid into her patient.

'Dip the sponge and soak it through, now wring it until it is just damp.' She showed Simon how to gently wet the inside of Sir Robert's lips. 'That's right, son. Now can you pass my scissors from my bag?'

Her practised hands made short work of cutting through the stinking bandages on Sir Robert's chest and shoulder. As she lifted the dirty dressings, she noted a faint fruity scent.

'These dressings have been made with salad oil and rose water, I'll warrant,' the midwife said, looking up from her work at Sir Robert's servant, who nodded in confirmation. 'Good, that's as it should be.'

''Ods blood,' Simon gasped as he saw the raw and angry burn emerge from under the dressings. Lucie shot him a look. 'There is no occasion for that language,' she reprimanded him, while continuing to work methodically with her scissors to remove the last vestiges of fabric from Sir Robert's weeping chest.

'We'll require some items from the kitchens, if you please,' Lucie said to the steward who had been hovering in the doorway this whole time.

'Of course,' said Friswell. 'Please provide a list and I will see it is brought up presently.'

'Beaten egg whites, with the egg yolks mixed with melted butter in a separate pot are the most urgent.' Lucie was surprised to see the steward turn on his heel and go to make the arrangements himself. While they waited, Lucie stroked her sleeping patient's hair as she had for her own sons as boys when they were sick. 'We'll have you feeling much more comfortable very soon,' she said in a low, comforting tone.

'He can't hear you if he sleeps, can he Mother?'

'Perhaps,' Lucie answered. 'He is not in a true sleep, but drowses from the medication.'

The eggs and butter were brought in by a housemaid moments later. Lucie had already taken the poppy oil from her bag. She set to work mixing a few drops into the beaten egg whites.

'Now this won't hurt my dear, just keep lying still for me,' she told the sleeping Sir Robert as she began to dab the mixture on the worst of the wounds. Out of the corner of her eye she noticed her son's colour draining as she touched the nasty injuries. 'Simon, could you get the burn ointment from my bag and treat your hands for me please? They are overdue an application.'

Lucie exchanged a glance with Sir Robert's servant who had been standing at the opposite side of the bed. He bore the pained look of a man who would rather have been anywhere else but felt dutybound to remain in place. Her lips and eyes crinkled into a reassuring smile.

'We'll have your master feeling much more comfortable very soon. Could you possibly see if there is some lemonade or other cordial in the kitchen, do you think?'

'But Sir Robert won't be able to drink it. Lord knows we have tried these past days . . . '

'No, I mean for me. The heat is troubling me, and I should like to carry on with my work.' Lucie ran her hand over her forehead to emphasise how much she needed the refreshment and smiled to see the servant nod and head out of the room. With both young men away for a few moments at least, Lucie could turn to the smaller blisters which needed attention now. Picking her scissors back up from the coverlet, she gently snipped the clear bumps to let the translucent humours drain into a clout. She was just finishing mixing the melted butter and egg yolks with a little rose oil when Simon, along with Sir Robert's servant, James, came back into the room.

'That was quickly done,' she commented as the servant placed a tray with a pitcher and some cups down on a small walnut table.

'Cat, the housemaid that is, was coming up the stairs with some small beer herself. The cook had sent her in case we were thirsty.'

'Ah that was well met then,' Lucie replied. 'You help yourselves, I have just to apply this salve to some small burns and I shall join you.' She walked back to the bed. 'The one good thing we can say about the heat is it kept the butter nice and liquid until I was ready for it.'

The men smiled at her. They weren't to know, Lucie thought, that she had decades of experience keeping folks' spirits up in difficult times and had more than one distraction technique up her sleeve. Satisfied that the wounds were tended, the midwife supped heartily on her beer.

'I'll be needing some warm water, soap, and linen shortly

if you please,' Lucie announced. She placed her cup on the tray, and helped herself to one of the warm biscuits that the cook had sent up with the beer. 'Our patient won't recover as well if left in the sorry state I found him.' She sat for a minute in a plush armchair near the bed, chewing her biscuit while she waited for someone to act on her request.

'You may leave me to my work gentlemen, when the water arrives,' she told her onlookers. 'Go and take some air and I'll call when I am finished. And you,' she said, looking directly at Sir Robert's man. 'You are exhausted. That is plain to see. I expect you have slept but little since this happened, but you can rest now. I'll tend to your master, and Simon can assist me in moving him.'

As tenderly and thoroughly as she cleaned many an ailing or deceased body over her long career, Lucie gently washed Sir Robert, believing he needed both cleanliness and dignity to aid his healing. Simon assisted in holding and manoeuvring his friend's limbs, and then running a comb through his friend's short hair. From a cupboard he produced a cap and placed it on his friend's now clean head. They then gently rolled the dirty, wet sheet out from under him.

'Hush, hush,' soothed Lucie as a small groan came from Sir Robert. 'You try and rest, dear, we are almost done here.'

'Have you finished with the tray, Widow Smith?' Cat asked. She came into the room and automatically started to tidy without really being aware of what she was doing.

'Yes, thank you. And this water may be disposed of too now, but before you do, could you bring some clean bed sheets and help me get this bed freshly made up, my dear?'

Between the three of them, Sir Robert was soon laying in a pristine bed of crisp white linen. His eyes flickered and he made the occasional groan as they worked but had not awoken fully at any point. Lucie then lay a single linen sheet over Sir Robert, so his body didn't overheat under the coverlet again. Cat left carrying the bundle of dirty laundry, saying she would come back for the tray straight after she had taken all that down.

'Will he recover?' Simon whispered, his face a picture of concern.

'Most likely, son. His wounds are deep and will leave scars, I'm afraid. But as long as they don't become infected, and if it's God's will, he should return to health before too long.'

'Here, let me do that, Mother,' Simon said as Lucie began packing up her things. 'You'll stay until he is well, won't you?'

'I will nurse him a day or two longer, but then I must return to the Three Doves. Now come here and give your old mother a hug.' As they embraced, Lucie was pleased Simon could not see her face, for a flush of shame passed over it when she thanked God it was the young man in the bed injured and not her precious son. A polite cough interrupted their reverie. Sir Robert's manservant was in the doorway with a glass bottle and a small silver spoon in his hand.

'It is time we gave Sir Robert his sedating medicine, Widow Smith. Doctor Thomas was most insistent that my master be given a spoon of this liquid every four hours to keep him drowsy and temper his pain.'

Lucie frowned and glanced over at Sir Robert who had indeed opened his eyes, but was staring blankly, as if he had not yet returned to a full consciousness.

'I think it best we limit this to the night-time only, James. It is better that Sir Robert begins to regain some awareness. It is not good for him to lie still for too many days. He will begin to waste away for want of proper nourishment too,' the midwife replied.

The servant shifted from foot-to-foot as if uncertain what to do.

'I understand. You are reluctant to discard an order from the Calstones' physician. Let me assure you that I will assume full responsibility for this change of treatment.' She saw the younger man's posture relax. 'Now if one of you gentlemen could take me to the steward's rooms, I need to make a report to him of how things stand.'

Life in the Manor settled into a regular pattern over the next few days. Lucie attended to Sir Robert's wounds several times a day, finding his recovery encouraging. Simon slept on the rug in the outer chamber, refusing to move any further away from his friend. Luckily, his hands were soon healed thanks to his mother's tending. By and by the seriously injured man's colour began to return, as he accepted spoons of caudle and other nourishment, patiently administered by Simon. While physically he was making progress, his humour was constantly foul. Every movement of his torso caused searing pain as his skin tried to knit itself back together. Lucie knew even with a good result and a complete recovery, Sir Robert would be disfigured by these wounds.

On the fourth evening, Lucie was sitting in the kitchen opposite the cook, Mabel Houton, with whom she had just taken supper, as had become a custom over the last days. Lucie had not forgotten the kindness Mabel had shown her when she had arrived at the Manor in a bedraggled state the previous year.

'You have scarcely touched your meat, Mabel,' Lucie said. 'Is something amiss?' The cook seemed a little agitated, wriggling uncomfortably on her seat. Mabel signalled with her eyes towards the young kitchen maid who was clearing the table and Lucie understood. When the girl had gone to the scullery, Mabel took a deep breath as if steeling her resolve and rose from her chair.

'I have something distressing to show you, Widow Smith,' she said. She reached behind a metal pail at the side of the dresser and brought out a linen parcel with one hand. 'I found this in the privy this evening. It was crudely wrapped and hidden behind the bucket of rags.'

Lucie took the parcel and opened it up. She gasped. The form of an infant, not much more than a hand's span in length, appeared from beneath the layers of cloth.

'Why did you not seek me out as soon as you made this discovery?' Lucie demanded, peering at the infant, born much too soon.

'I did not know what to do rightly, and you were so busy attending to the young master. But you're quite right, I was wrong not to send for you presently.' The cook looked down, wringing her hands in her lap, while Lucie examined the navel string which was still attached to a tiny purple after-burden.

'Oh Mabel, who could have done such a thing as this? We must find the woman for it is the action of either someone desperate or someone wicked. She might be in urgent need of my help too. Have you a notion who we must seek out?'

Lucie wrapped the creature back up and held it in the crook of her arm. She found herself swaying back and to in her seat as she had with countless infants over the decades.

'It was a man-child of about five months in his mother's womb,' she said. 'If this was a deliberate act to destroy the child, then the consequences are very severe, as you know.'

Mabel threw up her hands, 'Who could have done this? The Mistress will have to be told and we shall all be in trouble. What calamity has been visited on us?'

'Calm yourself Mabel. Sit down and take a sip of your wine,' Lucie instructed her. The Justice will have to be told, she thought as her stomach churned. She decided not to say anything aloud with Mabel being so overwrought but found her mind racing. She knew if they found the mother and she was unmarried, she would be presumed guilty of infanticide and hanged.

'I have been thinking about nothing else since I made the discovery, and there's only one person I can think of. But it can't be. Oh, my goodness, when his Lordship learns of this . . .' Mabel's hand shot to her mouth.

Lucie felt a flash of annoyance shadow her face. It was enough she had to deal with this and try and find a mother who could be in need of her skills, without the cook taking on so.

'Who do you think might be responsible?' she asked.

Since the household was running on a minimal number of servants there were only three women in addition to the cook and Lucie. Susanna the young kitchen maid, the chambermaid, Cat, and the married housekeeper. Without answering Lucie, Mabel got back up and marched out to the scullery to ask Susanna, who she'd apparently discounted, to summon Cat.

The plump, fresh-faced young woman who Lucie had always found so accommodating came into the kitchen a matter of moments later, looking puzzled.

'You're not still cross with me for taking that extra slice of apple pie, are you Cook? I've said sorry, I swear I didn't know it was spoken for.'

'No, it is me who wanted a word, Cat. I think you might have something rather more serious to tell me and it would be better for us all if you were truthful straight away,' Lucie answered.

'I don't understand, Widow Smith. Is there something wrong with Sir Robert's chambers? Or yours? I have begged Mister Smith to let me make him up a bed in another chamber that he might rest properly, but he'll not hear of it.' Cat wrung her hands on her apron and seemed genuinely puzzled.

Lucie bit her lip in irritation. It would do no good to react angrily. The young wench was certainly a good little actress if she was indeed the one they sought. The midwife composed herself and took a breath.

'No, there is nothing amiss with your work. May I ask if you have your flowers, Cat?'

The housemaid looked shocked. 'Why'd you ask that? My monthlies finished the day Sir Robert arrived home. I always keep a reckoning.' Her demeanour changed and she placed her hands on her hips as she answered. 'What a personal thing to drag me down the stairs for. What is going on?'

Lucie opened her mouth to speak severely to Cat to press her some more, but Mabel interrupted.

'You may go, Cat. Thank you,' she said. When the two were alone again, the cook explained herself. 'I've known the lass for more than three years and can tell when she's being less than truthful in a heartbeat. I reckon she is in earnest. I must have been mistaken,'

Mabel slumped back on her chair, resting her elbows on the table and putting her head in her hands. 'I just don't understand. You know yourself that Susanna, my kitchen maid, is not yet fully grown. She is only eleven and I am certain she has not had her courses yet and could not be with child. That only leaves Mistress Clopton the housekeeper; she's married to the head groom. If she was big bellied again, she wouldn't destroy it, nor suffer it to be born early without calling for a midwife. I'm in a maze Widow Smith.' She shook her head even while it was clamped in her hands.

'We'd better speak to Dorothy Clopton immediately,' Lucie replied with a weary sigh.

Cat was recalled and dispatched to the cottage next to the stables to fetch Mistress Clopton. When the housekeeper marched into the kitchen moments later, she was red faced and furious. It was clear her choler was high.

'What's the meaning of this? Cat here says you have been scolding her about her courses. Is this true?' Mistress Clopton gave Lucie a stern look. 'You had no business questioning one of my servants at all. You should have referred any concerns to me.'

'You're right Mistress Clopton. Please accept my apology.' She and Mabel had not adhered to proper custom in their haste to get to the bottom of this mystery. 'You need to see this, I am afraid.' Lucie placed the bundle that she had held close this whole time onto the kitchen table and unwrapped it once again.

Mistress Clopton's eyes widened in horror as she looked at both Lucie and Mabel, before turning round to stare at Cat. 'You knew of this?' she asked in an accusatory tone. Cat shook her head, looking pale and close to tears. She pointed to the corner of the kitchen where young Susanna was standing, trembling, with tears running down her face. The three older women turned, following the direction of Cat's stare.

'Oh child,' gasped Mabel. 'I had not seen you were still here. I thought you had retired to your bed. Do you know anything of this sorry business, my girl?'

Susanna could only shake her head nervously.

'Quickly pour her a dash of brandy, she looks like she might go into shock.' Lucie went to guide the girl into a chair by the fire. 'Look away from the table lass, what's there is not fit for young eyes.'

'You're quite sure this is not her doing, Cook?' Lucie caught the housekeeper's low tones asking Mabel while she was tending to Susanna. 'I know she is not in years but we have all known girls not much more than her age be mothers made. Stranger things have happened.'

'Quite certain, Mistress, but who could have done this wicked thing? You see why our thoughts turned to Cat at first. Who else is there? I am sorry, Cat, to have thought ill of you. I hope you will forgive me,' Mabel replied.

The housekeeper raised her hand to her chambermaid, signalling that there was no need for her to say anything further.

'Are we certain this happened today?' she asked. 'Yesterday the farmer's wife who serves as our laundress and her girls were here all day. I asked them to come especially because of the extra laundry from the care of Sir Robert. They travel from one of our farms three, sometimes four women of all ages. Goodwife Potton and her daughters. They have been doing the laundry here monthly for years.'

Mabel gasped. 'That didn't cross my mind. I should have

thought. I sent Goodwife Potton home with a beef pie because they all looked so done in. I knew the goodwife would struggle to cook for the farmer and the hands after all that work.'

Mistress Clopton's eyebrows shot up. 'I hope you have noted this in your account book, Cook. We cannot give benevolence every time the mood takes us. This must be deducted from their fee.'

'With respect Mistress Clopton, please can we keep to the matter in hand?' Lucie interrupted.

'I was just getting to that. We will have to inform Mister Friswell and he will no doubt ride to Grantby at first light to inform the Justice of the Peace and he'll make enquiries.'

Lucie and Mabel exchanged a glance. There was no denying the truth of the housekeeper's pronouncement but getting the verbose and self-important steward involved was not something they'd want if there was any other way.

'Indeed, Mistress Clopton. We have no choice but to follow the scheme you set out. However, it is my duty as a licensed midwife to give the infant a proper burial, making sure he cannot be accidentally dug up by an animal. Please have your husband send one of the stable lads to dig me a small plot in a suitable place. In the meantime, I will complete a full examination of the body.'

She scooped up the little parcel once again and sat back in a chair, resting it on her lap.

Under an hour later, in the clear light of a full moon, Lucie was accompanied by Clopton the head groom and Friswell the steward, both in their green satin doublets, to a small burial hole in the far end of the kitchen garden. The site was chosen as it was protected by a wall. There they interred the tiny body. The steward pontificated loudly throughout the whole operation. Lucie needed all her will to ignore the noise and knelt in the soil, gently laying the mite in its tiny grave, and bowed her head in silent prayer while the men filled in the hole. She put her hand out and Clopton helped her to her feet.

'Amen,' she said pointedly.

'Amen,' the groom replied.

'Yes, yes, amen. Now come along,' the pompous steward rattled on. For all his volume, Lucie didn't take in a word. Her prayers had included guidance to get to the bottom of this sorry affair and all she could think about now was the woman out there somewhere, possibly in pain, bleeding, and needing the attention of a midwife.

Chapter Four

In the six days Lucie had been at the Manor, Sir Robert had made considerable progress. He was now able to sit in his armchair for an hour or so each day and had become less prone to outbursts of temper than he had been in the early days of his recovery.

'I need to return home, son. Sir Robert is on the path to a full recovery. I should have gone a day or two ago were it not for that fever he ran, but that has passed now.' Lucie and Simon were taking a stroll around the formal garden arm-in-arm.

'Of course. I'll stay on here a little longer, Mother, but will help make arrangements for you to be taken home in the coach on the morrow. I will be forever grateful for what you have done here.'

'I've been experiencing night terrors, Simon, dreaming sore afraid that this happened to you not him, God forgive me,' Lucie admitted this in a low voice. 'You are all I have now, Simon.'

They walked on in silence a few moments more.

'Perhaps they will cease when I am in my own bed. But home is not the same without your father. Jasper *was* the Three Doves.'

'That's not how I see things Mother. You and he were the Three Doves. Your patients were the ones who moved in when in need of your constant care. Women and their husbands called for you all the time. Your work was as much a part of our lives as his when I was growing up with my brother and sisters.'

Tears brimmed Lucie's eyes. 'Those were happy days, son. I am surprised by how much you remember, for you were under ten years of age when that all changed.'

'Oh, I've many memories, and Martha and you have stories aplenty to add to the ones I forget,' Simon said with a smile. 'Mother, I am not going anywhere. I am bound to return to you like a bad penny you cannot rid yourself of. Now let's get you back inside.'

They walked back to the Manor, reminiscing companionably about the happiest of days when the Three Doves bustled with four children. Her two bonny maids and her two sons, along with Jasper, Martha their housemaid, and various animals. The happy tears continued to brim in Lucie's eyes as they talked.

'At times, the noise and bustle drove me to the very brink of madness, but oh, what I wouldn't give to live it for just one more day,' Lucie said with a sigh.

As they stepped into the dark entrance of the Manor, Lucie gave her son a quick peck on the cheek. She wondered if it was wrong after all not to have confided in Simon about the baby, but reckoned he had worries enough of his own. There had been a flurry of activity in the two days since the cook had made the grim discovery in the privy, but the steward had kept the women of the household in the dark, insisting he had matters in hand and they should refrain from idle talk about things which did not concern them. She took a deep breath as she knocked on Mister Friswell's door to inform him of her decision to return home on the morrow.

'Come.'

As she pushed open the heavy oak door, Lucie found herself entirely unsurprised to find he had company with him.

'Ah Widow Smith, do enter,' the steward looked up to see her in the open doorway. 'Your timing is excellent, for I was just about to send for you. This gentleman is Dr Somerton who has been sent by the Justice of the Peace in Grantby to search one of the laundry maids at Overwoods Farm.'

Lucie nodded courteously. The visitor, dressed in a pale blue coat and a smart, short grey periwig, bowed his head in return.

'A wench resides there who we believe to be the culprit who destroyed her own infant and concealed it here at the Manor.'

'That is the family Mistress Clopton first thought of. I know them a little for they sell their milk and white meat at Tupingham market from time to time. Oh their poor mother, those maids are very young.'

As Lucie spoke, Dr Somerton walked over to her and handed her his card.

Herbert Somerton, esq. MD.
Physician

Lucie took the card and read it carefully. It also gave the doctor's address in Grantby. She considered the information for a moment before opening her mouth to speak further, but the steward rose from his chair and told the midwife that there was no time for the pair to become better acquainted.

'We are leaving now. You, Widow Smith, will accompany us to the farm to make the necessary examination. Yesterday, Farmer Potton refused his permission for the physician here to search his daughter, and the Justice has determined a midwife should be engaged for the purpose. The farmer must now comply under threat of arrest.'

Within the hour Lucie was riding side-saddle the short distance to one of the tenanted farms belonging to the Calstone estate. Lucie had been surprised that it was the Pottons who did the laundry at the Manor, since their cheeses were popular and their stall always had a queue, but supposed that with a large family to feed, any extra coins were welcome. As they rode along the lane past the fields, Lucie saw men working the land, and assumed those were the older sons out with their father. In the farmyard, the physician and steward dismounted and tied up their horses before either appeared to remember that Lucie would need assistance getting down.

'Widow Smith,' greeted Goodwife Potton, looking up at Lucie. 'Wait and I'll fetch a stool. I was sorry to hear about your husband. A bad business, that. Taking the plague and dying so suddenly.'

'At least he did not bring it back to the country,' Friswell scoffed. Were people really saying that behind her back? Lucie wondered. She felt such a raw pang of grief that she almost gasped. As she helped Lucie down, Goodwife Potton spoke to the men in a stern tone 'I trust you'll find the journey wasted and you will be on your way soon, gentlemen.'

The kitchen was that of a busy family. Once again, a fleeting picture of the Three Doves in happier times flashed before Lucie's eyes. Two middle-sized girls were busy peeling vegetables and an older one was covered in flour to her elbow as she appeared to be making dumplings. The youngest child, a boy, was looking at the letters in his hornbook, tracing the shapes with a podgy finger.

Jane Potton had dark circles under her eyes, and her expression darkened to match as the steward and physician walked into the kitchen some moments later. If she had to guess, Lucie would say Friswell had been gossiping about her husband to this new doctor. The farmer's wife did not offer them any beer but instead turned to the gentlemen. 'Prudence is sick in bed,' she said. She turned to Lucie then, her voice softening. 'My daughter has done nothing amiss.'

Lucie caught the desperation in the mother's eyes and tried to force her lips into a reassuring smile.

'My lass is in her bed sick,' she dropped her voice before continuing, 'from her first of *those*. When we worked at the Manor this week. You know how it makes some girls sicken? Prudence is suffering appallingly. No doubt her body will become used to them in time.'

Goodwife Potton turned back to the men. 'Her father consents to her being searched by Widow Smith but will not allow men in the chamber. We are a God-fearing family and Prudence would have nothing to do with a man before she was wed. Hester, show Widow Smith up to your room, and stay with her until she has completed the tasks she has been charged with.'

'Be assured Goodwife Potton, I will be swift and gentle in my dealings with your daughter,' Lucie gave the worried mother a squeeze on the shoulder. She turned to follow Hester. She rather admired the way the goodwife had spoken of women's courses in front of the men without flinching, but her face fell when she saw the farmhouse did not have a pair of stairs to the upper floor, just a ladder. My knees are too old for this, she thought. Taking a deep breath, Lucie pushed back her shoulders and gripped the ladder firmly, following Hester up with a show of confidence that belied her caution.

'At least there is room to stand up fully,' Lucie said to Hester when she stepped into the boarded attic. 'I've been to mothers in upper rooms where I was obliged to remain bent over for lack of headroom.'

There were two beds in the room she had stepped into and on her right was a partition wall with a curtain in the doorway. Doubtless that's the parents' chamber, Lucie thought. She was used to scanning rooms and working out what was what from her years of helping labouring women. Over in her bed next to the external wall, Prudence Potton was lying on her back staring up to the rafters as if in a trance.

'Has she been like this for long?' Lucie asked Hester, who merely nodded in response. 'I see.' She walked over and lifted Prudence's limp arm to feel for her pulse.

'Prudence dear. My name is Widow Smith. I'm a midwife. You know what that means? Of course you do,' her blue eyes smiled directly into the girl's own blank ones. 'I help women bring their children forth, but also help with all manner of women's matters. If your courses are painful, I can leave your mother instructions for a syrup that will give you ease.' She sat on the edge of the bed and tucked the girl's arm back under her blanket, patting it. 'Now tell me. Did you experience your first bleeding at Calstone Manor the other day?'

The young woman made no response, so Lucie tried stroking her hair as she had for her own children when they were sick. 'It is just me and your sister Hester here, little one. Let me help you.' Lucie decided that rushing the girl would not help and determined to treat her gently. She looked over at the other girl, standing at the foot of the bed, pale and shaking.

'Hester, your sister is in a swoon from terror. Please go back to the kitchen and ask your mother if she has some cinnamon in her cupboard. If she has, ask that she mix a pinch into a cup of warm wine and bring it up to me immediately with a spoon and we will try to revive your sister's spirits.'

'Yes, Widow Smith,' replied Hester, bobbing. She looked relieved to have been given a reason to quit the room.

Lucie sat quietly on the edge of the bed and bent her head to offer a quiet prayer in the hope it would help Prudence as much as herself. In just a few minutes, Lucie heard footsteps on the ladder, and soon both Hester and her mother were in the attic chamber. Lucie stood up to allow Jane to offer the medicinal drink to her daughter. Raising her daughter's head in her arm, Jane managed to get a little of the soothing liquid into her child.

'The men downstairs will become impatient if asked to wait much longer,' Lucie whispered to the goodwife. 'Their voices are becoming raised,' she nodded her head in the direction of the floor where light from the kitchen could be seen through the gaps, allowing the men's voices to be heard clearly. Jane helped Lucie roll up the coverlet and sheets from the bottom of the bed, leaving Prudence covered from the waist up. Immediately the women saw blood covering the girl's shift and bedding.

'See, Widow Smith? Her flowers just as I told you,' Jane

hissed.

'Indeed, but I must search her womb.'

Lucie greased her hand with oil of lilies and gently opened Prudence's legs. Feeling her belly as she performed the examination, Lucie's brow furrowed but she held her tongue until she was sure. After wiping clean her hands on a linen towel, Lucie pulled down the bedding and went to the head of the bed to look at the girl's chest. There was no need for her to ask the child to pull down her shift, for there were small marks of fluid on the linen over both breasts.

Jane noticed at the same time as Lucie and let out a scream, managing to muffle the worst of it by putting her fist into her mouth.

'God help us!'

'Hush, Goodwife, please. Prudence, do you think you might talk to me now? It is clear to me the child we discovered came from your body. You must tell the truth and shame the devil.' Even as the words left her mouth, Lucie knew that truth was unlikely to spare this girl from the wrath of the law which would presume her guilt.

'Mother, may I speak for Pru?' Hester asked quietly.

'How? What do you know of this? Has she confided in you?'

Hester's voice was shaky with nerves as she began. 'You recall I bled for the first time some weeks ago? Remember in the kitchen you said not to tell Faith lest she be scared, but that you were sure Pru should bleed any day too since we have done everything together since we came into the world at the same time?'

Jane nodded, her face now almost as pale as that of her prone daughter. 'I remember. It is true Widow Smith. Prudence and Hester have done everything at the same time all their lives.'

'When we were in the washhouse the other day, Prudence had this awful bellyache come on sudden. She went to the privy.'

'Where was I?' the goodwife asked, her voice barely audible.

'You had gone to the big house to get more soap, Mother. My sister was gone a long time and I worried so I went to look for her.

'I recall. The soap was not grated ready for me and I had to attend to that in the scullery and so was away from the girls. That's right,' Goodwife Potton spoke as if she was still trying to piece together events.

Lucie caught Hester's glance at her mother for reassurance before she continued her sorry tale.

'Pru was sitting with a bloody bundle in her lap when I found her. Neither of us knew rightly what this could be, but when I took it from her and untangled it, we saw the body of a tiny child and its navel string.' Hester was almost babbling at this point as the words spilled out in a rushed whisper. 'Pru were making these strange grunting noises, and clutching at her belly. She stood up and another bundle, still joined to the string came forth and was hanging from the body. Blood was running down Pru's legs, Ma.' Hester gave a sob. 'We were both in a maze, but it was me who wrapped it in the linen. I tore a length from my shift – I am sorry mother – I tied up the body into a parcel and hid it behind the rag bucket.'

The dam Hester was holding back broke and she burst into wracking sobs. Lucie could see the episode had shocked her deeply. *If only I'd known*, Lucie lamented thinking how it was probable she was just yards away, likely walking in the grounds at that time. Hester bolted to her mother and launched herself into her chest. But Jane caught her by the shoulders and shook her, demanding answers.

'You wicked girl. Why did you not come to me? What possessed you? I am at a loss to comprehend.'

'Calm your passions, Goodwife Potton,' Lucie said. 'We need to hear the whole of this story before the men downstairs are alerted and if you raise your voice they will likely come running up.'

To everyone's surprise, Prudence's head rose a little, and with a weak voice, she begged her mother not to punish

Hester.

'My sister acted to help me. Neither of us knew what to do. We panicked. I don't know how the child got there. I thought I had my first bleed.'

'If she had the composure enough to cover and conceal the body then she had the wherewithal to do what was right. As for you, Prudence Potton I have no words. A daughter of mine is naught but a common whore. This intelligence will kill your father even as he is working in the fields to provide food for us all. Who is responsible for ruining you?' Jane raged.

'Please Goodwife. Leave us. Let me interview Prudence alone. Pray, go find your husband and ask him to wait in the kitchen until I come down.'

Jane puffed out her flushed cheeks before slowly blowing out the air. She stared at the midwife and then each of her twin daughters. 'Very well. But no more dissembling, child. You must tell Widow Smith the whole truth. Come Hester. You shall account to your father for your role in this calamity.'

Ten minutes later Lucie backed slowly down the ladder to the kitchen. She nodded curtly to Mister Friswell and Doctor Somerton.

'Take your brother out to play in the yard,' she instructed the girls, the elder of whom was presumably Faith. Lucie's brows knitted in annoyance that no-one had thought to send the children out before. Goodness only knows what was going round in their little minds. She went to the bucket, washing her hands in the cold water, and drying them on a towel on a nail above it while the three youngsters hurried out the door.

'Your journey was not wasted. The child in the privy did indeed come forth from Prudence Potton's body. But she did not destroy it. I knew when I first saw the mite that it had never drawn breath.' Lucie chose her words with great care. She would not tell an untruth but would not reveal Hester's role in the matter unless there was no alternative.

'I see,' said Dr Somerton, rising to his feet. 'The Justice of the Peace will have to be informed and the wench taken to Grantby gaol to await trial. I will arrange for her to be collected by the constable without delay.'

'No,' Lucie said firmly. 'You must not remove this young woman from her chamber for at least a sennight from now. She must recover her strength.'

'She'll not stay under my roof a night longer!' roared the farmer, walking in the door and catching the end of Lucie's testimony. 'She has disgraced my name and my family and is dead to me.'

'There is no question of her remaining here, Farmer Potton. She will accompany us to the gaol. She will be charged with murder. The law is clear. Any unmarried woman who conceals a dead birth is presumed guilty,' Friswell announced, his chest puffed out.

Goodwife Potton groaned and sank to the floor in a puddle of apron and skirts. 'Quickly,' said Lucie, rushing to her side. 'We must loosen your mother's laces. Hester, help me please.'

As she knelt on the floor assisting Jane Potton, Lucie spoke to the men. 'The girl up the stairs is in no fit condition to be moved. If she may not stay here, then please show compassion and release her into my custody. I will nurse her back to health with the help of Midwife Thorne who resides at the Three Doves in Tupingham with me. Then when it is meet, justice can take its course. Dr Somerton, a feather if you please.'

The physician harrumphed but did as she asked, and Lucie heard him call to the children outside to find him a feather, followed by a squawk as a nearby chicken was called on to supply it. Lucie burned the feather on the kitchen fire, and held the stinking object under Jane's nose. While she worked, she heard the three men discuss her proposal in low tones. As Jane was helped to her chair, the steward announced that this request would be acceded to.

'You will be driven to Tupingham on the farmer's cart at twilight. You will lodge her at the Three Doves until the Justice orders her appearance,' Friswell decreed.

Chapter Five

Lucie jumped, startled as she was sitting in her armchair by the fire, too tired to do more than gaze into the distance. Someone was rapping on the scullery door. Heaving herself up, Lucie went to answer the call. Mary had been in bed for a long time, and Lucie didn't want either her or Prudence Potton wakened by the caller.

'Mother, it's Simon,' he said as Lucie pulled the bolt open.

'What a day this has been!' Lucie slumped into his chest before he'd even got properly over the threshold.

'Friswell informed me you'd left for the Three Doves. He said he'd send a boy with your bags in the morning, but I wanted to see you for myself. I borrowed a horse,' Simon's words came tumbling out as he returned his mother's hug. 'Mother, what's happened? Please look at me, I am worried.' Lucie looked up and saw Simon's face was flushed with the exertion of his late-night gallop.

'I'm well, Simon. I'm sorry to have caused you concern like this. It was not my choice,' she freed herself from Simon's arms, and walked backwards into the kitchen. She held the door wide open, so he could pass her to place her bags down. Then she went to the hearth and lit a taper to light more candles that she and Simon might see one another properly.

'I am pleased I did not cause you to have to get up from your bed, but you being up so late does nothing to lessen my concern,' Simon continued. Lucie began unpacking the contents of her bags onto the large kitchen table. 'Mother, talk to me, please. Mary is in bed up the stairs?'

'Yes, son. We must keep our voices down for her sake but also for a houseguest up in my chamber. A wench from Overwoods Farm. That's where I went this afternoon.' She put her hand up to halt Simon's next question.

'I needed to sit quietly to gather my thoughts and pray on what has come to pass. I knew I'd not sleep until I had unravelled it all to my satisfaction. I believe with God's help I have arrived at the truth,' she said with a long sigh. 'How I miss your father's counsel.'

Lucie continued to sort her items, checking jars and pots to see which were empty and which could go back in her midwifery bag. 'Before I tell you the story, and I do need to take you entirely into my confidence Simon, pray pour yourself a cup of small beer. I expect your journey has left you thirsty.'

Leaving her bags for the moment, Lucie went back to her armchair and flicked her hand towards Jasper's chair, indicating that Simon should sit there. He hesitated for a moment before doing as his mother asked.

'Something happened at the Manor, and I could not speak of it. I regret now not taking you into my confidence then, son. Despite your height, sometimes I forget you're a grown man and not a youth.'

Lucie gazed into the fire for a few moments. Where to start?

'One of the Potton twins, you won't know them, their father is a tenant farmer on the Calstone estate. The maids are about fifteen, I'd guess. They do the laundry for the Manor monthly.'

Simon's eyebrows knitted as he pulled a confused face.

'Let me tell the story in my own way, son. It'll make sense presently. They were at the Manor an additional time this week, to wash the extra linen from Sir Robert's indisposition. While there, Prudence, one of the twins, miscarried of a tiny babe. Well before its time.'

'I see,' said Simon letting out a low whistle.

'I am not sure you do quite yet,' Lucie said and explained how the girls had panicked and wrapped the baby in a piece torn from Hester's chemise and hidden it behind the rag bucket in the privy. Her eyes glistened with tears as she spoke, making them sparkle in the flickering candlelight.

'Simon, that maid was ravished and ruined at the Manor. On an earlier visit I mean. Her maidenhead snatched from her in a cruel attack.' A piece of spittle escaped Lucie's pursed lips as she spoke. 'By my reckoning it would have been in May. It will be easy enough to check the details from Mistress Clopton's housekeeping records.'

'What was she planning to do if she'd carried the baby its full time?'

'That's just it. She had no notion she was with child. Son, she had not yet had her courses. She was not fully a woman.'

Simon took off his cap and ran his fingers through his short hair, shaking his head.

'Did she name the rogue?' he asked.

Lucie shook her head sadly. 'No, only that her attacker was a man older than her father.' Lucie caught her son's eye and their gaze locked just for a moment.

'We are of the same mind,' Lucie said softly. That brief look had confirmed to her that Simon knew what this description meant. 'He'd promised her that what he was doing would not hurt her much. Said her maidenhead was but a toy worth discarding since it would heal him.'

'He deserves to hang!' Simon thumped his fist on the arm of Jasper's chair, colour flaring in his cheeks.

'He wore fine clothes, and a long black curled periwig. Said if she screamed or told anyone he would see to it her father was thrown off his lands and her family made paupers.'

'I bet he did. Calstone,' Simon spat the name. 'He was here in May. Robbie - Sir Robert - told me back then how much more pleasant London was without his father around.'

Lucie couldn't speak, she'd feared the worst, and Simon confirmed she wasn't being fanciful.

''Ods blood, Mother. He has whores enough in London,' Simon rubbed his fist. Clearly his hands were not yet sufficiently healed that they could take a pounding.

'Simon, this must go no further, but some foolish men believe that having their way with a virgin will cure them of the French disease.'

Simon's fist clenched and his jaw set in cold anger.

'Of course, he would be full of that. He has contaminated the girl?'

Lucie shrugged, dabbing her eyes with the corner of her apron. 'Quite possibly he's ruined her in more ways than one. You see why I pleaded for her to be released into my care rather than taken to Grantby gaol?'

Simon slipped out of his chair and knelt in front of Lucie. On his knees, their faces were almost level. 'Of course I do, Mother.' He took Lucie's hands and squeezed them.

'You're a comfort to me Simon,' Lucie said with a watery smile. 'We must find a way to convince his Lordship to intervene in this case. We must get word to him. If Prudence Potton is tried for her crime of concealing a birth it is she who will be hanged.'

Simon sprang to his feet and began pacing.

'But Mother, why would Lord Calstone agree to speak for the girl? He would not want his name brought into this case.'

'Keep your voice down,' Lucie chided. She reached over to Simon's chair and picked up his cup, taking a deep swig, before explaining that if Prudence was charged, scandal would visit the Manor whichever way the matter concluded.

'You know how fast rumours spread, Simon. We had our own taste of this last year. Calstone Manor will be the centre of gossip in Tupingham, Grantby, and beyond. News will surely reach the Court eventually and his standing will be diminished.'

Lucie quickly turned her head as she heard footsteps on the creaky stairs.

'Ah Widow Smith, I did not know you were still awake until I saw the lights. Mister Smith you are here too,' Mary pulled her shawl tight around herself. 'I went down to look in on our charge and found her sleeping soundly. I just came to get a cup of small beer for I woke with a dry mouth.'

'Who is Mister Smith?' Simon said, smiling fondly.

'I know, I know, but it feels strange calling you Simon.' Lucie caught Mary's blush in the flickering candlelight.

'Well if you do not, I shall start calling you Mother Chair, after your profession,' he teased.

'You will not,' Mary retorted. 'It is good to see you, Simon. I was so very worried when Widow Smith told me about the fire.'

Lucie smiled at her son and her former deputy, for a short moment feeling like it was old times. A sharp gripe in her tummy caused her to gasp, bringing her back into the present.

'Here, let me pour your beer for you.' Lucie reached up for another cup from the dresser. As she passed the drink over, Simon looked at his mother with a quizzical expression as if to ask how much Mary knew of the situation. Lucie shook her head fleetingly.

Simon sat down at the bench of the large kitchen table. 'Mary, you have the chair by the fire, keep warm. Mother come and sit back down. Lord Calstone is expected at the Manor any day to see how his son does.'

'I see,' said Lucie. She rose to her feet again even though she had only just sat down. 'We need to pray on the best course. It's surely past midnight, we must sleep. Simon, you'll rest here I hope?'

'No Mother, there is a good moon and the horse is strong. I left it tethered at the trough and need to collect it. I want to be back by Robbie's side before he wakes.'

Lucie walked to the back door with him, and as they embraced, heard his whispered promise. 'Don't fret, I will not say a word about this dreadful business, nor let anyone in the household think I have the least notion. I will return in a couple of days to see what you have decided must be done and I will be at your command, Mother.'

After she had redrawn the bolt across the back door, Lucie walked back into the kitchen, motioning to Mary to take her arm as they made for the stairs.

'Mayhap things will look brighter after some sleep,' Lucie said, her spare hand masking a yawn.

Chapter Six

'Widow Smith! Good. I find myself in the right place.' Dr Somerton stalked into the middle of the apothecary shop. Lucie started at the man's voice, spilling expensive pearl powder on the wooden counter. She'd heard the door open, of course, but hadn't looked up because weighing this fine powder required all her concentration. Gascoigne's Powder was complicated to mix, with fifteen different ingredients all currently assembled on the counter before her.

'Good morning, Dr Somerton, what do you lack?' Lucie took off her spectacles, trying to keep her voice steady.

'So this is the apothecary shop they call the Three Doves,' the physician opened his arms wide, hands in their expensive pale gloves facing palm up. 'How any man is meant to find it I haven't the least notion, for there's no sign hanging outside.'

'Well find us you did, and I am sure it was but the work of a moment to enquire where we are since the townsfolk here need no sign to guide them to our door.'

'Indeed, and a fine little town it seems. This is my first visit here. However, since it is within riding distance of the city of Grantby I shall make Alderman Robbins, whose acquaintance I made but a moment ago, aware that I intend to serve as physician to this town in addition to the city. It is true the town lacks an attending physician, and has not the service of an apothecary?'

Lucie nodded, 'But we manage with a fine sur. . . '.

Dr Somerton spoke over her before she could explain about Mr Collins the barber-surgeon.

'I shall ride over when summoned and also make visits on the first market day of each month, I think. Ah, I see you have a small room off the shop,' he looked towards Jasper's store which had also served as his study. 'Would that be a suitable office to write up my cases and draw up prescriptions? I may even see occasional patients there. Those who would rather see me in private than at their home. It will benefit you too for you shall make up the remedies I prescribe. This will prove sufficient recompense for any inconvenience especially as your widow's portion is already ample.'

This last appeared to be a statement rather than a question. Lucie bit her lip as she wondered at the doctor's forwardness and the speed at which he appeared to be formulating this plan. She swallowed an urge to tell him that between herself, Mary Thorne, and Timothy Collins the barber-surgeon, Tupingham did very nicely for care of the body, but stayed her tongue. Watching him stalk around her shop, she suddenly shivered as a cold wave travelled down her spine. He was come for Prudence. It was the only reason he would be here. Lucie's mind raced as she stood rooted to the spot, following him with her eyes only, but the physician seemed perfectly at ease. He paced the shop, examining the shelves.

Lucie was pleased she had the counter to grasp as she took a moment to consider the man before her. Tall and spare, he was approaching the ninth climacteric age of sixty-three at a guess, she thought. He was immaculately dressed in a frock coat of deep blue with a matching vest and lace collar. He wore a mid-length periwig under his hat, made from soft-grey coloured hair. Her fingers turned white as they gripped the wooden edge of the counter.

'The use of the Three Doves was not the purpose of your journey, I'll warrant Dr Somerton.' She tried to steady the tremor in her voice as she continued. 'But if you wish to engage in business of the type you propose you will need to make the necessary arrangements with the town councillors. I only agreed to keep the shop open temporarily and with much reduced opening hours until an apothecary to replace my late husband can be engaged.'

A look of amusement lit up the physician's face, increasing Lucie's ire.

'However, since you propose to use it, I might as well show you the storeroom,' she said, forcing her reluctant feet to move. 'This way.' He ignored her and Lucie found herself hovering midway between the counter and the storeroom.

'How goes the Potton girl? She is recovered I take it?'

It took all Lucie's will not to let her knees buckle. As much as she knew the question was coming, it still filled her with dread.

'It is not so clear, I fear,' she said, pleased her voice remained steady.

'How so?'

'She had a setback, and a fever that burned for three days last week. Mary, that's Midwife Thorne, was afeared for the maid's life and didn't leave her side for two days and nights.'

'Did you send for assistance?'

'Of course. Mister Collins the chirurgeon twice let blood from her arm.'

How dare he question my care, Lucie thought, walking purposely back to the security of her counter. She, Jasper and the chirurgeon had worked hand-in-hand for decades for the people of Tupingham.

'She is recovered now?' Dr Somerton pressed. 'No doubt your remedies here helped.'

Lucie bit her lip again; he needn't try and mollify me, she thought.

'I was pleased to do what I could, Sir. I undertook to care for the lass and that is what we have done.'

'Good. I am pleased to hear this.' He walked over so he was directly opposite Lucie on the other side of the counter and placed his hands on the wooden top, leaning in towards her.

'You are certain the child she bore was born without life, Widow Smith?'

'Entirely certain,' Lucie replied.

'I wondered that's all. It matters not now, except for the wench's mortal soul of course. It is most curious,' the doctor lowered his voice even though there was no-one else about and leaned further across the counter as Lucie took a half step backwards. 'I have been instructed to tell you the matter is closed. The girl is free to return to her family with no stain on her character, upon promising she and they will forever hold their peace. The Justice has determined you were mistaken when you thought you saw an abortive birth in that bundle.'

Lucie gasped. 'Who instructed you?' she demanded, spots of colour appearing on her cheeks. 'I know what I am about. I buried the child. I haven't worked as a midwife above thirty years to not know a baby when I see one.' She took a step back from the counter and his oppressive stare. 'You have papers to that effect?'

'There are no records, Widow Smith. My word should be sufficient for your purposes. I know nothing more than I convey.' The physician looked directly into Lucie's eyes, and she could see in his that he spoke the truth. 'The Justice of the Peace called me to his rooms and there I was received by Friswell, steward of Calstone Manor. I was instructed to convey this message to you personally as it is of a sensitive nature.' He cleared his throat. 'I have been given the same instruction as thou. There was a mistaken judgement and there was no child and no deflowered maid.'

'If that is so,' Lucie said, her eyes blazing, 'Dr Somerton, why is there a sick young woman up my stairs? How does the law account for this?'

'I have not the least notion but would suggest for her own sake that she accepts she was mistaken. This matter could have cost her neck, so she should consider herself fortunate. That is my last word on this sorry matter, Widow Smith.' Tipping his hat slightly, the physician turned on his heel and moved to leave the shop. 'I bid you good day. With some adjustments, these premises will suit my purposes very well. I will call again anon.'

Lucie had no chance to say more, for as the physician strode back through the shop, a goodwife with a brood of children about her skirts came through the door.

'Try not to worry, my dear, all children have worms from time to time,' she said as she escorted them back to the door, purchase made. Waving them off as cheerily as she could, Lucie locked the door, breathing a loud sigh of relief as Deb called through from the back kitchen to inform her that dinner was served.

Deb Healey had been employed as a housemaid at the Three Doves for several months. She was a good little cook, and not afraid of hard work. She was no replacement for Martha, of course. Deb could not live in as Martha had done because before she walked down High Street each morning, she was needed to work in her parents' bakery.

'How does our patient do today, Deb?' Lucie asked. She took her seat at the kitchen table, smoothing her apron down in her lap. 'I am sure it has helped her recovery to have your companionship. You are alike in age, and she must be missing her twin so.'

'She seems in fair spirits today, Widow Smith. I am just about to take this bowl up for her.'

Deb was not a curious young woman and as far as Lucie could tell, it had never crossed her mind to wonder more deeply than she had been told about the nature of Prudence's illness. She accepted that Prudence had had a hard time with an exceptionally violent flow at her first courses leading to her sickness. Mary knew more of the story, of course, but not the whole sordid mess. That would have to remain as secret as it could, she thought, clasping her hands in preparation for saying a prayer before her meal.

Lucie had scarcely lifted her spoon to her mouth when there was an urgent rattle on the shop door. Dropping her spoon onto the table, she rose to answer the call, but Deb came clattering down the stairs and shouted that she'd see who it was.

'You've been on your feet all morning, Widow Smith, sit back down,' she called as she went through to the shop. Lucie smiled to herself, what she wouldn't give to have half that girl's energy. Her smile faded when she saw the look on the face of the caller who followed Deb back into the kitchen.

'Widow Smith, is Midwife Thorne at home?' It was a rangy youth in a dirty shirt and leather breeches who she recognised as one of the tanner's sons. 'There is a mother at her time without the town walls. She is in a sorry condition. She has her pains, my Ma says, and is in need of a midwife.' He was out of breath, having run all the way to High Street.

'Mary is occupied at the shoemaker's. Dolly Barton is at her time this day too. I'll come presently. The distressed woman is at the tannery, yes? Deb, bring me my bag, would you? Mary has the chair at the Barton house, so we shall have to do without it.' Lucie looked around the kitchen, checking her bag was in its usual place beside the dresser. 'No matter. I need you to look after Prudence, Deb, and when Mary comes home if I am not returned, please bid her to come to assist me.'

As Lucie made herself ready, quickly taking a spoon or two of meat from her plate to give her strength for what she was to face, the youth, Tom Mallet, explained that the woman had a strange accent, and her husband said they were refugees from the fire in London last month.

'They've walked all the way from London,' Tom said admiringly. Lucie shook her head.

'But that is two days' ride on horse. Longer in a coach. They've walked you say?'

Tom nodded, taking Lucie's bag from her housemaid.

'Tom, you run on ahead with the bag, I shall follow as best I can. I am not as fast on my feet as I used to be, but will set off straight away. Tell your mother help is on the way.' As the tanner's lad barged out of the door, Lucie turned to Deb. 'Something about this tale sounds queer to me. Make sure Mary joins me as soon as she is able.'

Lucie stepped out into High Street and took a deep breath of air which was much cooler than it had been just a couple of short weeks ago. She hesitated just a moment on the pavement wondering if she should ask for her horse, Dapple, to be brought out from its stabling at the blacksmith's. Then she saw Dick Cobb standing looking in the shop window. The boy often passed the time taking in the sights and sounds of the High Street.

'Dick, will you let me take your arm and walk with me to the tannery without the town gate? It is a long walk for me, but together we can make it a merry one.'

Dick's face lit up. He seemed delighted to have such a task and walked alongside Lucie in good spirits the whole way. Before long the acrid smells of urine, faeces, and flesh hit their noses, and Dick coughed as the pungent odour caught the back of his throat. Lucie patted his back and bade him return to the Boar before his mother missed him. She reached into her pocket and pressed a small coin in his hand for his trouble. Inside the tanner's house a woman stood, bent slightly with one hand braced against the wall. Goodwife Mallet was rubbing her back and speaking encouragingly to her.

'Good afternoon, goodwives. It was fortunate this poor woman made it to your door before her travail began,' Lucie said brightly, untying the bow of her cape and shaking it off.

'Before you start, Widow Smith, a word please,' Goodman Mallet grabbed her arm and pulled her to one side. 'I know my wife's sent for you, but I want to know if coming from London they're like to be carrying the contagion?'

'No, no, most unlikely. The King's been back months and

we all know he'd not stay if there was a chance of the plague. No, my son tells me it is quite abated in London, even if not in the whole country. Fear not Goodman Mallet.' Lucie spoke in the practised, firm voice she'd employed at births for decades. 'Now if you'll excuse me.'

She walked over to the woman who was gripping the mantel shelf for dear life. Her young face contorted. Lucie waited next to her for the pang to abate.

'What's your name my dear? I'm Widow Smith, a midwife.'

The woman, whose tears of pain had left wet trails down her dirty, weary face, was only able to whisper in her thick accent that her name was Adela, Adela Poole, before the next pain came, and she let out an agonised scream.

'It doesn't look like I arrived a moment too soon. If your pangs are so close the baby will be here any minute.' Lucie took out a bottle of lily oil and greased her hands liberally with it.

'I need to search you, Adela. You can stay standing just as you are my dear. Goodwife can you assist me, and hold up her skirts?'

The examination took only moments, for the child was ready to be born. Adela grunted as Lucie removed her hand. 'We need to get you into the bed chamber right away.'

The bed was in an alcove off the main room and was a humble one. It was apparent that whoever normally slept in it lay directly on the rough linen case of the straw mattress without sheets. One filthy bolster ran the length of the head end.

'This is the lads' bed. You know how boys are. They sleep here, and our 'prentice, and a brace of dogs,' Goody Mallet looked down in shame, and suggested that Adela would be more comfortable in the Mallet's best bed on the next floor. 'You know the bed, Widow Smith. You've lain me on it more than once,' she said with a chuckle. Lucie caught the terror in the young mother's eyes, which had widened into dishes at the thought of climbing the stairs to the upper floor in her condition.

'Pray look inside my bag, Goody Mallet. There's a pair of sheets at the bottom and some clouts. We will be perfectly well accommodated in our current situation, and I am sure Adela here is grateful for your hospitality,' Lucie smiled, noting the slight relaxation on Adela's face. Then Adela bent over screaming, as the next pain wracked her whole body.

An hour later, Lucie came out to the kitchen wiping her hands on a clout. She smiled at the guilty look on Tom Tanner's face as she caught him red handed helping himself to some pottage straight from a pot hanging in the grate.

'Don't mind me, Tom. Pray go and find Goodman Poole and tell him he has a new daughter, born a little too soon but lusty enough, and his wife does well.'

Lucie stayed on at the tannery a while, taking a cup of beer which had to stand in for the groaning ale traditionally served after a happy delivery. The tanner's wife broke into a fruit cake she had been saving and asked her daughter Cissy to hand it round to everyone.

'We weren't expecting to be celebrating this morning, but here we are,' the tanner said.

'You're a good man, and you too Goodwife. When I think of the story Adela told me while I was settling her. No wonder her pains wracked her so. She's exhausted, the poor thing.'

'Aye it is a terrible business, to lose your home like they and lots of others like 'em have.'

'Simon told me there are thousands displaced. Living under canvas without the city walls. My heart goes out to them,' Lucie said.

'Makes me feel a bit guilty that we're sitting here enjoying this cake and ale,' Goodwife Mallet said. Her sons had no such compunctions and were using licked fingers to pick up every crumb from the plates and table.

'No, us not celebrating a new life would not benefit them. We should pray for their relief. Perhaps we could see if

Reverend Archer might have a collection to send to the camps,' Lucie suggested.

'We've nothing to spare, like most round here. The Pooles are welcome under my roof for as long as they have need, but we won't be able to do the like if there's a load more homeless on the road following.'

Sitting precariously on the tanner's horse while Tom led it a short time later, Lucie gripped the reins tightly. The tanner didn't have a side saddle, so she had to make the best of sitting awkwardly with her legs astride the wide horse. Anything was better than trudging back to the Three Doves on foot.

'This day took an unexpected turn, Tom,' she said with a smile. 'Your parents are good people, offering refuge to the Pooles like that.'

'Well, we've not got much but we have a roof. Not many'd want to sleep under it with the stink of our trade,' Tom laughed.

'I'm sure they are most grateful. Imagine if Goodwife Poole had had her little maid on the road, or in those dreadful camps.'

'My father reckons he had his wits about him getting her out of there, that Poole.'

Lucie thought of the little tablet of new soap in her pocket. Francis Poole had produced it as she was leaving.

'A soap boiler by trade, he told me,' Lucie said to Tom.

'Aye.'

The conversation petered out as the young lad bowed his head and concentrated on leading the horse. Lucie smiled to herself despite her discomfort on the horse, guessing Tom had come to the end of his desire to make small talk with a woman old enough to be his grandmother. Thank goodness I am nothing like his grandame, she thought, remembering the woman who'd been too fond of the liquor and in her cups the night his little sister was born. Funny to think Cissy Mallet was the last baby she'd attended at the tannery before this one. Suddenly, she felt herself falling.

'Help, Tom!' Lucie's voice was high, but Tom had noticed and grabbed her leg, heaving her back into the seat.

'My fault, sorry. I was just lost in an old memory for a second.' Lucie didn't want to share the nature of the memory with her young escort. Tom's sister was left without an eye because of her drunken grandame's rough handling of his mother in her delivery. Concentrate, Lucie Smith, she reprimanded herself.

As the horse turned onto the cobbles of High Street, with the shop windows lit up with candles and lamps, she could just make out a light in the window of the Three Doves halfway up the street. Deb must've lit it to light her home, for the Three Doves only opened in the mornings nowadays, and certainly not when Lucie wasn't home. How thoughtful she was. Lucie smiled to herself.

'Let me down here Tom. I don't need escorting to the very door.'

'If you're sure? Poole gave me a penny to see you home safe.'

'Quite sure. Goodman Poole paid me in full for my service too. I'm ashamed to say I thought as refugees, they would have no money, but of course they were forced out by the conflagration, not poverty.'

Tom made light work of lifting the midwife down and onto the street. The horse whinnied as if relieved to be free from its awkwardly seated burden.

'Here Tom, let me add another penny to your purse,' she reached under her apron to her own purse. 'You'll have another when you return the linen I left at the tannery with Goodwife Poole to the Three Doves. No rush, she needs to rest these next few days.'

Lucie had a swing in her step as she walked up High Street. This afternoon had been quite a tonic. And how she was going to enjoy telling Mary about her afternoon, and the story of the

Pooles naming their little maid. Adela had looked up with the babe in her arms and held her out for her father to meet her, whispering 'Ma petite Marguerite'.

'Mes belles filles,' Francis had beamed as he took hold of the infant. What a proud father he had made.

'Welcome Marguerite, but I think it prudent you grow up with an English name outside the house. Daisy, it is. Perfect like her mother.'

The couple had shared a chuckle together, but Adela had caught Lucie's quizzical look and laughed before explaining that this was the same name.

'She will be Marguerite to her maman but Daisy to her father.'

That's a moment that'll stay with me for a long time, Lucie thought, as she turned into the ginnel at the side of the Three Doves.

Chapter Seven

Lucie stepped back over her threshold the next afternoon, shaking out her wet cloak. Despite being soaked she was cheered from visiting new mothers Adela Poole at the tannery and Dolly Barton who Mary had delivered of a lusty son late yesterday. Both mothers and babies were doing very well, and she'd called into the rectory on her way home and arranged to take the infants to All Hallows on the morrow for their baptisms. It'd been some time since she'd last had the privilege of standing in place of the mother at the font but tomorrow she and Mary would go together to perform that office.

'That's better,' Lucie said to herself as she settled in her armchair in front of the dancing flame in the hearth, feeling its warmth wash over her. Those two babies were born into quite different lives with one a homeless refugee and one in the security of the shoemakers, she thought, as she bent to untie her pattens, but both had loving parents. As she sat back up a pair of neatly darned stockings on the table caught her eye. Deb has been busy, Lucie thought. She's getting better too, that work is much neater than usual.

'Deb, are you still here? Mary?' The candles were lit and the fire well banked, but it was past four o'clock and Deb had normally left for home by now. Lucie got up from her chair to go and pour herself a drink.

'Prudence, do you require anything?' she called up the stairs, puzzled that none of the women were answering her calls. Prudence must be sleeping. I haven't the strength to climb the stairs to check. Not after a morning serving in the shop and an afternoon on Dapple, Lucie thought, rubbing her sore lower back.

'Just me for a cup of beer,' Lucie announced to the empty room. 'Then I'd best get the chickens locked up for the night since it's getting dark. But first a minute or two in the chair,' she smiled ruefully as she snuggled into her favourite seat and cupped her drink. Lucie and Mary had stayed up late into the night last evening, swapping stories of the deliveries they'd both attended. Then Lucie had confided almost the whole of Prudence's story to her former deputy. What choice did she have? After Dr Somerton's visit decisions needed to be made quickly, and without Jasper to talk to and Simon still at the Manor, Lucie needed Mary's counsel. Still, she'd not been able to tell of his Lordship's guilt.

'Mother, wake up!' Lucie felt Simon's hand gently shaking her by the shoulder.

'Son, whatever is wrong?' she asked, squinting her eyes as she tried to focus.

As she roused in her chair, she saw the kitchen was filled with several people.

'I was riding home from the Manor when I passed Hester Potton walking in the same direction. I pulled the horse up in order to offer my services and she rode here behind me. Hester, please tell Widow Smith what you told me,' Simon urged the girl forwards from the shadows in the kitchen. Mary was home now too, Lucie noticed, and it was clear from her expression that something was amiss.

'If you please Widow Smith, I need to speak to my sister urgently. My family have gone. That man who came with you when you took our Pru, he came back and said my father must relinquish his tenancy, no matter that he has paid all that is due in a timely way for two decades.' The girl was shuffling from foot to foot as she spoke, clearly agitated. 'There was this long, harsh meeting between them. My father and brothers, and the man I mean. They've given him the lease on a new farm several day's ride east, and some money. But they made it clear he had no choice but to agree. They're left already. The men are walking the cattle and my mother and sisters are in the cart with everything we could carry on it and the chickens.'

Hester seemed to run out of breath at that point, giving Lucie a moment to absorb this intelligence.

'You've been sent to collect Prudence and follow along?' Lucie asked, easing herself up.

'No, Widow Smith. They've abandoned her. I was in the cart too but waited until my mother was occupied with one of the little ones. Then I jumped to the ground while it was moving. I waited in the hedgerow until they were out of sight and began to walk towards Tupingham. I need to speak with my sister.'

'Mary, could you go up and see if Prudence is awake please? We will have to break this news to her gently,' Lucie said.

'I am afraid I cannot. I arrived at the Three Doves at the same time as Mister Smith and Hester. I've been out looking for Prudence; she's disappeared.'

'I beg your pardon?' Lucie frowned. 'She's not left the house in over a fortnight and should not be out alone. Why didn't Deb stop her?' Lucie waved the stockings that were on the table. 'Too busy with these? That makes no sense,' she said with a shake of her head.

'Prudence had got up and dressed in a suit loaned from one of the Healey girls. Deb's mother brought it over just after you went out.'

'That's my sister's work,' Hester said, looking at the stockings.

'Yes, Prudence offered to help Deb. You know how poor a sewer the girl is. I left them to pay a quick visit to Goodwife Higgs in Warley Lane. One of the children has a fever, you see.'

She had been out for just over an hour, delivering some medicaments.

'I explained to Martha that I couldn't tarry this day for I needed to get back for Prudence. I met Deb on High Street, as I came home. She said Prudence was well enough and was working with her needle in the kitchen.'

'Excuse me,' Hester interrupted. 'Why would Prudence leave without telling anyone?'

'I think Mary and I can explain that, and Simon you need to hear this as well, then we shall have to organise a search. Prudence must not be out on her own and in this weather too.'

Lucie absentmindedly ran her hand across her brow, the kitchen seemed hot and crowded, and she had a headache coming on. Sitting back down, Lucie explained about the visit from Dr Somerton and how she'd been informed that there were no charges to be pressed. She looked up at Mary, who took the hint and carried on the story.

'I spoke to Prudence this afternoon. We took a turn around the garden, and she had a little colour in her cheeks for the first time since the day she came. She soon lost that when I told her she was free to return home, on condition that this whole summer be forgotten. Then she sobbed as if her young heart were breaking,' Mary sat down in the armchair opposite Lucie. 'I shouldn't have left her. This is my fault.'

'Hush, it is certainly not,' Lucie reached over and patted Mary's arm. 'Like you say, she was darning with Deb.'

Simon had clearly heard enough. 'I'll organise a search. I'll go to the blacksmith's and get his lads to ready the horses at the stables. My horse from the Manor is still tied up at the trough. We should have maybe half a dozen men out very soon. Hester, do you know where she might have headed?'

Hester shook her head. 'My sister knows the town quite well from our visits to market, but I have no notion where she could be. I'm coming to look for her too.'

'No, you stay here. She will need you when we bring her home, as surely we will,' Simon said.

'Yes, my son is right. Come sit down and I'll get you a cup of beer. You've had a shock,' Lucie grabbed the arms of her chair to heave herself up. She could tell by her son's tone that he was speaking with more confidence than he felt.

'Here have this chair, Hester,' Mary said. 'I'm joining the search.'

Lucie and Hester tried to keep busy while they waited. Hester offered to catch up on the heap of linen waiting to be ironed and Lucie showed her where the blanket they placed on the table while ironing was, then helped her pull the dried linen from the rack hanging from the ceiling. She found a paring knife in the dresser and sat at the end of the kitchen table peeling some root vegetables to add to the pottage pan.

'When everyone comes back in with your sister, I shall have many hungry mouths to feed I expect,' Lucie said, trying to keep her tone light.

The door slowly creaked. Hester didn't notice but Lucie was attuned to the squeaks and groans of the Three Doves and felt her heart rate speed up. Let it be good news, she thought.

'Oh Dick Cobb, it's you.' The lad hovered in the doorway. Lucie could see the rope in his hand, which must surely mean that enormous wolfhound, Lad, from the Boar Inn, wasn't far behind. 'What can I do for you Dick?'

Dick came into the kitchen followed by Lad and tugged hard at Lucie's sleeve. 'Where do you want me to go Dick? I can't leave the Three Doves at present.'

Dick's tugging became more urgent, and he hopped from foot to foot as if frustrated he couldn't make himself understood. Lad seemed to sense Dick's distress and joined in with a loud howl.

'Very well. Let me put on my pattens and cloak and you can show me what's ado. Hester, I am sorry to leave you, but it seems I am needed. Please do not add to the confusion by leaving here. I will find out what troubles Dick and hurry back.'

Moments later, Lucie found herself walking in the direction of All Hallows, struggling to keep pace with Dick and the wolfhound on the cobbles.

'Why are we going to the church, Dick?' Even though she knew there would be no answer, Lucie could not stay her worried tongue.

As the pair walked up the churchyard path, Dick's eyes widened and he pointed to the porch. Lad started barking. Lucie's eyes strained ahead, as she peered through the lowering dusk and the light drizzle. Then suddenly she saw what Dick was showing her. A figure curled in the corner of the porch near the door. Lucie's pace quickened. As they approached she saw it was Prudence, icy cold and insensible.

'Oh Dick, you are a good boy,' she fell to her knees in the porch and checked Prudence's pulse. The girl was frozen, lying on the cold flags in damp clothes. 'This poor maid needs to be carried to the Three Doves immediately. Will you help me?' Lucie looked up at Dick, and held out her hand so he could help her back to her feet.

'Now, can you lift Prudence, Dick? We must act in all haste. Here, let me show you.'

Lucie bent and rolled Prudence over, and picked up the girl's feet, indicating to Dick to do the like at the girl's shoulders. Dick surprised Lucie by reaching down and lifting Prudence clean up by himself. He was remarkably robust for one so undersized. Lucie stepped back so he could adjust the maid in his arms.

'Prudence needs to be warmed up with all haste. God forbid but she might have caught her death.' Lucie fretted all the way back to the Three Doves. 'It is a mercy you and Lad came across her and thought to fetch me. You shall be well rewarded.' She ignored the curious looks from shopkeepers leaning through their serving hatches, and even the offers of help that were called out. All she could think of was getting Prudence safely inside the warmth of her kitchen. For once, the bad weather was in her favour and the High Street was relatively quiet.

As they sat around the kitchen table later that evening, Lucie reflected that it was the second time in just a few weeks that she, Simon and Mary had sat together to try to determine the best course for the Potton girls. The first time they had only one twin in their charge, now the pair were both tucked up in Mary's bed. When she had been revived and warmed through, poor Prudence told them how she'd been taken with a desire to sit in the church to be in God's presence and seek divine guidance. When she got there, she'd not been able to bring herself to open the door and go in. She wasn't sure if she needed to be churched after the miscarriage and suddenly became paralysed with fear for her immortal soul. The last thing she remembered was standing with her hand on the large ring latch of the ancient door.

Mary tipped the cooked sausages from the pan onto a dish on the table, and the three ate in companionable silence for a few minutes. Lucie put down her knife.

'I had thought to keep Prudence here as a new housemaid, if she had been agreeable. Deb's a pleasure, and her work is most thorough, but I know the Healeys can hardly spare her from the bakery, and labouring there before working a day here is not fair to the lass. Prudence's skills in laundry work are ideal in our trade, Mary, but we can't afford or provide occupation for two maids.'

'Mightn't Farmer Potton not return to collect Hester? It won't have taken them any time to have guessed to where she fled,' Mary asked. But before Lucie had chance to answer, Simon interjected, his brow furrowed.

'It is a terrible thing for a father to have driven out his daughters like that Mother. It's no secret that Father and

I struggled to stay on good terms, but he would never have treated me like that, I'm certain.' He speared his last piece of sausage with more force than was necessary. 'While the Three Doves is filling up with waifs and strays, I must beg you find room for one more.'

What now? Lucie's stomach twisted.

'I cannot go back to the Manor. Lord Calstone is returned and in a foul humour too. He raged when he saw me attending to Sir Robert and demanded I leave.' Lucie caught the cloud pass across her son's face, and at the same moment had a realisation about how the events of the past couple of days had come to pass.

'Lord Calstone must have intervened in person with the Justice in Grantby and made him halt the investigation. Presumably a purse was given or other promise made in exchange.' She paused, giving her company a moment to absorb her conclusion. 'The despicable man was doubtless saving his own skin, not the girl's.' She pushed her plate away, shaking her head. 'I am pleased Lady Calstone is at their estate in the North and not at the Manor while this disgrace is happening.' Simon nodded, and Mary looked anxiously from one to the other.

'Yes, Mother, that is the conclusion I reached too. I'm afraid that since losing everything in the London fire, my purse is too empty to fund lodgings at the Boar Inn, or I would not impose like this.'

'Simon, after tonight, you should have my chamber and I will take a room at the Park Street boarding house if they have one. This is your home, and it is only proper,' Mary rose and started clearing the dishes.

'No,' Lucie replied. 'This night we will make do as best we can and then tomorrow we will arrange a bed for Simon in my chamber. In the cellar there is the folding screen we used to partition the shop in the old days before the storeroom was built on the back, and there is a bedstead too.' Lucie reminded Mary that their late neighbour Henry had bequeathed this to her for the day she married. Mary had nursed him with such care in his last days.

'We have ample linen. Who knows how long any of us shall remain at the Three Doves, for we only have but a temporary lease until a new apothecary is found for Tupingham, but until we are turned out, or matters change, we shall all muddle along.' Goodness knows what Jasper would've made of all these comings and goings, she thought. She took the key from its hook in the kitchen and went through into the apothecary shop. There she unlocked Jasper's storeroom. On a shelf in the corner was a pile of woollen blankets and bed tyes. Taking the larger of the tyes, Lucie stuffed several blankets inside and carried another over her arm.

'There, Simon,' she said on her return to the kitchen. 'This mattress will make for a tolerable repose for you in front of the hearth tonight. Tomorrow, we will begin to determine how we are to proceed. Now to bed, come Mary.'

Chapter Eight

Lucie was putting the finishing touches to a belt for the itch. She was refreshing it with some of the paste she had watched Jasper blend countless times. This saved the customer the cost of a whole new linen belt, and so was a staple part of her work in the Three Doves. She folded the belt over itself before handing it to her grateful customer. Waiting in the queue next was the postmaster's boy, who handed Lucie a pile of letters. She gave him a coin, then slipped the letters in her pocket under her apron to read at dinner time when the shop closed.

'Anything for me?' Simon poked his head around the doorway of the storeroom. He was filling his days sorting through his father's things. If Dr Somerton was to use the room from time to time, they were all in agreement that he would do so without valuable apothecary equipment at his disposal. Lucie had put off clearing the space. It was piled high, not just with equipment and apparatus, but a lifetime of papers. Jasper had known where everything was and had a system he alone could fathom, but little by little Simon was making progress.

'I didn't look through it all but think not,' Lucie replied, turning back to what she hoped was the last customer of the morning. Goodman Trotte had requested a cordial for his elderly mother. Lucie put the one shilling payment into the money box and walked out with the goodman to lock the shop door. Another day supplying the service that her late husband no longer could to the townsfolk of Tupingham was done, she reflected. She drew the bolt and turned the key.

When Lucie went through to the kitchen at dinner time, she saw a striking portrait on a scrap of paper. Picking it up, she saw it was drawn on the back of part of a printed sheet. It was of a young dark-skinned woman, with piercing black eyes which had an intriguing glint in them.

'Who's this?' Lucie asked.

'Kate, Mother. Kate who perished in the London fire,' Simon replied. 'I was thinking about her and just started scribbling with my pencil.'

'It's beautiful. She was beautiful. Look girls, isn't this lovely? Simon has such a talent,' Lucie's cheeks flushed warm as she showed the portrait around.

'It is not good enough to do her justice. She had such wit, and her tales were the tallest and the best.' Simon smiled. 'She told us her ancestor came to England from Africa as a trumpeter in the court of old King Henry. Her family legend says there is a painting in one of the palaces of the court musicians with him drawn in. She said her family swore by it.'

Lucie smiled too, and squeezed her son's arm. 'She sounds like good company, son. I will pray for her. May I keep this sketch?'

Simon nodded and wiped his left eye with the back of his hand. Lucie gave him a moment as she set the table, placing a pewter plate and wooden spoon down for each of the family. When she was finished, Deb carried a pot of steaming stew over from the fire and carefully placed it on a pad of linen so it didn't scorch the table.

'Take care, it is very hot,' she tucked her linen cloth in her apron. 'Come on you two.' Deb called the Pottons from the scullery where they'd been folding sheets. With the family seated, Lucie said a short prayer of thanks and then signalled for Deb to begin spooning out their meal.

'Do you think of the fire often, Son?' Lucie asked in a low voice.

'How could I not? I still have night terrors, I don't mind admitting it.'

'I don't think I have told you; we have others who experienced the fire staying in town. A number of folk fleeing the terrible camps have found our town, but the first was a young family. The wife was at her time. She delivered in the tannery.'

'That cannot have been a pleasant experience, Mother.'

'They have been well accommodated there, while the goodwife, a French woman called Adela, recovers.'

'A French woman?' Simon's interest seemed to pique.

'Yes, what of it? She's a lovely woman. They are soap boilers. It is they who supplied that lavender soap I have in my chamber.'

'He's English? No wonder they fled London,' Simon went on to explain about the trouble the fire's aftermath had caused. The suspicion and unrest. Dutch and French nationals had been targeted especially, as rumours about who started the fire ran around the city. Colour rose on his cheeks as he told how he'd seen the Duke of York personally intervene as one foreign family had been surrounded by a chanting mob. Prudence Potton's eyes went wide and her face paled as she listened to Simon's impassioned words. 'The Duke said he'd have the crowd whipped if they didn't disperse.' Some spittle escaped the corner of Simon's mouth as his choler rose.

'Oh, the poor family. Like you say, it is little wonder they removed as soon as they were able. What is this country coming to?' Lucie's eyes felt dewy at the thought of the family's plight. 'After all we have experienced, you'd think we'd have learned to show some Christian compassion.'

After the family had finished their midday meal, Prudence and Hester jumped up and began clearing the table. Deb also rose, lifted the cooking pot, and declared that there was enough stew left to fill a pie for tomorrow's meal. When the table was cleared, and only she and Simon remained seated, Lucie took the letters out of her pocket.

'Ah, Simon, there *is* a letter for you, I'm sorry. One of two from the Manor. One for you and one for me.' She passed Simon's over with a raised eyebrow. She called to Deb. 'Could you run and get my spectacles please? I must have left them on the counter in the shop.'

Simon tore open the seal on his letter.

'Oh Mother, Sir Robert writes that he has a daughter,' Simon grinned. 'He's received word from my Lady Calstone that Lady Eleanor has been delivered of a lusty maid.'

'What a blessing, a sister for little Charles. This happy news will have helped improve Sir Robert's humours and so aid his recovery, I'm sure. Does he say what they have named her?'

'Yes, I have just got to that, she has been baptised as Barbara Cecilia,' Simon let out a low whistle, shaking his head. Lucie frowned, unable to fathom Simon's reaction.

'I sincerely hope Lady Eleanor has not named her for the Countess of Castlemaine. Her Christian name is Barbara,' he explained catching Lucie's uncomprehending look. 'Lady Eleanor will have served alongside Castlemaine as one of Her Majesty's ladies, but Castlemaine has not let her position stop her from giving the King a nursery full of lusty children.'

Lucie felt a wave of disgust run through her. She could just picture Jasper's glowering face at mention of the loose morals of the court.

'Well, her second name is after Lady Calstone,' Simon said quickly, glancing at his mother.

'I just hope Lady Eleanor had an easier time than she did with Charles. It was a wearisome three days for the girl, if I remember rightly.'

Simon's brows furrowed as he read the rest his letter. 'Sir Robert sends his gratitude to you, Mother. He says he doubts not that you saved his life and says he will pay any sum you request in respect of your time and service.' He paused, his frown deepening. 'He has left the Manor.'

'He's well enough to ride north?' Lucie glanced up from her own letter, surprised.

'He is not headed to meet his daughter, but to Calstone House in London. He cannot be in the same residence as his father. I do understand that, but he should not be travelling yet.' Simon's jaw tensed. 'I must go after him.'

'Now is the time for you to be thinking of your own future, Simon. It is not seemly to be chasing about the countryside.' Lucie chided him in a low voice. 'Sir Robert is a grown man and father of two. You should trust your friend knows what he's about.' Simon's face flushed, and he hastily changed the subject.

'What does your letter from the Manor say?'

Lucie offered it over to Simon to read for himself. It was from Friswell the steward, and had contained three crowns. She placed the shiny silver coins in a row on the kitchen table as Simon read. Her son let out a long sigh.

'So you are to take this sum in payment for your services to Sir Robert *and* for the tabling of Prudence Potton. Sir Robert clearly was not informed about this settlement, for he has just undertaken to pay you himself.' Simon's voice rose with his indignation. 'Is it not customary to await receipt of a bill informing you of the fee payable? Friswell is too high handed for his own good. You wouldn't think him a servant who walks about in green livery, dependant on the whims of his master for his authority.' Simon's eyes glistened and the choler he'd displayed earlier was rising once more. 'And there is more ... an instruction, if you please.'

'Simon, hush, we will discourse on this later with Mary,' Lucie lowered her voice as the Potton twins came in from the garden with a basket of dried linen between them.

'Of course,' he gulped down his ire, his lips thin as he asked who the third letter was from.

Lucie smiled and her face softened. 'This is in Alice Wallis's hand. A treat, I'm sure. I think I will take it to my chamber to read where the light is better, and I can enjoy it at my leisure. I will let you know how she does, Son.'

Simon stood up, declaring he was going to Hearne's Coffeehouse to read the latest news about the London fire. He held the kitchen door open for the Potton twins.

'Girls, leave the ironing for another day, please. Take advantage of this fine afternoon to take a turn about the town for air,' Lucie said. Her voice trembled. Unseen by the company, under the table, her hands were so tightly knitted together that they'd turned white. She needed the young women out of the house. Looking back from the doorway, Simon searched his mother's face questioningly, but she answered with a small shake of her head. How could she tell him that the sight of the girls sorting linen next to him in the kitchen of the Three Doves had given her a wave of nausea and grief so strong it made her want to run outside and scream until the pain abated? The realisation that this could have been her everyday life if Sarah and Hannah had lived to reach the twins' age brought a pain beyond endurance. Using all her will, Lucie steadied her breathing and continued. 'Look in the tin box in the dresser. Take ten shillings. Yes, that drawer Hester, towards the back. Go and see if there is any German serge to be had. Get two yards each. The seamstress generally has fabric for sale, and you both are in need of a new skirt. Prudence's must be returned to the Healeys before long, and yours, Hester, is now short on you.'

'Come girls, I'll show you out,' Simon must have noticed the glance that passed between the girls and like Lucie, had sensed they were about to object. He was clearly bemused by what he had just witnessed. 'Mother, I'll stay at home, for you don't look at all well.'

'No, please, you go too and divert yourself with the company at the coffeehouse. I am quite well.' Lucie had an overwhelming longing to be alone. As soon as she heard the door bang behind them, she rose unsteadily from the table and poured herself a cup of beer. As she turned towards the stairs the basket of linen again caught her eye. Before she knew what she was doing, she swiped at it and knocked it clean off the table. The sight of the scattered cloths on the stone flags brought her back to her senses. She took a deep swig of her beer, overcome by a wave of remorse. Through a veil of tears, she knelt down, ignoring the throb as her stiff knees protested, and picked up the linen and righted the basket. Have a care, Lucie, she chided herself, using the edge of the table to haul herself up. Slowly, she climbed the stairs.

Settled at her desk near the window of her chamber, Lucie made herself comfortable in her chair, pulling her shawl more tightly around herself. She straightened her cap, tucking in some escaped strands of grey hair, waiting for her breathing to settle. Pushing her spectacles up her nose, she tore open Alice's letter, feeling the smile arrive on her face as she did so. A lovely long missive, oh how she'd enjoy hearing Alice's news.

My dearest Widow Smith,

I thank you for sending me word that Simon is home. I was pleased to learn he's safe, and you can be assured that he remains in my prayers. I have been following the newssheets, it seems much of that City is raised to the ground. Does Simon have plans yet for his future? My husband bids I send his humble duty to you and says he will be pleased to help raise finance for Simon to rebuild his business if that is his wish. He has many associates in London.

For my part, I have two pieces of news for you. The first concerns Dr Somerton who I believe you to be acquainted with. He has recently set up as physician in Grantby and is already much called for. On a separate sheet within this letter is an exact copy of the entry in my case notes of a woman I delivered recently at which the good doctor was also in attendance, at my request.

Lucie put the letter down and turned to the supplement.

I was called to the home of Goodwife S__ across St Philip's Plain behind the cathedral. She had been in pain a night and a day, of her first child, but when I touched her, I found her only just at the beginning of her labour. I gave her an anodyne that night and returned home. When I saw her again the next day, I found little alteration, and so I left the same medicine to abate the pain and told her to send for me if the pain got worse. They sent for me again the following day, but her labour was still not yet advanced enough for my assistance. The day after that her pangs were worse so I touched her again and found the womb open the breadth of a sixpence. The child lay very high, which surprised me as she had been in pain for four days now. She told me she'd been in violent pain from one of the clock in the morning and it was now about five. I endeavoured to dilate the Womb, tho' to little purpose, nor could I get the child's head off the share bone. I suspected that although the child was head down, it was still presenting wrongly. I asked the husband of the woman to send for the physician for I wished to reliquish my position being unsure how I was going to achieve a happy delivery in this case.

Dr Somerton arrived about six of the clock but the woman would by no means suffer him to touch her. I then lay her across the bed pillows and a bolster to give the more liberty to her belly to lie hollow. I searched her again and found as I suspected that the child's head was facing upwards. It was a prodigious long-headed child. I despaired of delivering this child without instruments, and again pleaded with her to allow the physician to take my place. The doctor spoke encouragingly to her, but she would not submit. Dr Somerton and I had a private conversation and it was decided I should try to turn the child to bring it forth feet first, as we feared we could not deliver it alive by the head. It was a very difficult operation which took about fifteen minutes and all my strength, but eventually I found a foot and tugged the child round. Half an hour later the child was born alive.

Lucie put the sheet down and picked the letter back up. Alice was seeking Lucie's opinion of the way she managed the delivery. Lucie resolved to write back about the tales she'd heard of women who had been ruined when incompetent surgeons or unskilled midwives had forced babies out with hooks and the child destroyed. She was entirely satisfied that Alice with, it seemed, good counsel from Dr Somerton, had taken the right course and shown great forbearance. Now she could read on and learn what Alice's second piece of intelligence was.

She'd barely finished reading when she heard the Potton twins' chatter from down the stairs. Lucie pushed back her chair across the wooden boards to go down and see if their trip was a success. The girls were excitedly talking about cutting the coarse but warm-looking red woollen cloth they'd bought and were showing it to Deb, who had stopped scouring the kitchen table with sand to look up.

'I didn't hear the door, girls. But it looks like your outing was purposeful.'

'That would be because I had the door open when they came back, Widow Smith,' Deb explained. 'I'd just popped into the garden to give the hens the boiled peelings.'

‘That’s quite alright, Deb,’ Lucie smiled. ‘The ladies are well, I hope.’

‘They are as noisy and greedy as ever,’ Deb chuckled.

‘It looks as if we shall shortly be able to return the clothes your mother kindly supplied for Prudence, Deb,’ Lucie said with a smile. ‘It does my heart good to hear you girls chatter and see Prudence with colour in her cheeks at long last.’

Lucie’s burst of passion earlier had abated and she was feeling much calmer.

‘Come ladies, there is no time like the present. Mary is still out but we four can start cutting out, and we shall have two new skirts in no time. If we go through to the empty shop, we can lay the serge out on the floor there.’

Lucie looked over the supper table that evening much more contented than she had been in the same seat some hours earlier. The table was somewhat merrier than of late, with the Potton girls having benefitted from their outing.

‘Jemima was throwing her hoop in the air and baby Jasper giggled so to watch it,’ Mary told them. ‘He’s such a sweet baby, but a handful. The whole time I dandled him he was jiggling.’

‘He reminds me of Oliver, our little brother. He’s four now but was the same as a baby, wasn’t he, Hester?’

Lucie and Mary exchanged happy looks. Prudence had joined in the conversation for the first time unbidden.

Mary had been to the Higgs’s cottage for the afternoon. She and Martha still maintained the close friendship they’d formed over the years that they were bedmates at the Three Doves. Mary had been an apprentice midwife and Martha was the housemaid. Mary walked there whenever she had a free afternoon, and always had funny tales of the children’s play to recount when she came home.

‘I expect they weren’t at their boisterous games long before their father chased them out of doors,’ Lucie commented.

Anthony worked at his loom all the day long in the one-roomed cottage.

'Martha had them playing outside before Anthony could get cross,' Mary said.

'She has taken to motherhood like it is all she has ever known,' Lucie replied. Pride softened her voice.

'I never had our Martha down for a wife and mother,' Simon slathered butter on a hunk of bread. 'I know not why, since she mothered all us Smiths for so many years, didn't she?'

Lucie had another nostalgic moment, watching her son sitting at the head of the table, giving off the same aroma of coffee and tobacco as Jasper had done on many an afternoon throughout their long marriage. Although his father had better table manners, she thought, smiling fondly.

'Not just that, but she said that since having Jasper, she'd reflected how if she had her time again, she might now have considered midwifery.' Mary said. 'She feels she has perhaps been wrong to dismiss the notion all these years.'

'Good heavens above,' Lucie felt her eyes widen in surprise. 'That is not something I thought I'd ever hear. Well, well.' As she reached over to cut herself a slice of cheese, she shook her head.

'Could you pass the salt dish, Simon?' Mary accepted it from him and sprinkled a little on her pickled mushrooms.

'What's the news from Hearne's, son?'

'The newssheets are full of the size of the camps outside the city walls. Thousands of souls are living under canvas and in cobbled together shacks.'

'It is a double tragedy for them,' Lucie sighed. 'They've lost their homes and goods, and now must live like this. Something must be done.'

'I wish there was something we in Tupingham could do,' Mary said.

'I wouldn't suggest that outdoors, Mary, some of the aldermen were grumbling about the refugees who have arrived here already. The overseer of the poor has been making representations to the parish council that he needs an assistant, for his workload has risen so much. There isn't work enough in Tupingham for even our few incomers.'

'I doubt many more will arrive. The papers report families are trickling back into London town, and that means they are living several families to a room, sometimes. It's a scandal,' Simon said.

'What a calamity,' Lucie sighed again. 'We must trust in God's plan while praying for the swift relief of these poor souls. And I had better not see anyone being unwelcoming in Tupingham. I came here from Deptford as a young bride and have worked hard for the townspeople for over thirty years. No-one can say this outsider has not benefitted the town, and doubtless other incomers will do the like in time.'

Hester and Prudence jumped up as soon as Lucie stopped speaking. She hoped she hadn't unsettled them. Goodness it was like having scared kittens in the house, just when you won their trust, they became skittish again.

'Thank you, my dears,' Lucie said brightly. She was relieved that they smiled back at her in unison. The two girls made light work of taking the used pewter plates and spoons into the scullery to wash. When all was set to rights, Lucie sent the girls to their room with their sections of cloth.

'You have enough light to sew a seam each by my reckoning,' she told them. 'Take some hot coals on the shovel up with you to light a good fire. This was your first trip abroad, Prudence, and we do not want you catching a chill. You may show me your stitches in the morning, if it pleases you, but I am sure your mother taught you well and you need no instruction from me. God bless.' Lucie dismissed them.

'Sleep tight,' Mary called out.

Hester and Prudence bowed their heads and wished the family goodnight. Once their footsteps could no longer be heard, and Lucie was confident they were in their chamber up the two flights of stairs, she asked Mary to pour more ale, before summarising the letter from the steward at the Manor.

'He what?' Mary looked scandalised. Simon and Lucie exchanged glances and Simon reminded Mary that the girls would hear if she raised her voice. 'I can't believe he is telling you who may and who may not lodge in your own home, Widow Smith.'

'Well, that is just what the letter says. The three crowns are in respect of my service to Sir Robert and the tabling of Prudence Potton until the date of his letter, two days since. He says we are to turn her out and insists she makes her own way from now on. Then her name is never to be mentioned by anyone under this roof again.'

'Monstrous. Not to be borne,' Simon's lips thinned. He had read the letter at dinnertime and Lucie knew his anger had been simmering ever since. She'd seen his brow furrow whenever the Potton girls were looking away, when he did not have to keep up a sunny air for their sakes.

'It occurs to me that the Manor have no notion that Hester is here too,' Mary said.

'Quite, and that means we have some advantage at present while we determine how to proceed. But there is more intelligence which neither of you know yet.'

A candle on the table guttered and Lucie started to rise to replace it, but Simon jumped up to do it.

'Mary, I received a very long letter from Mistress Willis in Grantby. She wanted my thoughts on a recent delivery she had attended which you and I might discuss on another occasion.'

Lucie paused as what she had to say next was difficult but also confirmed as much as anything ever could that Lord Calstone was the rogue responsible for ruining and defiling the poor maid under her roof.

'Alice informs me that there is a lot of talk in Grantby about the strange behaviour of Lord Calstone on a recent visit. It seems he and the Justice of the Peace took a private dining room at The Fox, the coaching inn that Martha and I lodged in last summer, but during the course of their meal, raised voices could be heard before Lord Calstone pushed over the table with all their meat upon it, and punched the man serving them straight on the nose. It seems he was due to stay in the city over night but instead he had his chariot prepared. He thundered out of town in a foul humour.'

Lucie picked up her spectacles and took Alice's letter from her pocket. 'This accounts for why Friswell was in Grantby for the meeting with Dr Somerton. No doubt he had been sent to smooth things with the magistrate. But there is more,' she pointed to the passage in the letter. 'Alice writes describing the talk of Sir Robert's injuries, and of how I was at the Manor to nurse him, which is the occasion of her passing this intelligence on. She also says there is chatter about Farmer Potton and his family leaving abruptly and no-one knows why or where they have gone. Of course, Alice knows the Pottons a little from the markets here at Tupingham and at Grantby, and she is quick witted enough to wonder if a connection might be made between their flight and his Lordship's ill temper. It is well-known Friswell and the Justice have had several meetings.'

Mary groaned, 'His Lordship defiled Prudence? How dreadful. I'd thought it an irresponsible youth, someone working for the Calstones, not a man of quality. Oh no, no, no, the poor girl.' Tears spilled from Lucie's former deputy, causing Lucie's stomach to convulse in jabs of pain. How clumsy she was. She'd quite forgotten that she and Simon had kept their suspicions from Mary thus far. Simon let out a long, low whistle.

'It seems there is little chance of this scandal being private now, Mother. No, not because of you, Mary!' he had clearly caught the look of horror on the young midwife's face. 'But people are gossiping, and others will start to wonder at the connection between the Pottons' flight and his Lordship's temper. They will perhaps not guess rightly at what has happened but that will not stay their tongues.'

'No, and it seems my name is brought into this gossip too. It is almost more than I can bear to be subject of idle chatter again. When word reaches Grantby that the twins were lodged at the Three Doves, what then?'

Mary dried her eyes with her handkerchief and walked to the dresser to pick up the last of the day's bread.

'Widow Smith, let me make you a poultice of toast for your belly. I can see it is paining you. Why don't you retire, and I'll bring it up presently?' Mary was already slicing the bread.

'Thank you, Mary,' Simon smiled at her. 'Let's sleep on matters and discourse further on the morrow. Come, Mother, let me help you up.'

Chapter Nine

Lucie cast an admiring glance over the dinner table on which today's meal of roasted chicken with slices of neat's tongue was laid out.

'You always set out such a fine board, Mistress Archer.'

She'd become accustomed to dining with Dr Archer and his wife after the service at All Hallows each Sunday morning. The rector and his wife had provided unwavering support during her troubles last year. Now Simon was home, the invitation was naturally extended to him, and Dr Archer and he conversed about the camps of homeless families outside London.

'Thank you, Widow Smith. It is my pleasure,' Phillipa Archer said. 'The Potton twins looked very smart at the service this morning.'

'Yes, they are lovely little dressmakers. Their mother has taught them well.'

Lucie felt a pang of guilt. The Archers had done nothing but help her this past year, but Lucie could not bring herself to be entirely frank about the reasons for the twins' sudden stay at the Three Doves, and knew she needed the rector's counsel, but for now she changed the subject.

'I hear Goodman Poole has bought a disused grain store without the town walls, not far from the tannery,' she said brightly.

'Yes, he's told me all about his plans,' the rector replied. 'He is ambitious. With some careful alterations it will make a fine home for his family and a serviceable manufactory for his trade.'

'I heard in Hearne's that the council and Alderman Robbins have worked hard to negotiate approval for the plans submitted by Goodman Poole with utmost speed,' Simon added.

'I thought they were opposed to incomers?'

'Not when their trade is one which will profit the town, Widow Smith,' the rector explained. 'In any case, it is better to have two noxious trades hard by one another to save stinking out two separate parts of town.'

'That's true enough,' Lucie said. 'Could you pass some of the plum pottage, Mistress Archer? It's delicious with the meat.'

'The soap boiler is more fortunate than many in his position,' the rector said. 'I had a ride out to his premises earlier in the week, and he kindly showed me around. I learned several new names for things I'd never seen before.' The rector smiled fondly and took a sip of his wine.

'Do tell,' Simon prompted.

'It was all still tied to his cart, but there is a large bucket which he calls his leeching tub, a vast cauldron, and several diverse implements whose names and functions I do not recall, but may come back to me anon. He is a very engaging young man, I enjoyed his company. I'm sure he will do well here.'

'His wife, Adela, I think she is called. Is she of the old faith?' Mistress Archer asked.

'I brought their daughter, Daisy, to be baptised into our congregation myself,' Lucie frowned. She was not sure all this talk was helpful.

'Well that's what the Londoners who harassed her and other French folks would have thought,' Simon said.

'Then they would be wrong,' the rector's voice was firm. 'Her family came to England because they were of our faith, and uncomfortable across the Channel.'

The conversation died out as the four concentrated on their meat and waited for the awkwardness to abate. Presently Dr Archer swigged back the last of his wine and called to his servant for more. 'Goodman Poole told me a little of their flight, while I was there. The older child and his big-bellied wife had to walk alongside the cart with him for there was only room enough for the two-year-old to squeeze in alongside the tools and a small number of household items: all their food and apparel, gathered in haste.'

'How awful,' Lucie said. 'It's but little wonder the child she carried came early now I hear this. I must confess, with all the haste at the tanners I had not realised there was yet more family. I saw the infant on his father's lap, of course. Are they staying with the tanner still?'

'No, indeed. They are removed to rooms on Park Street while their new home is made ready. I believe his horse is at the new premises. He hopes to start up his trade almost immediately, but his wife is still abed and so he is obliged to tend his brood until she is on her feet.' Spearing a piece of tongue with his knife, the rector continued, 'I am in full agreement with the Council that the Pooles will make a fine addition to our town.'

Lucie felt a warm contentment at this news, but her joy was short-lived as Mistress Archer returned to the topic of the Pottons.

'Widow Smith, speaking of new residents to the town, how do your young charges do, aside from sporting new skirts, of course?'

'They go well, I am pleased to say. Although I wish to keep Prudence under close watch for a little while longer. In fact,' Lucie put down her spoon, 'I would welcome your judgement, Rector. We have received instruction from Mister Friswell, steward to Lord Calstone, that we are to turn the maid out and send her on her way. I fear this is not a Christian thing to ask of me, for the child may still be labouring under an indisposition.'

'I thought you said she was quite well, Widow Smith?'

'Indeed. However, there is more to the story. She has been turned out by her parents who have disowned her, so she has nowhere to go. And what's more, her twin is lodging with me too, as you know, but the Manor have no intelligence about this yet. Hester ran away when her family was turned off their farm by Lord Calstone, and no-one has enquired after her although they must know where she made for.'

The rector's cheeks flushed, and Mistress Archer's eyes widened. Lucie knew they both would know of the family, like most town residents did, but his ability to intervene would be limited because they weren't his parishioners.

'Why does the steward of the Manor involve himself in this matter? No, no don't tell me. Women's business and tattle at its root no doubt. Do you have an address to where a letter to Farmer Potton might be sent?'

Mistress Archer met Lucie's eyes, and Lucie understood. She would not challenge the rector. After all she needed his help. She also knew Philippa would want to hear the whole story once the men stepped into the rector's study for a cup of port and a pipe of tobacco.

'Are you minded to write to the girls' father, Rector?' asked Simon, while Lucie nodded to confirm she had a rough address. Hester had told her approximately where the new farm was and a letter to the local postmaster would see it reach Farmer Potton.

'Yes, I think it my duty. I will inform him that the second twin—' he paused.

'Hester,' Lucie prompted.

'Yes, I will inform him that Misses Hester and Prudence are safely in your custody and that he may send one of his sons to collect them at his earliest convenience. I do not want to know the occasion of Prudence being disowned, and pray inform me no further,' he said, raising his hand, 'but my hope is that Farmer Potton will be of a calmer disposition and ready to welcome *both* his daughters home. It is for God to judge our sins, not man. Isn't that so?' With that he pushed back his chair and gestured to Simon to follow him.

Lucie bristled at the idea that women had caused the ruin of young Prudence. *If only he knew.* But nevertheless, she felt some relief at the rector's plan. Should the Manor ask why she had not yet acted on their instruction, she could in all good conscience now explain that the rector's letter had been sent.

'This is very tasty,' Lucie complimented Mistress Archer again, as she took a spoon of apple pie. She found her appetite quite restored.

It was just after three of the clock when Lucie and Simon stepped out of the rectory. Lucie pulled her cloak tight against the light drizzle now falling. She took her son's arm and turned to give a cheery wave to Mistress Archer, standing on the threshold to see them off. When they were comfortably down the lane, Simon turned to his mother.

'Dr Archer had news of his own to share.'

'Really? I had thought between the Pooles and the Pottons we had covered all available topics this day.'

'No, this is major news for the town. The council have announced they've finally raised the funds necessary for the long-planned new town hall.'

'Goodness me. Your father thought that unlikely to be raised for years. He'd be pleased at this turn,' Lucie smiled at the thought. Simon described the plans as Dr Archer had to him. It was to be a brick building, he said, sitting atop Tuscan style stone pillars, and reached by stone steps. Underneath would be space to hold the new butter market. Atop was to be one large room where the town's aldermen would meet around a grand table.

'When we get out of the wet, I can show you a rough sketch the rector drew for me with his quill and ink. It is thought the town hall will help make Tupingham more prosperous.'

‘How was the money raised?’ Lucie was curious, as these plans seemed more elaborate than any Jasper had told her about.

‘I’m not sure you want to know that, Mother,’ Simon pulled his hat down as the rain became a little heavier. When Lucie didn’t respond he continued. ‘The council had half the eight hundred pounds. A donor has promised the balance.’

‘Calstone?’ Lucie felt her face set hard.

‘You guess correctly. Father is not forgotten, though, there are plans to name the council chamber for him. How do you like that, Mother? A fitting tribute to a man who served Tupingham above thirty years, is it not?’

‘We already have the marble memorial plaque you have commissioned for the chancel of All Hallows, Simon. It will be in place by Christmastide, you said the stonemason agreed.’

Simon had corresponded with both the stonemason in Grantby and the rector several times while nursing Sir Robert at the Manor those three weeks in September. He’d agreed a design, modest and unadorned, save for the three small doves above an inscription. Lucie had insisted on meeting the cost in full. At ten pounds from her inheritance, it was a substantial purchase, but Lucie was sure it was the right thing to do with the fire having destroyed her husband’s final resting place in London. Jasper had been baptised in that church like all their four children, three of whom who lay in its very grounds.

‘We will decline the offer to name the chamber for your father,’ Lucie’s voice was icy cold.

‘I was astonished like you at this news, Mother, I had no notion Calstone had such spare wealth,’ Simon said.

‘He’ll be looking for something in kind. I want nothing to do with the scheme.’

‘If that’s your wish, Mother.’ Simon looked a little crestfallen, as if he had thought this good news. He has misjudged me if so, Lucie thought a little bitterly.

‘Apparently Calstone’s bragged that his investment in the Company of Royal Adventurers Trading to Africa has already turned a handsome profit. It’s a new trading company set up by the Stuarts.’

Lucie harumphed, but Simon pressed on with his story as they walked, taking care to avoid the puddles that were forming. ‘Remember that portrait in Sir Robert’s room of the family’s founder, the wine merchant? Calstone was boasting that his grandsire would be in a maze at how he had turned the family’s fortunes around since the King’s return. The business was concluded on Calstone’s recent return here, but the initial talks were held in May when, of course, you and I know he was at the Manor too.’

Lucie’s stomach knotted instantly. What a horrible end to a pleasant afternoon. The rector wasn’t to know, of course, of Lucie’s deep antipathy to Lord Calstone, nor could he find out, but how relieved she was that he told Simon this out of her earshot. She took a deep breath, determined not to let this news spoil her whole day. Since they were just about to pass the end of Warley Lane, Lucie changed course.

‘Come Simon, let’s wait out the rain at Martha’s home. I should like to see the children. I confess to being a little concerned, since Martha was not at church this morning, it’s most unlike her.’

The pair walked up the dirt track round the back of the cottages, to the only door each cottage had.

‘I was going to make myself a warm poultice for my sore belly as soon as I got home, but perhaps a cuddle with baby Jasper will do just as much good.’ Lucie smiled in anticipation of the warm child in her arms. The communal yard was quiet with the rain having driven the many children who lived in the cottages back indoors.

‘Widow Smith, I was so hoping you would call,’ Martha swung open the cottage door. ‘Jemima is troubling us. She has a fever which returns every few days. Just as we think her recovered, she is taken ill once again.’

Lucie untied her damp cloak and hat, handing them to Simon. She rushed over to the bed where the child lay, and touching her forehead, found her alarmingly hot.

'What have you tried for her? She has taken the verjuice with syrup of raspberries that Mary brought, I trust?'

'Yes, all of it over the last few days,' Martha's brows were knitted together, and her cheeks were flushed. Lucie knew Martha was disquieted because she'd allowed red tendrils of hair to fall out of her cap and onto her face, something her former maid could not normally abide.

'I think we must now apply leeches. Two behind each ear, the poor love. And she must have small beer with rhubarb essence. I will send word to Mister Collins and he will attend without delay. I am sure we will get your daughter set to rights, Goodman,' Lucie turned to Anthony Higgs, Martha's husband. She saw a shadow pass over Martha's face, too. 'I'll settle his account, please don't concern yourself about that.'

'We couldn't ask that of you Widow Smith, you are too kind as it is, what with the school fees for her and George.'

Lucie held her finger to her lips. She and Mister Collins the barber-surgeon worked hand-in-hand on many cases and charged each other fairly for their respective services, there would be no inordinate charge for the application of the leeches.

'Say no more, Martha. You know you're kin to us after all the years we lived together. I want the best for these children just as surely as if I were their grandame. If the leeches don't provide a cure, we shall ask Dr Somerton to call too. George is well?' The boy was riding on Simon's back, playing horses. 'Ah there is not much wrong with him,' Lucie laughed, as the child urged Simon to *giddy up*. 'Now where is baby Jasper?' Lucie opened her arms. 'Pass him here Goodman and let me dandle him on my lap a few moments, and Simon can tell you all about the plans for Tupingham. We are to have a grand town hall after all, it seems.' She rolled her eyes.

Chapter Ten

Rain bounced off the cobbles and soaked the bottom of Lucie's petticoat and her stockings with mud and goodness knows what else from the filth of the street. It had done nothing but rain for days. Lucie pulled her cloak in tight and walked head down as briskly as her iron over shoes would allow.

'Oh, Mistress Robbins, I am so sorry,' Lucie hadn't noticed the school mistress until she almost knocked her over in her haste. She adjusted the cheesecake in her arms and peeped inside the paper to check it wasn't broken. It was a favourite dish of Simon's and it was meant to be something of an apology for her ill temper with him as they had walked back from the rectory.

'Not at all Widow Smith, this was my fault, I was in a world of my own. You're not hurt I hope?' Susanna wiped a wet strand of hair off her face, and tucked it behind her ear.

Lucie ushered her under the eaves of the nearest building.

'My dear, I see you are big bellied again. This must be a comfort to you after losing Jeremy. How long until your time?'

'I want but two months from my time,' Susanna stroked her belly protectively under her cloak. 'I am still stricken after our firstborn was returned to God, but I am in hopes of a lusty child to comfort us.'

'Indeed. I will inform Mary that you will be in need of her services after Christmastide. You know,' Lucie patted Mistress Robbins' arm with her free hand, 'Goodwife Jones is still grieving the loss of your son. My Martha tells me so. It was the will of God and not our place to question His ways. Anne does not take drink and so it was an accident, the will of the Lord, I hope you know this in your heart.'

Jeremy Robbins had been living as a nursling at the Jones's cottage on Warley Lane from a few days after his arrival in the world until his death at five months old. Lucie's eyes filled with tears at the memory. The midwife lived in the presence of death, but always found it hard to lay out an infant cut down before he had a chance to bloom. She'd brought the babe into the world, taken him to his baptism, and had to ready him for his return whence he came, all too soon after. Susanna shifted awkwardly from foot to foot.

'I'm sorry I have to go, it does not do well to stand in this wet weather,' she sounded curt. 'And if you please, I will not be in need of a midwife, my husband has engaged Dr Somerton for my delivery. Good day, Widow Smith.'

The schoolteacher walked off at pace. Lucie turned on her heel and strode after her, struggling to draw level.

'Pray, tell me again. Did you say you are to be delivered by the physician from Grantby rather than engage the services of the experienced midwives on your threshold?' Lucie clutched Mistress Robbins' arm to stay her and spoke loudly to be heard over the driving rain.

'Indeed, this is my husband's wish. He thinks it fitting. Please release my arm.'

Lucie stood in the middle of the cobbled street in a maze, rain and tears mingling down her face as she watched the teacher's figure recede.

'Oy, out my road,' called a carter. His horse whinnied in protest at his master's yanking of the reins, as he tried to avoid the midwife. The carter shook his fist at Lucie, who picked up her basket and hurried for the Three Doves, her heart pounding uncomfortably.

The shop was in darkness. It struck Lucie that at this time last year she'd been at the Robbins' gossiping, with Simon and Jasper. On that occasion when she'd returned home, the leaded windowpanes had been glowing with twinkling candlelight, and she remembered standing a moment and watching the shadow of Ned, their former apprentice, as he served a customer. So much had changed. And was changing still, it seemed. Lucie grabbed at the wall of the ginnel as she walked through it, suddenly lightheaded.

'Oh Mother, you are soaked through and dirty. Why did you not ask me or one of the maids to run your errand?' Simon helped her off with her clothes and crouched to unstrap her pattens. 'Hester, please fetch some dry woollen stockings, and a towel for my mother. Oh, and a new cap.'

While Hester ran for the items, Prudence put some spiced wine into a pot on the fire to make Lucie a warm drink, and the room filled with the scent of ginger and cloves. The girl had clearly observed it was Lucie's custom to take a cup of this restorative.

'I had a duty to personally inform Mistress Healey that we will be letting Deb go. It wouldn't be proper to do that through a message.' Lucie pulled on her clean, dry stockings. Wordlessly, Prudence handed her the wine and she took a sip. 'Thank you, that is just what was required,' she smiled up at the nervous girl. She related the conversation she had just had with Mistress Robbins to Simon.

'Ah, I have some intelligence to add here, Mother.' Simon sat down in his father's chair directly opposite Lucie's. 'Alderman Robbins has submitted a petition for a coat of arms. It has been all the talk at the coffee house this past week. He fancies himself a gentleman. This fits with him wanting his wife delivered by the physician, acting man-midwife.'

'Goodness. A coat of arms is an expensive pursuit I imagine, son. I did not know him to be so well-to-do,' Lucie sipped her drink and felt its warmth spread through her body.

'As I understand it, the alderman has made a successful investment in the Company of Royal Adventurers on the recommendation,' he lowered his voice to a whisper so the Potton girls who were sitting nearby at the kitchen table sewing clouts wouldn't overhear, 'of Lord C. Those with money to put down are reaping the reward.'

Simon returned his voice to its normal pitch. 'I can quite see why father was addicted to passing his afternoons at Hearne's. Mother, I've a second piece of news. Collins was in there this afternoon. He asked me what I'd think if he were to put in an application to take the lease of the Three Doves. He would conduct his barber-surgeon trade from here.'

Lucie nodded slowly. She'd half-expected this for a number of months, indeed, she and Timothy Collins had skirted around the topic several times over supper.

'In many ways it makes good sense. Mister Collins is skilled at the healing arts and knows a good many cures in addition to his surgical abilities.'

There was no indication an apothecary could be found to replace Jasper in the near future after all. The time to pack up the Three Doves and move on might well be approaching.

Her cup was halfway to her lips again when the back door banged open. Prudence and Hester started and pulled closer together. Simon began to rise when a bedraggled and flustered Mary burst into the kitchen.

'I'm so glad you're here, Widow Smith. I need some advice please.' The younger woman pulled off her soaked cap. Lucie indicated to Prudence to prepare a cup of warmed wine for Mary too, and Hester rose unbidden to run up the two pairs of stairs and fetch Mary some dry stockings and a clean cap. While Mary took her wine, she explained to Lucie that she had been out nursing Joan Horden. After being delivered of a dead child the previous week, the goodwife had been taken with the most debilitating stomach cramps and scourings.

'I gave her a decoction of the inward green bark of an oak with cinnamon and blanched almonds boiled into sweetened milk, as you've taught me. She's been taking this at regular intervals, half a pint at a time, but she isn't improving. Her gossips and I are troubled. I wonder what you might recommend trying in its place?'

Lucie frowned. 'I have seldom known that to fail. But I do know an effective alternative which has proven its worth. We can prepare it now for you to take to her.' She used the arms of her chair to push herself up. 'We'll need half an ounce of white Spanish, cinnamon in the stick – just the smallest amount, perhaps 1/8 of an ounce – and an ounce of fine wheat flour,' she counted off the ingredients on her fingers. 'It is my custom to boil the cinnamon in milk in a separate pan from the rest of the milk with the flour and white Spanish. The first can be blended in the second once it has cooked to a thick custard. We can then sweeten it with sugar from the loaf to make it more appealing.'

In the kitchen, Lucie set to pulling two pans down from the shelf while Mary went through to the shop to find the liquorice root and a cinnamon stick.

'Mary, see if there is any dried charity on the shelf too. A blend of that in oil rubbed on her belly will offer comfort too. It helps me when my own belly is griping.'

As they worked Lucie watched Mary. She found she didn't have the heart to relate the news about the expected Robbins child. Mary was so caring and so very capable, why would Mistress Robbins consent instead to be delivered by a physician with whom she wasn't acquainted?

'Would you like me to accompany you back to the Hordens, my dear? The girls here have been busy today boiling and preparing us some beautifully fresh lampreys for our meal. They've been baking in that pot this past hour and have at least the same to go until they are fit. I am not required here.'

'No, you stay dry, Widow Smith. There is no sense in us both getting another soaking. Thank you for the remedies.' Lucie was not minded to argue further. She willingly settled back into her armchair beside the fire. As she started to doze, Lucie caught sight of the Pottons, darning and whispering just out of her eyeline. A cold shiver ran through her. Surely someone has just walked across my grave, she thought, and shuddered again. She closed her eyes, but sleep alluded her, and her thoughts were crowded with memories of this very room in days long gone.

Chapter Eleven

Lucie was busying herself in the Three Doves, looking up anxiously each time the door opened. She knew when Dr Somerton called for his customary monthly visit she would have to have it out with him. Last month he had appeared just as Lucie was closing up at dinnertime and so she had been able to let him in without obligation to work hard by him. The clock ticked past noon without his appearance.

'Today is the day Dr Somerton's due is it not?' she asked Hester, who had just put her head around the door to announce their meal was about to be served.

'I reckon so,' Hester looked down as she spoke.

Lucie squeezed out from behind the counter and turned the key in the front door, then went back to the counter to reckon up her takings. It was a dull overcast day, so she was obliged to have a pair of candles on the counter even at this early hour. When she had tallied the money and written a shopping list of items in need of replenishment, Lucie retired to the back kitchen to join the girls. Mary and Simon were abroad, so it was just the three of them. A simple but filling meal of bread, cheese and pickles was today's fare, but at least Lucie was able to enjoy it without interruption.

'Would you like to try this pickle, girls?' She spooned a little of the pickled Alexander buds and sliced ginger on her plate, but both twins screwed up their noses. 'A bit sharp for a young palate, eh?' Lucie's ready smile slowly slipped from her face as the twins kept their heads down, concentrating on their bread and cheese. The girls lacked the easy good humour of Deb, and Martha's familiarity with the rhythms of the household, but their skills at housewifery were beyond compare.

As she watched the girls clear the table, moving in synchrony, she wondered if Dr Archer's letter had reached their father yet. She felt fortunate that no enquiry from the Manor had arrived to see if she had carried out her instruction to turn them out. Perhaps the steward assumed his word was law, and that Prudence was long gone.

The afternoon drew on, and yet more candles were lit. Lucie was sitting beside the hearth reading with Hester and Prudence nearby knitting stockings for the poor, when the three of them started in unison at a loud rapping on the shop door.

'Goodness me, whoever that is will have the door off. They'd better not waken Mary,' Lucie grumbled as she pushed herself out of her warm chair. She popped a candle in the crack in the door jamb and turned the front door key before drawing back the bolt. The door pushed in towards her before she could pull it open.

'Ho there, have a care,' Lucie called out.

'Widow Smith! Did you not hear the commotion at the town cross just before noon?' Dr Somerton did not trouble himself with the formalities of a greeting.

'Good day to you too, Sir. I can't say I did hear anything, but I have been in the back kitchen since noon. Do step inside,' Lucie moved out of his way that he might pass into the shop. 'What was to do?'

'The butcher, Cordel. He met with an accident when his horse threw him.'

'Is he badly hurt?'

'He will recover in time. It is as well Tupingham has a capable chirurgeon. This Cordel had a basket of meat on the back of his horse. Something spooked the beast, and the butcher was unseated. He fell backwards and he tore his cods on the basket. It made for a very bloody scene.' The physician's eyes glistened as though the events of the afternoon had excited his passions.

'Mister Collins performed an operation on him?'

'Yes, yes. With my oversight, of course,' the physician boasted.

Lucie guided him to the storeroom and lit the candles there from her own, while he explained that he had been journeying to Tupingham at the time of the accident, but when he rode into High Street he saw the butcher being carried by a group of men towards Mister Collins's house.

'Why did no-one send for me?' Lucie frowned.

'I know not. I jumped from my horse and the men slung Cordel over the saddle. He was faint from loss of blood, his vital heat draining from him,' he added pompously. 'Naturally, once we had arrived at the chirurgeon's place, I introduced myself, and directed the mission to save the man.'

I expect Collins will have a different account of this tale when I see him next, Lucie thought.

'The chirurgeon will tell you himself it was a fortunate day for the butcher that it is the day of my regular visitation in this town.'

Lucie grimaced. The doctor's condescension was more of an annoyance than ever this day. She was pleased the physician had his back to her as he settled himself at Jasper's now bare desk.

'We removed a rotten and pulpy testicle which weighed four pounds and a quarter. Can you believe that Widow Smith?' He turned and held open his hands in imitation of the size of the tumour. 'Scarce wonder he caught it on the basket, the cove must have been labouring under the disease of his stone for several seasons. The accident seems to have been a blessing, for Collins's swift action has affected a perfect cure if it please God.'

Lucie's chest relaxed; she hadn't realised just how tense she had become during the story. Praise God, she thought.

Cordel was a family man whose dependants required him to be in good health.

'I seem to remember Joseph Cordel having long standing trouble with his privy parts, and my husband supplying medications for it,' she shook her head. Could it really be that the man had allowed matters to come to this point from a stubborn disinclination to seek hers or even the chirurgeon's counsel these last months.

'I'll leave you to your business now, Dr Somerton. Pray call out if you require anything. When you're finished, I would be grateful for a moment of your time to discourse on another matter before you leave,' Lucie backed out of the small room.

Just half an hour later, the physician walked through to the kitchen with two prescriptions in his hand which he placed on the large table.

'This is a wonderfully cosy chamber,' he said, his eyes surveying the whole room. They stopped at the shadowy outline of the painting Simon had drawn on the wall depicting the High Street many years earlier. It was just visible in the flicker of candlelight. 'That's a view up from the river is it not?'

Lucie smiled and nodded, beckoning the physician to take a seat opposite her in front of the warm hearth.

'I trust you won't think it amiss, but I have sent the girls to Goodwife Cordel in the butcher's shop with a sleeping draught to help the injured man get the rest he needs.' After pouring herself and the physician a cup of small beer, Lucie steeled herself, remaining standing to have a small advantage over her addressee. 'Dr Somerton, as you know, Midwife Thorne has taken over my women now that I am mostly retired from that calling,' she found herself speaking rather too quickly with nerves and willed herself to slow down. 'Tupingham has work enough for one midwife only.' She sipped on her beer, hoping to stay the griping in her guts, while at the same time the physician raised a quizzical eyebrow at her. 'There's no occasion to look at me like that, I've heard how you're engaged to deliver the Robbins baby. Am I to understand you mean to practise as one of those man-midwives of which I hear, while you are acting as physician to this town? Because if this is the case you will not only be acting unnaturally in my opinion, but will be taking work from Mary.'

Dr Somerton roared with laughter, slapping his thigh. Lucie slammed her cup on the table, her choler rising rapidly.

'Oh, my dear woman. My dear, dear woman. It is true I've a moderate degree of proficiency in this art from when I lived in London between '58 and '59, but that was mainly among the meaner sort of women.' He took out his handkerchief to wipe his eyes. 'I don't mean to continue in that trade routinely. I hold that it is a good and fitting thing that every woman should have her midwife with her at the time of her delivery.' He raised his hand to stay Lucie's attempt to interrupt his flow. 'Although I do say this is not absolutely necessary, for that many be delivered without the help of midwives. We both can tell stories of women delivered by the sole assistance of Dame Nature, Eve's midwife.'

Lucie nodded slowly. She decided to ignore the jibe about her profession, before asking in a cold voice, 'So, pray, how did it come to pass that you have been engaged to deliver Alderman Robbins' next infant?'

'That is explained simply. The alderman is a puffed-up man who labours under notions of grandeur. While he and I were in discussion about my scheme to act as physician to the town, the subject of his wife's big belly was chanced upon, and he asked that I attend. It does not do well to refuse a man of influence. It is my hope that Midwife Thorne will attend with me, and that she takes no slight from my commission?'

'I see.'

Lucie decided to take the physician at his word, for the moment at least. Mary was so good natured that she had not taken the least offence when she heard the news, commenting that it was not as if she was short of work. Lucie walked over to the hearth and stirred the meat simmering in the caldron over the flames. The aroma of mutton filled the room.

'You'll stay for some supper, Dr Somerton?' Lucie hoped he would refuse.

'Very kind. I would be honoured. Do you mind if I light my pipe?'

Yes, I do, Lucie thought, but shook her head. She took the bread which had been drying out in front of the fire, sliced it, and laid it in a dish. She could sense Dr Somerton's eyes upon her the whole time and bit her lower lip as she worked, finding the whole situation deeply uncomfortable.

'Perhaps it might please you to repair to the Boar for a tankard of ale before we eat?' She kept her back to him as she spoke.

'Ah no, if my presence distracts you not from your work my good woman? I find myself most comfortable here, it is many years since my wife died, and my younger daughter married two years ago.' He tapped out the contents of his pipe on the hearth stone and reached into his waistcoat pocket for his pouch of tobacco. 'I have sorely missed sitting in a kitchen conversing like this.'

Lucie felt a brief pang of empathy for a fellow widow and assured the physician that he was welcome to continue sitting in that case. She ladled the cooking liquor on to the bread and popped it on the coals, before sitting in her chair, ready to add more liquid each time the bread absorbed the last.

'This will just take a few minutes more, Dr Somerton. The Potton girls should be home by now. I hope they are not delayed much longer, or the meat will spoil.'

'The Potton girls? The maid who was caught up in that unfortunate business at the Manor? She is still resident here?' the physician sat upright from his slouch in the chair, a frown on his face. 'I understood you to have been instructed to send her to her father.'

A hot coal rolled from the fire, so Lucie bent to flick it back with her ladle; she was rather glad of her excuse to attend to the flames rather than meet the physician's eye.

'I have not turned them out, nor will I, while they have nowhere to go.'

'They?'

Lucie quickly related how it was that she now had two Potton girls under her roof and how the rector was interceding with their father to bring about a reconciliation. She waited for the physician to think on this while she stood over the cauldron and fished out the bundle of thyme, chives, and sweet marjoram that had been flavouring the meat.

'Excuse me while I go up and rouse Midwife Thorne, she has slept three hours now and won't sleep well tonight if she doesn't rise soon. I'd rather hoped the smell of this meat might alert her senses,' Lucie smiled at her guest.

'Certainly, Widow Smith. I will watch the pot if I may, a fine meal awaits us. Just before you leave, I was so good as to answer your question earlier, and before I leave after sampling this generous hospitality, I must beg an answer to a question of my own.'

'Of course. After supper though. I must get on,' Lucie answered.

As she looked around the crowded table, Lucie was relieved she'd bought such a large cut of meat from the butcher yesterday. And to think, at the time she had thought it likely to provide several meals. 'Who knows what our getting of meat will be like with Butcher Cordel laid up? He has a couple of good apprentices though, mayhap the place will run as normal,' she mused aloud.

Simon had returned and was eating the mutton broth, baked bread, and peas with great enthusiasm.

'Come along everyone, eat up, don't let good food go cold,' Lucie's light tone masked the impatience she felt. She dearly wanted to know where Simon had spent his day, but would not ask in front of Dr Somerton. She knew he had gone out on Dapple this morning, for he'd told her so as he breezed out of the shop. Naturally, she was attending to a customer so hadn't had the opportunity to learn where he was headed. He'd had a spring in his step then and had returned home even cheerier judging by the good-humoured way he was spooning food in his mouth. By contrast, Hester and Prudence were polite but subdued, clearly intimidated by the physician's presence. The girls jumped up and gathered the pewter dishes and spoons as soon as the party had finished eating and took them to the scullery to clean.

'Widow Smith and I were discoursing on the Robbins delivery earlier, Midwife Thorne,' Dr Somerton said, leaning back slightly so that Hester could place the remains of a fruitcake down in front of him. The physician repeated what he had told Lucie, and assured Mary he was not here to take her trade. Lucie asked the physician to pass the fruit cake to her and she cut into it, offering a slice each to Dr Somerton, Mary, and Simon before cutting herself one.

'Prudence, there is a Cheshire cheese on the shelf in the scullery,' she called out. 'Could you bring it in for us to have a piece with our cake? And you maids are welcome to finish your meal before cleaning the dishes if you'd like.'

Hester Potton brought the cheese in and bobbed her head as she put it on the table, 'If you please, Widow Smith, Pru bade *me* bring in the cheese.'

Lucie patted the girl's hand. 'The rector is in correspondence with your father, and I have some hope this whole sorry business will be resolved soon, do go comfort your sister.'

Lucie caught the physician's raised eyebrow. 'They come from a dairy farm. I presume asking for the Cheshire has set the timid lass off again. She is terribly nervous.'

As the party finished their cake, Dr Somerton offered to relate the story of a patient he had treated in his hometown of Birmingham.

'I received word from my daughter of her lately passing. 'Tis a wonder she lived as long as she did, after what happened,' he remarked, piquing the interest of the midwives.

'A poor woman by the name of Faith Raworth had suffered what we physicians call a *lapus uteri* upon lifting a bucket of coal which was beyond her capacity.'

'She's not the first and won't be the last,' Lucie commented, having no doubt that the Latin meant the woman's womb had prolapsed.

'Perhaps my story is not to Mister Smith's taste?' the physician remarked, upon Simon's grimace.

'You guess right, Sir. I will sit by the fire and read this newssheet, if you'll not think me ignorant,' Simon replied.

'My son has been raised on stories of women's business and has evidently had a surfeit. Pray continue, if it pleases you.'

The physician explained how Goodwife Raworth had sought no assistance. He grew animated and loud as he continued his tale, obviously enjoying the attention. Lucie rather wished he would hurry to the end and take his leave.

'One day the goodwife grew to such an ill humour about her indisposition that she went into her garden, and laying hold on her womb drew it, and cut it forth with a knife.'

'What?' Lucie's eyes flew open. Mary's hand went to her mouth as she let out a gasp. Simon looked up from his paper.

''Ods blood, Somerton. This is too much!'

'Thy mother finds the case of interest I dare say, so unless she instructs me to the contrary, I'll proceed.'

Now he had Lucie's interest, he grandly took a swig of his wine, and then started tapping out his pipe on his plate.

Mary spoke up, 'Please conclude your tale, Sir. I should like to know how the poor woman did.'

Lucie put her hand to her mouth to stifle a yawn. She wanted to speak to Simon before she retired. Somerton was clearly telling a tall tale designed to show off his skills.

'The goodwife lost so much blood. A bit like the butcher today, if I might say,' he continued, while puffing out clouds of smoke. Lucie coughed but Somerton showed no sign of noticing.

'Everyone thought it impossible she should survive, but recover she did thanks to me. She'd cut through the neck of her bladder and was forever more doomed to dribble piss insensibly by day and night, but my skill with a needle and some double silk thread provided some months of relief.'

'The poor woman,' Lucie said. 'If only she had sought some assistance from her midwife before butchering her own body.'

'I can assure you, I provided all possible assistance, Madam. The woman would've had no relief at all but for my actions.'

Neither Lucie nor Mary spoke, only looked at each other in disbelief. The physician was casting himself as the hero of his story, yet Lucie could only think of the woman's pain and embarrassment.

Dr Somerton cleared his throat and went to rise up from the bench. 'I fear I have imposed upon your hospitality long enough. I am deeply grateful for a delicious meal in homely surroundings. It has done my heart good. Just before I go, I beg leave to ask if it is thy belief that the chirurgeon will proceed with his plans to acquire this shop from which to trade?'

Mary looked startled.

'Oh I am sorry, my dear. Simon told me this just last night and I haven't had a chance to talk with you about it,' Lucie said.

'I have spoken out of turn. My apologies, Miss. Collins imparted his intentions to me as we operated on the butcher. I am curious as to whether such a scheme would receive thy blessings.'

Lucie stood up. She passed the physician his heavy winter coat and explained that the arrangement she had brokered with the council to remain in the Three Doves was only ever a temporary one.

'And if the next tenant is Chirurgeon Collins, then he has my blessing, not that my opinion will be sought.' She passed the physician his hat. 'Our situation on High Street is certainly a more convenient location than his house on the edge of town.'

'You would not miss the hubbub of commerce, Widow Smith, or feel a wrench to leave thy home after a lifetime here? And you, Simon, if I may, how does this sit with you?'

'I am a master printer, not a healer Dr Somerton. I have a life to rebuild after the London fire which destroyed my home in September. Now if it pleases you, I will walk down to the Boar and take a tankard of ale and tell you about my print house if you wish to hear it.'

After the men had gone, Mary and Lucie were left sitting at the table.

'We have much to think on, Mary,' Lucie said, as the twins joined them at the table again. 'But no one has approached me about this plan, so I suppose we will carry on waiting to be informed when the men have decided our fate amongst themselves. Girls, you have some cake,' Lucie cut the last fragment of it in two and pushed the board towards the end of the table. 'There is no occasion for you two to be worried. Whatever comes to pass, I'll make sure you have a roof over your heads.'

Unseen by the other women, Lucie rubbed her knotted tummy under her apron. She spoke with more certainty in her ability than she felt.

'I'll warm a little spiced wine, and then take it to my bed. Mary, will you take a cup too?'

Chapter Twelve

'I have to say, Widow Smith, that the way the Three Doves gleams make me feel like a slattern the years it was in my care.' Martha looked around her former home, smiling in wonder. She had always prided herself on being a good housewife, but now the house was spotless.

'Wait until you see the master's storeroom, Martha.' Lucie took the key down from its hook. 'Simon's cleared and sorted his father's papers. The girls then got to work, and it too is a wonder to behold.'

Lucie walked Martha to the small room at the back of the shop. Dr Somerton now had ample room to write up his cases, prescriptions, and make out his bills. Martha's jaw dropped when she entered the tiny room, which appeared to have doubled in size. The walls which had been scarcely visible before had been given a coat of whitewash and with the light coming in from the large window at the front of the shop the little room, normally crowded and cluttered with chemistry equipment and papers, appeared completely different.

'Of course, we have to keep the spices chest in here. Its contents are too valuable for it to be on view in the shop.'

'I confess, this makes me a little sad, Widow Smith. It truly is the end of an era.'

'I know,' said Lucie. She slid her arm around Martha's waist and the two women stood quietly for a moment. 'I feel the same way, but better to prepare to leave the Three Doves little by little. Now why don't you go into the kitchen and fetch us a cup of beer each while I hold onto this young man. Come here baby Jasper, now what do you think about your namesake's study? Would you like to sit in his chair?'

'The Potton girls are at their sewing at the table. Has there been any word from their father yet? Martha asked when she returned with the drinks.

'Nothing. Dr Archer has received no reply to his letters. He is minded to take a trip out as his next course of action. Simon has offered to accompany him,' Lucie made a funny face at Jasper and was rewarded with a giggle. 'The girls are sewing the last of Mister Smith's shirts into clouts for me. Their stitching is beautiful,' she said. She turned her attention back to Martha.

'Is Mary abroad?' Martha asked. Lucie nodded, giving the baby a kiss on his little nose.

'I should have liked to have thanked her for the care she gave to Jemima,' Martha reached over for Jasper as he was starting to fret, not caring to be kissed. 'I think he is ready for feeding. He has a little pap about this time, so I'd better set out for home.'

Lucie saw the pair out the door and hugged Martha as best she could around the fussy baby, who was now seeking his mother's dug. 'Are you sure you don't want to nurse him in the kitchen a little before you walk home?'

'No, but thank you, Anthony will be wondering where I have got to, and it won't do this tiny glutton any harm to wait a while for his food.'

Lucie waved them down the street, and then returned to the counter. A few minutes later the door opened and George Rowley limped in.

'Has Alderman Robbins sent you for something this morning?' Lucie asked of the alderman's servant.

'No, Mistress, I'm come for myself. I have had a fall from my horse and got a terrific sore bruise down my thigh. May I show you?'

'That won't be necessary,' Lucie waved a hand at him as he began to untie his breeches. 'I've seen enough bruises in my time.'

She went over to the shelf to look for some yellow salve. The door went again, and Lucie thought it was shaping up to be a busy morning. 'I'll be with you in a minute,' she called, without turning to see who it was. It required all her attention to climb safely on a wooden box to reach the shelf.

'Here, let me get that Widow Smith, yellow salve is it?' said a very familiar voice.

Lucie looked round sharply and had to grab at the wall as she wobbled on the box. She felt her face light up in delight. A tall young man with a full beard stood next to her.

'Ned! Well, isn't this the best surprise?' She scarcely believed the evidence of her own eyes. He seemed to have grown a full six inches in the eleven months since she'd last seen him. Her husband's former apprentice. He had a new suit of clothes with a dark blue woollen coat. So mature. Ned took down a small pot of yellow salve and handed it to Lucie with a bow of the head. He clearly remembered his way around the shop in which he'd trained for many years.

'I can't tell you what a relief it is to know you are safe. I wrote to the last address we had for you, at Mister Battersby's. Did you not receive it?'

'I expect it got lost in the disorder after the fire. I'm most remiss for not writing, forgive me, Widow Smith.' Ned bowed his head again.

'Come now. It matters not. You are here and looking like a fine young man. Let me finish serving Rowley, then you must tell me what brings you here. It is good to see you Ned,' she could feel her eyes smiling. 'That will be one shilling, please,' she said to Rowley. 'Apply twice a day and it will soothe your bruises.'

'Thank you kindly, Widow Smith. Eh, tell young Ned here what happened to the butcher. My fall was nothing compared to his, the coxcomb. I'm grateful a bruised arse is all I have to show for my trouble.'

Lucie shook her head, still smiling, 'I'll thank you to keep that language out of my shop.' Ned's grin was fulsome, as Rowley limped out.

'I only keep the shop open until midday Ned. If you come back then you can take some meat with us and tell me all your news. You were not hurt in the fire? How does your mother do? And your sisters? And I want to hear all about your new master,' Lucie put her hand to her mouth, her cheeks flushing. 'Forgive me Ned. All in good time.' The door swung open again and a flustered young mother came in with four children about her skirts. 'Come back at noon, Simon will be home then too.'

'Good morning, Widow Smith, was that the 'potecary's 'prentice?' said Winifred Bumstead.

'It certainly was, Goody, it certainly was,' Lucie's eyes still watched the door Ned had left through, 'and if he had been but half an hour earlier, Goodwife Higgs would have been here to see him too.'

'He looked full of good cheer. Let's hope he's not here bringing more bad news to your door like that son of yours keeps doing.'

'Excuse me?' Lucie's eyebrows shot up.

'Begging your pardon Widow Smith,' Goodwife Bumsted flapped her hands as if to bat away her ill-chosen words. 'Perhaps I shouldn't have spoken of it, but it can't be denied that Mister Smith brought news of the plague, and his father's death. And is now back in town quite ruined in the great fire, they are saying.'

'I think you have said quite enough,' Lucie's hands were on her hips, her expression sour. 'Did you come to make a purchase?'

After the Bumstead family had left with their itch girdles refreshed, Lucie's mood continued to darken as she went through the motions of reckoning her takings with slumped shoulders. She now knew without a doubt that Simon was the talk of Tupingham, and Ned's arrival would be all around the town within moments.

At ten past noon Prudence Potton placed a large dish of toasted cheese on oiled bacon and onions on the kitchen table. The rich, nutty smell filled the kitchen, and just before they were given leave to dig in, Prudence reached over to scorch the top of the food with the back of the coal shovel.

'This looks delicious girls, but we need one further place at our table, for we are expecting a guest.' Lucie had little appetite, and hoped the wobble in her voice had gone unnoticed.

Simon looked at his mother quizzically, head on one side. 'Pray who calls, Mother?'

The scullery door creaked open, saving Lucie the trouble of explaining. Everyone looked up, and Simon turned around in his seat to see the visitor properly, seeming to take a moment to register who it was.

'Edward Brocke. As I live,' Simon jumped up from the bench and almost toppled Prudence over as she was sitting down. He bounded to the door, and hugged Ned hard, thumping him on the back. 'You rogue, you're taller than me now.' Mary rose too and waited to greet Ned the moment Simon released him. She took his smart new coat from him and hung it on the hook.

'Let the lad come inside properly, you two. Ned, come and join us for some toasted cheese and bacon,' Lucie felt her smile reach her eyes and her mood lifted at the presence of Ned back in her kitchen after all this time. She patted the seat on the bench next to her. 'You'll recognise Prudence and Hester Potton from the dairy stall in Tupingham market, won't you?'

Ned looked across the room. He evidently saw Prudence first and bowed briefly, and then he saw Hester. When their eyes met, Ned blushed to the roots of his hair. Hester bent her head, biting her lip.

'You are acquainted, I see,' said Simon with a roar of laughter. He slapped his thigh as if this was the best amusement he'd had in a long time.

'Simon, hush. Come everyone, let's take this food while it is hot,' Lucie elbowed her son, and moved along the bench so Ned could sit on her other side. Settling herself, Lucie led a prayer of thanks for their food, and added a silent prayer of her own that she might be given the forbearance to deal with any bad news Ned might be bringing with him.

During the mealtime chatter, Ned revealed that he had lost his mother and two of his sisters to the plague in January. Lucie rubbed his arm, soothingly. Losing the master with whom he had lived almost six years and then his mother and sisters a mere month later must've been almost unendurable for the youth. He's not even twenty-one yet, Lucie thought, feeling her eyes brim.

After the meal, the Pottons jumped up to take the dirty plates and dishes to the scullery and Ned took his chance to ask how the girls came to be at the Three Doves.

'We'll perhaps come onto that, Ned,' Lucie replied. 'But first I must know what brings you back to Tupingham?'

'I bring good news,' Ned said brightly, puffing his chest out ever so slightly. 'I am released early from my indenture.'

'Good news? Tell me you were not dismissed for bad behaviour?' Lucie and Mary exchanged glances. Ned had been a rowdy apprentice in Tupingham, but surely recent events had changed him?

'No cause for alarm, Widow Smith. Apothecary Smith taught me so well that my new master said I was as well prepared as any after just a few months with him. He freed me to seek employment as a journey man.'

'Then why did he not keep you in his employ? We paid over a purse for the remainder of your training,' Lucie looked to Simon for confirmation that the agreed fee was paid. Ned wriggled in his seat, trying to get to the inside pocket of his doublet.

'I have the whole of the fee to return to you.' He placed a full leather purse on the table. 'And a letter,' he reached back into his pocket.

'Let me see,' Simon leant across his mother and took the letter. He glanced quickly down the paper. 'Ned speaks true, Mother. Apothecary Battersby has returned the whole fee to "the relict of his dear and much missed Friend, for her continued comfort". Mother he has returned the money, that is most Christian.' He passed the letter to Lucie.

'I don't know what to say. I will read this later when I have my spectacles. I am sorry to have doubted you, Ned, but you must confess you led us a merry dance more than once when you resided here.' Lucie squeezed the young man's hand.

''Tis I who must apologise. I've had this money kept safe for you some weeks, but with starting a new position I couldn't ask for leave to bring it. My sister has a strong box in her house in Deptford, and kept your purse for me there. There is a shortage of apothecaries since the plague. I've taken a position with a chemist by the name of Neville. We were at Cheapside.'

'You've done well for yourself getting a place in a chemist's there,' Simon said admiringly. Ned had secured work on one of the most prestigious streets for commerce.

'Had done well,' Ned said sadly. 'The lot went up on the Tuesday of the fire. Nothing we could do.'

'Aye, we thought they'd save Cheapside. I heard how they dug down into the great conduit, hoping the water would gush out. Damn it, Ned. We must have been but yards apart at times, fighting the fire. I at Paul's and you at Cheapside.' The men looked at each other for a long pause. Mary and the girls gazed at their hands, but Lucie felt no desire to reprimand Simon for his curse.

'We've lost everything bar our lives and a few portable goods. You?'

'Everything. Nothing was saved. We put our books and goods in the crypt at St Paul's ...'

'Oh no,' Ned closed his eyes. 'The noise when that went up.'

'Aye it was like cannon fire, and with it all I owned.' Simon rubbed his ears, closing his eyes briefly. 'None of that compares to losing Kate. The Millers' housemaid.'

'The maid who suffocated? She was in your household? So few lives were lost, it was terribly unfortunate about her. I'm so very sorry,' Ned wiped away a tear with the back of his hand.

'You two have much to discuss, it seems,' Lucie said. 'And my prayers will be evermore filled with gratitude for the delivery of you both from the horror.'

No one spoke for a moment, then Ned cleared his throat.

'Apothecary Neville's receipt book was a large one like Mister Smith's own. But it must have fallen from our cart. Like Mister Smith, Mister Neville guarded his book fiercely and is very melancholy at its loss.'

'That will have complicated your master's plans to establish a new apothecary shop.' Tears now stung Lucie's eyes. She shuddered to think how Jasper would have reacted to a similar loss. Ned shifted on the bench.

'The thing is this, Widow Smith. I'm instructed by Apothecary Neville to request he might be allowed to purchase Mister Smith's receipt book. It will be the key to his successful re-establishing of a business and you have not need of it, or so I thought when I set out. I did not know you had continued trading, Widow Smith.'

'Oh Ned! I cannot part with my husband's book for any price,' her hand shot to her mouth in shock. She pushed herself up from the table and went to the mantel to light a pair of candles, for November drew on a pace, darkening the room even though it was early afternoon.

'Come, Ned,' Simon regarded his mother with concern. 'Let's you and I walk to Hearne's and we can learn the rest of one another. We can compare notes on the fire, and you can tell me the story of you and the pretty maid.'

'Simon, I am sure Ned does not care to be teased.' Lucie had heard the scullery door opening and presumed the girls had discreetly withdrawn to the garden after cleaning the cooking pots. She had often observed them through the window, tending to the chickens or turning the compost heap unprompted. They were such hard workers. It had crossed Lucie's mind more than once that these wenches didn't seem to have been raised to expect much carefree time, or the sort of silliness other maids of similar age enjoyed. No games or gazing at fripperies on the market for them, it seemed.

When the men had left and the two women remained at the table, Mary said, 'I think the offer to purchase Mr Smith's receipt book may be worth considering.'

'Never,' Lucie's voice was firm. 'Now Mary, call those maids indoors will you? It is not fit weather for them to be loitering in the garden.'

While Mary was gone, Lucie sank into her armchair and replayed the dinnertime conversations in her mind. She hit on an idea as the kitchen door creaked open and the three young women entered the room.

'Mary, before you sit down, would you go up the stairs to the chest with Mister Smith's papers in please? Here is the key,' she took a small key from the pocket under her apron. 'In there you will find a new calf-bound book. It is yet empty. If Ned wishes to avail himself of some copied receipts, he is welcome to have that new book as my gift.'

Before Lucie could tell Simon the story of the notebook that evening, he surprised her by producing a paper of his own from his pocket.

'Mother, it seems that as well as your spectacles, there was one further surprise Apothecary Smith had for his wife. I found this deed several days ago but before telling you, I wanted to take measures to ensure it was a true one.'

'Son, are you in your cups? How much did you drink with Ned?' she asked.

Simon laughed heartily. Lucie looked at his sparkling eyes and high colour in amazement.

'Look at this deed, Mother. Do you know what it is?'

Lucie studied it blankly. Her husband had hundreds of papers, but this one looked like a legal document of one sort or another. Simon explained that it was a deed for a parcel of land, twenty minutes' walk from the Three Doves, which his father had purchased two decades earlier.

'You see Mother? That's what I have been doing when I rode out on Dapple the last couple of times.'

'You took my horse to see some land around the corner? Simon, I am not following you at all, perhaps it will be better to continue this conversation when you have slept the liquor off. I thought you left for Hearne's, not the alehouse.'

Simon grabbed his mother's hands, crumpling the paper in his haste. He bobbed down to look in her eyes.

'I am not drunk, Mother. I'm ecstatic. Father left you all his property and so this land is yours. Don't you see?'

'My spectacles are on the counter in the shop, or on my desk up the stairs, I know not which,' was her only answer. Simon set off at great speed, bounding up the stairs two at a time, returning moments later with the eyeglasses in his hand.

'I went to see the builder who renovated the soap-boiler's place. Francis Poole gave me the directions and an introduction. The builder has been to inspect the site. He says he can build you a timber-framed house, large enough for all your needs, for a very good price. Do you see now?' Simon took Lucie's hands, pulling her to her feet. She stumbled as he spun her around. 'You won't need to lease rooms; you could be a lady of property. A householder!'

'Are you sure, Simon?' Lucie's mind was spinning, and not just because of her son's vigorous embrace. But his enthusiasm soon infected her, and the pair sat and talked over a cup of warm wine.

'Of course, it's coming back to me now I see the paper properly,' she laid the deed down on the kitchen table and placed the candle she was holding on the hearth.

'Your father bought this when we were still a family of six. It had been his intention to save and have a house built with a dispensary within. He thought it would be healthier for us all to be in the country away from High Street. Of course, that was not to be,' Lucie sighed. 'Losing the three children at once changed your father, like it would any decent man. I don't think either of us paid any mind to that scrap of land ever again.' How strange that he had kept the title of it and not sold it on, she thought. Lucie let out a sigh as she felt her spirits sinking. 'We'll have to sell it of course. I am too old to think of such a scheme and will remove to rooms as I planned when the time comes to leave the Three Doves. The money raised will help you recover your losses from the fire.'

Chapter Thirteen

The scratching sounds from Jasper's desk were regular and urgent. Ned was in there noting down recipes as fast as he could write. His hands were almost as ink stained as his blotter.

'Don't you damage your eyes, sitting scribbling hour after hour,' Lucie called from behind the counter.

'This is as near to having Mister Smith's book as possible, and I fear to miss out anything which might be important to Apothecary Neville and me.' Ned barely looked up from his work. At that moment Sam Jones burst through the shop door as if rushing to put out a fire.

'Widow Smith, please if you will, I need you to come with me presently. The women have sent me to fetch you. Goodwife Hatch's baby is half out, but it seems stuck and the young lass who's the midwife now said she's in need of your opinion. Please come now, the women said it was life or death.' The man shook as he delivered his message.

Lucie put down the little linen parcels of herbs she had been measuring out and rushed to find her midwifery bag.

'Simon, please shut up the shop after me. I have to go to Warley Lane to attend one of the combers' wives. Mary is waiting for me.'

'No need to close, Widow Smith. I am here and willing to serve. It is the least I can do,' Ned jumped up immediately, much to Lucie's relief. Winter was always a busy time in the

Three Doves, with everyone seemingly suffering all manner of seasonal ailments.

Lucie sent Goodman Jones on ahead. Simon, having pulled on his coat, offered to walk with his mother that he might carry her bag. When they arrived at the cottage, Lucie sent Simon back to the Three Doves.

'You know how matters are between Ned and Hester Potton, neither one can look at the other without blushing or giggling. They must be supervised.'

Inside the small cottage, Judith Hatch was lying on her bed with part of a baby's head between her open legs. Mary crouched in front of her, holding the child back.

'I wasn't sure whether to send for the chirurgeon or yourself first, Widow Smith. I am so sorry to have troubled you so.'

'Didn't I say this wench was too young for a midwife?' one of the older gossips who Lucie could not place remarked. Lucie saw the women, who included her own Martha, exchange worried glances, and knew she had but a moment to restore their confidence.

'All was progressing well and the crown was born in a seemly fashion, but it is fast. I didn't want to force it and injure it,' Mary explained calmly.

'Mary has been doing splendidly, as has Judith here,' Martha spoke up for her friend and the labouring mother, who remained calm while Lucie greased her hand. 'She was right to call for help when she reached the limits of her experience.'

'Ah, I see the problem,' Lucie adjusted herself so she could move her arm into a better position. 'The navel string is stretched too tight for this child to come out any further. Mary, you did exactly the right thing supporting it within the womb until I arrived. If you had tugged on it, you'd have surely destroyed it.' Lucie kept her hand firmly in place but turned to bestow a glower on the woman who had spoken earlier.

'Goodwife Hatch, you are to do exactly as I instruct,' Lucie winced as her patient let out a groan. 'Yes, I know it is sore, but with God's help we'll have you and the babe out of this predicament afore much longer.'

Lucie slid her fingers deeper into Judith's vagina and kept tight pressure on the child's navel. She then adjusted her position once again and slid her left hand behind the child's back. Easing him out, she kept tight her pressure on the child's belly.

'Quickly, Mary, cut through the string where it is, can you see? It is right next to the goodwife's privities, so take extra care.'

The shortness of the cord meant the child could only be brought out a little way. The string was so tight a movement from the baby could have caused it to injure itself. Mary leaned over. In three firm snips the child was free of its mother. The babe let out a lusty yell.

'Your son is displeased with the manner of his arrival I fear,' Lucie felt her face crinkle with joy.

'Let's hope he has not reason to curse us in future,' joked Jane, one of the gossips. 'You know what they say about cutting a boy's string long enough that he may grow into a fine man.'

The women laughed but Lucie was not listening now. She had handed the baby to Mary to attend to with one hand as she held the cord clamped tightly between the fingers of the other. All her attention was now focussed on bringing out the womb cake. She worked with the mother's body to guide it out on a tightening, and it took just seven minutes more for the episode to be brought to a happy ending.

'No need of Mister Collins, and Mary will have seen what I did and have no need of assistance should this happen again. It is very rare though, so worry not. Now ladies, if you'll excuse me, I will leave you in Midwife Thorne's capable hands and bid you well. God bless.'

Lucie's aching knees had stiffened at being forced to kneel. Martha rushed over to help her up. 'Won't you stay for a celebratory drink, Widow Smith?'

'No, thank you very much my dear. I will just pop my head around the door of your cottage to see the children, and I'll have a cuddle with baby Jasper. They are with their father?'

'Of course, come, let me take you there. Ladies, I will be back in a few minutes. Congratulations Judith, you have a fine son!' Martha picked up Lucie's bag and walked with her out of the cottage.

Instead of going straight to the Three Doves after her visit to Martha's home, Lucie took a detour to All Hallows. She lowered herself into her customary pew and said a prayer of thanks for the safe delivery of Goodwife Hatch, and for the continued good health of baby Jasper, who was such a comfort to her.

'Ah Mistress Archer, well met,' Lucie spotted the rector's wife at the back of the church as she walked back down the aisle. 'Will you inform Dr Archer that we shall be in need of his services for a baptism in the next day or two?'

'Oh how lovely, Widow Smith. Are you free to step into the rectory for a drink with me and tell me all about Tupingham's newest resident? I have some of that fruitcake you enjoy.'

The parlour was warm and welcoming with the fire well banked. The Archers' servant brought beer and cake for the women.

'This is most kind,' Lucie rubbed her sore knees. 'The warmth will help settle my painful joints afore long. I am too old for kneeling before groaning mothers, Mistress Archer. But it's unlikely Mary will see another such presentation for years. I can only recall a few. The first time was awful. Mother Henshaw,' Lucie rolled her eyes at the name, 'was at the heart of it, of course. The mother resided without the town walls, before your time here. She'd been delivered at one o'clock in the afternoon, but they thought not to send for me until eleven o'clock that night. Jasper walked me there and held the lantern, and Martha watched my own young family. A lifetime ago.'

Her feelings must have shown on her face. Phillipa Archer patted Lucie's arm comfortingly.

'We've lost five ourselves. Two as dear babes, three afore they were fifteen, with three married and living their own lives,' she dabbed her eyes with her handkerchief.

'I find my thoughts turning to my pretty maids a lot these days. Do you think me sinful, Mistress Archer?'

'God's will was done. But can a mother forget the baby at her breast?'

'Amen,' Lucie responded. 'We lost our son, Peter too. All three gone in little more than a sennight.'

'Smallpox?'

'Smallpox,' Lucie confirmed.

'Console yourself, they all rest in God's bosom, their father too now.'

'My husband, he would not talk of them. I believe it pained him too much, but I find comfort in remembering them,' Lucie took a sip of her beer, hugging her free arm around her tummy. 'My husband would say excessive grief was an affront to God, a challenge to His holy will.'

'I know, my dear, I know it well. I think it no sin to remember our babes and to weep sometimes. Now come, tell me the rest of that story. They did not send for you until the night. Too late to save the mother I'll warrant.'

'You know what the hand woman is like. She makes all her women bear standing up if they will endure it. It was too fast, and the baby's own weight caused its tight navel string to snap. Ripped his very bowels from his guts. The poor bereaved mother had violent floodings all afternoon.' Lucie shook her head at the memory.

'Mary Thorne will know how to deliver a woman safely in the like circumstance in future thanks to your diligence, Widow Smith. Take comfort in that.'

'You know who I have heard no word of for months now?' Lucie said as she arrived back in her kitchen. Simon lifted his head from where he was sitting in his father's chair, Ned turned to her from the table where he was busy with his quill, and the Potton girls glanced up in unison from their sewing, all waiting for Lucie to answer her own question.

'Agnes Henshaw, that's who.'

'The old hand woman?' asked Ned.

'Yes, Mother Henshaw, as they call her,' Lucie took off her cloak and hung it on the door hook. 'She was forever interfering with my women, but Mary has not made mention of seeing her this year.'

'She delivered all my mother's children, Widow Smith,' Prudence mumbled, blushing from the effort of speaking up.

'Yes, she attended on many of those who live in the countryside, and plenty of those she attended were glad of her help, I know,' Lucie lowered herself into her favourite armchair. 'For all she has done, the good and the bad, she is an ancient woman, and I ought to seek news of her and see how she goes. She might be in need of charity if she isn't able to work.'

Chapter Fourteen

'It's surely gone a little quiet this morning, not that I am complaining.' Lucie turned to Mary and took both her hands in her own. 'My dear, is something troubling you? It is not the comber's wife, is it? For you did exactly the right thing in seeking my help.'

'Oh Widow Smith,' tears sprang to the younger woman's eyes. 'If only it was that. No, it's that my parents have instructed me to return home to them on the occasion of you leaving the Three Doves. My father visited a number of days ago. The shop was crowded and so he asked me to offer his greetings but did not feel it appropriate to disturb you.'

Lucie squeezed Mary's hands tightly.

'But why would he do such a thing?'

'My mother is ailing, Widow Smith. She fell from a stool when she was cleaning the outside of our windows, and she hasn't risen from her chamber since they put her to bed.'

Lucie dropped Mary's hands and drew her into a hug. 'Mary, whyever did you not tell me? Of course you must go to her.'

'It is not so simple. My father says the villagers are caring for Mother, so it is not a nurse he seeks, but for me to remove back and keep the house for them all.' She ran a palm across her wet cheek.

'I understand, Mary. Truly I do,' Lucie sighed deeply. 'Tupingham will be a lesser place without you to care for its teeming women though. We must make the most of you while we have you, for no one has said a word to me about Mister Collins or anyone else taking over the Three Doves even yet.'

'I don't want to go. I love my art and wish to continue in the trade I am trained for.'

'I could try speaking with your father, but we women have so little say in our paths for most of our lives.' Lucie's stomach churned furiously. Those young maids in her kitchen had been abandoned by their father, and now another father was playing fast and loose with another young woman's hopes for her future. Her choler rose and her cheeks burned. There was not much comfort to be found in widowhood, but at least she herself no longer had to answer to any man. As suddenly as her temper had risen, it waned. She grabbed at the counter, a wave of grief for Jasper threatening to knock her off her feet. With her free hand she rubbed her belly. How could she have had such a thought?

'Excuse me, Mary.' She dashed out the shop to the privy. Sitting on the wooden seat, resting her head against the cold brick walls, her breath came in jagged gulps. Would she have to come out of her retirement? She couldn't leave the women with no midwife, that would contravene her oath. Over the low door of the privy, Lucie saw the twins across the garden, scattering grain for the hens. She shuddered as the ice-cold sensation she had experienced weeks ago spread down her back. 'My girls,' she whispered, slumping forward, her head in her hands. Her breathing slowed and steadied. ''Twas just the shock of Mary's news,' she said to herself.

'Mother. Mother are you ill?' Lucie heard Simon's voice calling.

'Just coming,' she wouldn't tell Simon of the unsettling experience she had had more than once now; he'd think she was losing her mind. Taking a moment to rise slowly, Lucie walked back to the scullery and washed her hands, calling for some warm wine to sooth herself.

'I took the liberty of preparing your customary poultice, Widow Smith,' Mary handed Lucie a linen parcel containing warmed bread and various spices.

'Most kind,' Lucie lowered herself into her armchair and tucked the remedy under her skirt, over her shift. Immediately she felt its warmth spread across her belly.

'I collected a letter from the postmaster while I was out.' Simon handed his mother a letter in Alice Wallis's hand. Lucie took it and tucked it into her pocket beneath her apron to save for later. Ned walked into the kitchen from the shop, ready to join them for what was to be their last meal together. He was due to return to London the next morning.

'It's been good to see you lad, and looking so well,' she stretched to squeeze his hand across the table. Ned squeezed back, and held on to her, while with his free hand he mopped the meat juices from his pewter plate with the last of the bread.

A loud rapping sounded at the door.

Lucie startled, letting go of Ned's hand. 'Who can that be?'

Mary went to answer it and Friswell from the Manor burst in with a face like thunder. His oiled leather riding coat dripped water onto Lucie's floor.

Hester dropped the pewter dish she was carrying, and Lucie noticed the panicked expressions she and Prudence exchanged.

'It's true then.' He shoved past Mary into the kitchen. Lucie ignored his rude entrance and rose to greet him politely, holding out a cup of beer. He brushed this aside.

'I am not here on a social call, Widow Smith. I'd be grateful to know why you have disobeyed my clear instruction to have the Potton girl removed from your household?' The man's choler was high, and red blotches appeared on his face. 'Not only have you failed to take the necessary actions, but you have added a second Potton girl to your disobedience,' his words were peppered with spittle. Shaking off his coat, he held it out, seemingly expecting Mary to take it. Out of cordiality, she did. He then walked to the fireplace and dropped into Jasper's armchair in front of the hearth.

Simon drew himself up to his full height. 'See here, Friswell. You cannot force yourself into my mother's home and speak thusly!'

'It seems I have, Mister Smith. And what's more,' Friswell's thin smile didn't reach his eyes, 'I will be taking matters into my own hands forthwith. This pair of conniving wenches will be leaving with me, and I will do what you have singularly failed to do.' He grabbed the cup he had rejected earlier and took a deep swig. Ned also rose to his full height and stood beside Simon.

'You'll have to get past the two of us before you lay a hand on either of these maids,' Simon spoke angrily, but Lucie noted his satisfaction at Ned's show of support.

'There will be no cause for violence, gentlemen. Mister Friswall, I will not have such coarse language under my roof.' Lucie ensured her tone was firm, even as her bottom lip trembled. 'You should know that Dr Archer, the rector of All Hallows is, as we speak, on a trip to speak to the maids' father to seek a reconciliation.'

'He has had a wasted journey in that case. I happen to know that the lease Farmer Potton has signed states he has no contact with this ... *maid*,' he pointed at Hester, mistaking her for her twin.

Lucie sank into her chair, opposite this disagreeable man. It seemed the Manor's steward had thought of everything. To her surprise Ned spoke up.

'It is of no consequence. The Pottons are coming to London with me.'

Prudence let out a gasp, her hand flying to her mouth.

'I am sorry, Widow Smith. I wanted to ask your permission first, but it seems events have overtaken us. My elder sister Scrawbrook is in need of help. She asked me to look out a suitable maid. Miss Hester Potton and I discoursed upon whether she might like to take the position, if I can persuade my sister to engage both twins. I consider this a formality, as my sister has a large house and her sea captain husband is away for months or years on end. She is in need of both help and company.'

'Mister Friswell, please leave us now,' Simon said. 'As you see, we have plans in hand to place the Pottons.'

Friswell scowled, but reluctantly allowed himself to be ushered towards the door by Simon and Ned. Mary pushed his coat into his arms. The steward growled that they had a week's grace and no more, or he would send the constable to arrest the girls.

'He has no grounds for seeking your arrest, girls,' Simon reassured them after he had shut the door and slid the large iron bolt across it. 'But the power of the Manor is in the ascendency once again in this town, and so we must take his threat seriously.'

Lucie shifted her gaze from Ned to Hester, wondering how long they had been cooking this scheme up.

'Prudence, would you be content to follow your sister into service in Deptford?' she asked. The girl nodded. 'Ned, is this offer of employment genuine?'

'Yes, Widow Smith. I swear I spoke the truth about my sister Scrawbrook's condition. She is a godly woman. She and her husband, the seaman, follow the Quakers.'

Lucie's brows knitted while she considered Ned's words. 'Quakers, you say? Good people. We had a group of Quakers travelling through Tupingham, about six years ago. Martha will know when exactly. Do you remember Ned? You were newly here and very young.'

Lucie's eyes cast upwards to the left as she remembered, and she rubbed her lips with her finger. 'I delivered one of their women, a gentle soul, but they do speak in a strange way. They said the child was born on the third day of the eleventh month, it being a second day. That's how they discourse,' she smiled at the memory. 'But oh my goodness, she had the most awful scars on her back, I can see them now,' she said with a wince.

'You have never told me this story, Mother.'

'Nor me,' agreed Mary.

'Their leader, I forget his name, went on to make a great nuisance of himself in Grantby,' Lucie felt a twinkle in her eye. 'My husband fetched home a newssheet – I expect I used it for lining of a pie dish soon after we read it – but I remember the funniest thing was this man claimed to have heard the Lord instructing the party that they should go into Grantby and that the Lord commanded he put off his shoes. It was the middle of winter! It gives me chilblains just to think on't. He stood in the market square barefoot, hollering "woe unto the bloody city of Grantby,"' she chuckled. 'Your sister, I take it, makes no objection to the wearing of shoes, Ned?'

Although she did not agree with some of their practices, Lucie felt they were good Christian folk. Ned nodded and kept his head bowed, as if suppressing a smile.

'Very well,' said Lucie. 'Simon, I'll need you to ride back to London with Ned and verify there is a position for these maids and that it is in a suitable household. I'm sorry Ned, I don't doubt you, but I must satisfy myself, you understand. You will have to leave on the morrow to be back before we have another visit from that dreadful man. She turned to the twins. 'You two go and sweep the floors upstairs, will you?'

She could hear their whispered conversation as they climbed the two pairs of stairs to the attic. Simon and Ned began discussing the arrangements they'd need to make if they were to travel together. Lucie took Alice's letter from her pocket and broke open the seal, moving her candle closer to give her better sight of it. It contained some news she had been hoping for, and the timing was perfect. She passed it to Simon.

'Some news I was expecting. You'll see I have another reason to ask you to visit London,' she said. 'Mistress Wallis's husband has been informed of a property available to lease which might suit you very well, son. He has first refusal and so if you agree it meets your needs, we can place a down payment through him.'

'I doubt I can afford the terms, Mother. A friend tells me that a lease on a shop which was within my means a year ago now goes for treble. There's no money in that for the likes of me.'

'This is a little way from your former property. Near Westminster Hall. Perhaps that is not a convenient location. I know not, but it must be worth considering.'

Simon studied the letter a moment. 'The message from Alice says the property has no accommodation, so I would need lodgings, which is an additional expense. But you're right Mother, if I am to make a go of printing alone, I must not tarry longer over leasing new buildings.'

'We'd best go to the Boar to arrange another horse,' Ned said.

'Yes, you better had,' Lucie smiled fondly at the young man, a riotous apprentice but a year ago. The men put on their coats and headed out, letting in a blast of cold air. Lucie doubted they'd be back before dark, as they'd surely go from the Boar to Hearne's for the afternoon.

'It seems events have made our Ned grow up these past months. It'd warm my husband's heart to see him so, Mary,' Lucie said.

'Aye, I can't believe how tall he is become. Let's hope his scheme is genuine for the girls' sake,' Mary nodded her head towards the stairs. The women's eyes met. It was clear they both had the same concern that Ned and Hester were conniving to be together. Then Lucie's eyes crinkled into a smile.

'Mary, you'll never guess what else was in Alice's letter. She told the tale of a birth she attended last week for one of the curate's wives. You know, from the Cathedral. Apparently, it was a Sunday morning and the husband burst into the chamber and asked that his wife quiet her grumblings, for he was struggling to do God's work and write his sermon for evensong!'

'I am only a little acquainted with Mistress Wallis, but even I know she would not have taken this rebuke to a woman in her groanings kindly,' Mary laughed, but her face was still unnaturally pale.

'No, indeed not. He was sent away with a flea in his ear, he'll not forget for a long time. He was left in no doubt that it was his wife who was doing God's work at that moment,' Lucie laughed too, thinking fondly of Alice.

Chapter Fifteen

'You take good care, Simon,' Lucie gave her son a final hug as he put his foot on the mounting block. 'You are the joy of my life,' she whispered, as he climbed on the hired horse.

'And you Ned. It's done my heart good to see you, and so altered too. If you were but half a dozen years older, you could have taken over the lease of the Three Doves with my blessing, and that's not something I thought I'd say a year ago, my lad.'

Simon and Ned exchanged glances. Lucie thought she saw Simon wink.

'Dick, come and bid farewell to the men,' Lucie urged. The lad had been hovering in the doorway of the inn but appeared wary.

'I think the apprentices of the town are a bit noisy for Dick, Widow Smith. I was as guilty as the rest,' Ned rummaged in the pocket of his coat. 'Here Dick, look what I have for you.' He held out a small paper packet filled with sugared almonds. 'A peace offering.'

Dick moved a little closer, while staying near to Lucie.

'Perhaps Widow Smith will be so kind as to pass them to you?' Ned swung himself onto his horse. 'Farewell!'

Lucie put her arm around Dick's shoulders, waving the men off. She prayed Simon would be back within the week with good news for the Potton girls, and perhaps for himself.

'Have you chores to do, Dick, or would you like to come with me to watch the builders assembling the treadwheel crane in the square? Shall we ask your mother?'

Ten minutes later Lucie and Dick were standing in front of the crane. Dick's mouth fell agape. Now assembled, the crane was big enough for two men to stand side-by-side on the wheel to lever the large stones of the new town hall into place.

'Goodness, doesn't that look hard labour, Dick? I shouldn't care to try and turn that wheel.' Dick was pointing at the crane in amazement.

'See the way the men have tied string to these pegs, Dick? That marks the shape of the new building,' she pointed out the markers and how the carts that were rumbling down High Street contained the gravel and stone for the footings.

'You looking for work, Dick?' one of the builders called out playfully. 'I could use a hand.'

'I've never known him so animated,' Lucie called back. 'I can't wait to tell his mother.'

Dick was bright-eyed as he pointed to the various elements of the building site, and Lucie did her best to explain each one.

'A momentous day in the history of Tupingham, Widow Smith.' Alderman Robbins had appeared, looking exceptionally pleased with himself. Lucie jumped, she hadn't heard him approach. 'We will be on the map when this hall and butter market is complete, mark my words.'

Without waiting for a reply, the alderman, with his rolls of paper tucked under his arm, marched off to bark at the foreman.

'I must say, Dick, I never thought the Town Hall would go up so very quickly.'

I'll warrant this is in a bid to impress Lord Calstone, she added under her breath.

'Sometimes women do become melancholic after having a baby, Goodman Malkin. Your Grace is far from alone,' Lucie reassured the worried husband at the counter of the Three

Doves, as she walked over to the shelves to find some Venetian treacle.

'Let your wife take a spoonful daily, fasting, and in the evenings give her two spoons of poppy syrup. Just five nights at most. You will have to make sure someone else minds the baby those nights; Grace needs sleep for her body to remove the poison of melancholic humours. The treacle will see her right in no time if she rests herself too.' As she explained the dosage, Lucie poured some of the thick syrup into a smaller bottle, sealing it with a cork.

'Just 1s 8d for the two items today,' Lucie said. She handed Goodman Malkin the change from his two shillings. As her customer left, Lucie's face lit up. Martha had walked in with George and Jemima.

'No baby today, Martha?' Lucie stood on tip toes to see.

'He is with Anne,' Martha shook her head. 'I am just collecting this pair from school and need to ask you something.'

'Children, why don't you run through to the kitchen and see if there is a warm biscuit for you each while your mother and I talk?' Lucie gave them both a smile. 'Isn't the commotion outside wearisome? Dick Cobb was in raptures watching the crane earlier. He and I took a walk to survey the process after I'd seen the men off from the Boar. Oh Martha, his face was a picture. Now what's ado?'

'It's these rumours going round, Widow Smith. Some are saying that physician who comes here means to be a man-midwife and deliver the local women. Is this true?'

Lucie screwed the cork back on the Venice treacle as she listened, hearing the agitation in Martha's voice. 'How was this rumour begun?'

'Schoolmistress Robbins told one of the parents that Dr Somerton will be delivering her soon. The women won't stand for it if he tries to take Mary's place.'

Their conversation was cut short as the door slowly opened. Martha went over and held it for Goodwife Lydia Johnson, whose shoeless left foot was wrapped in a piece of linen.

'I've scalded it badly,' Goody Johnson winced as she stepped forward.

'Come and have a seat. Let me see what can be done to give you some ease. Martha could you untie the bandage? I'll go and get a mixture I've recently had delivered from the apothecary in Grantby.' She soon returned with a bottle of linseed oil in which crayfishes had been boiled and dabbed some on the burn before wrapping it in a clean bandage. 'You'll need to call into the Three Doves each morning for the next few days to have this process repeated, my dear,' Lucie said gently.

'I can guess what Goody Higgs here was saying, Widow Smith, and she's right, we don't want no man acting midwife here.' She raised herself from the stool with a grunt. ''Tain't proper,' the goodwife paused to add as she limped from the shop. Another family had already bustled in. Thomasina Shepherd needed something for her back tooth, which was tormenting her.

'You need a cordial made with oil of cloves. Three spoonfuls morning and night, if you wish to be cured,' Lucie handed over the mixture and accepted the shilling payment. Martha closed the shop door after holding it open for the Shepherds, and Lucie asked her to slide the bolt so they would not be disturbed again.

'It's as near noon as makes no difference. Come through to the kitchen Martha, and have a cup of beer. I have both good news concerning the matter you raise and some less than welcome information.'

The kitchen was busy. The children were standing beside Prudence and Hester at the hearth, cooking biscuits on the griddle. Prudence spoke first, and Lucie's heart grew to see the young woman gain confidence daily.

'There was no cake or biscuits, Widow Smith, so George and Jemima helped us mix some. They have had a fine time.' The girl was smiling, but suddenly frowned. 'We should have asked if that was the right thing to do. We haven't neglected the meat; it's bubbling well in the pot.' Prudence wrung her hands in her apron as if fearing a scolding.

'If these two are happy, I am,' Lucie reassured her. 'If we had no biscuits for them what else would you do?' Her eyes crinkled as she felt her smile reach them, and she was pleased to see the nervous maid's body relax. 'You've made a fine batch. When they are cooled, Jemima, you and George shall take a parcel of them home to share among your friends in Warley Lane.'

Hester chuckled. 'There are rather a lot. Forgive us Widow Smith, Pru and I are used to cooking for a large family which includes many hungry farmhands, so even when we reduce the quantity of our paste, we still make too much.'

'They won't go to waste in Warley Lane,' Martha said.

'No, indeed. Girls could you go and clean the shop, sweep the floor and give the countertop a scrub with sand? The Venice treacle made a stickly mark this morning. We'll eat when Martha and I have finished our discourse.'

She set about pouring a cup of beer for herself and Martha.

'George, would you like to run outside and see if you can find any eggs? There's a love.' The restless boy had a look of mischief on his face. He was unlikely to find any eggs as the Pottons would have collected them already, but he'd look hard knowing Lucie would insist he kept any he found.

'He is full of life that boy,' Martha commented. 'He never seems to tire, does he Jem?'

'Remember when Peter was of an age with George? My boy was just the same. He and Simon were quite different weren't they? Simon so quiet and always drawing, Peter with his perpetually scraped knees and that football pounding the scullery door when he couldn't persuade Sarah to kick about with him.' Lucie's eyes drifted to the childish painting of the High Street Simon had done twenty years before. In the bedroom window were four dots the size of a child's fingerprints.

Martha's gaze followed Lucie's, 'The four of them peering out the window for you to come back from one of your women, Simon said.'

'How many times have you and I whitewashed this room over the years, Martha, always so careful to go around that picture. It's part of the fabric of the Three Doves now. Even Dr Somerton recognised it as the view up the High Street when he was here last.'

Martha lifted Jemima up onto the bench so she could try and see the faded grey marks representing Peter, Simon, Sarah and Hannah.

'About Dr Somerton,' Lucie took a sip of her beer, 'he's made it clear that he does not plan to work as a man-midwife. Indeed, he thinks women would manage just as well under the care of "Dame Nature" as he puts it.'

'Well, that wouldn't have happened at Judith's son's birth would it? This Dame Nature would have carried her and her boy off, if it weren't for yours and Mary's skills.'

Lucie shifted in her seat, putting her cup down 'This brings me to the bad news. Mary has been summoned home. Her mother ails and her father needs her to keep the house. He's a gun maker as you know, and never short of trade,' Lucie rolled her eyes at Martha. 'I always assumed Mary would take over my women, but I shouldn't have.' She rubbed her belly. Martha appeared shocked, as she wiped her mouth with the back of her hand.

'But Widow Smith, how will we manage? And it is surely more reason to fear this Somerton might want to take your women.'

'A little bird told me you might have trained as a midwife if things had been different.'

'Oh no, not I. I might have said a few loose words to Mary at a birthing. Grace's, baby I think, but no, I could not have that responsibility.'

George was back in the kitchen, rosy checked and triumphant, holding two eggs, one between the thumb and forefinger of each hand. He grinned broadly. Lucie eased herself from her chair and went to the dresser.

'Here young man, let's add one more and you, Jemima and baby Jasper shall have an egg each today. Martha, pop these in your basket with this pile of biscuits. Let's pray on the other matter and see how things stand in a few days.'

The midwife bent down and pointed to her cheek, and each of the children planted a kiss on her. She slipped a halfpenny to each child. Martha shook her head as she shepherded the pair out through the scullery.

'Martha, make sure the children have a care around those building works. They are very dangerous.'

As she heard the door shut, Lucie sank back in her seat and rubbed her sore belly. In that moment her grief for Jasper was a physical pain, a ball in the centre of her body.

'How I long to receive your counsel, Jasper,' she said to herself. 'Thirty years a wife and almost a year a widow,' she closed her eyes in a vain attempt to hold back the tears that were never far away these days.

Chapter Sixteen

'Butcher Cordel does very badly, I fear,' said Dr Somerton, looking up from his paperwork in what Lucie would always think of as Jasper's study. 'He's not recovering as Collins and I hoped. You've been providing him with remedies, Widow Smith. What is thy opinion in the case?'

Lucie was busy with a jar of *sal prunella* from Jasper's chest and tipped a number of the balls into her mortar, locking the chest after she had returned the jar.

'I am ever hopeful, Dr Somerton, but concede that Joseph Cordel is unlikely to recover. His wound weeps so. I have tried all I can to find a remedy which would help but to no satisfactory end thus far. We're in need of a miracle, I fear.'

'Indeed.' The physician turned back to the prescription he was writing up, dipping his quill.

'You'll eat with us at noon, Doctor, will you?' The physician would appreciate her hospitality, and it was undoubtedly true that their arrangement had enhanced her income from the shop, mainly because he drew up prescriptions for cures made from more expensive ingredients than Jasper would have recommended in his place.

The table was hearty with slices of bacon and a fruity pottage. The Potton twins were subdued as was normal in the presence of the physician, and so the conversation was stilted.

'If you are finished, girls, leave the plates and go tidy the apothecary shop, would you?' Lucie asked. The twins must have been grateful to have been excused and Prudence quickly fetched a broom from the scullery. The pair went through to the shop.

'I hope thy son goes well on these cold, dark roads Widow Smith. I spend half my life on horseback these days and it does not offer much joy in the winter season.' The physician rubbed his chapped face. 'This reminds me to purchase a balm from you, against these rough winds which are making my lips sore.'

'Certainly, Dr Somerton, let me go through to the shop and bring you one presently, lest we forget. Would you mind pouring us a cup of wine each and we can finish our meal with a slice of this apple pie the girls made yesterday. I shall miss their cooking when they leave me, although my waistline will be happier. I have grown quite fat these last weeks.'

When they were settled back at the hearth, each taking an armchair to sup their wine, Lucie explained the plans to remove the girls to Deptford.

'I am pleased they have been placed within a good home, Widow Smith. They have earned their tabling with you, I think, but have been a burden you did not seek, I fear.'

Lucie said nothing. If only you knew, she thought. How often had the sight of those maids put her in mind of her own pretty ones? How often had her heart been broken afresh? The physician paid no attention to Lucie's silence but launched into one of his tales.

'It was on the ninth, there was a poor fool by the name of Mary Baker, wandering for sustenance in this chill weather, lacking clothes to keep her warm. She had clearly gone barefooted for many years, for her feet were thick and callused. She was found in an open, windy, cold place, nigh to a house of office, on the north road out of Grantby. There she was delivered by the sole assistance of Dame Nature,

Eve's midwife we might say. Don't look at me like that, Widow Smith.'

'I was not aware I looked a particular way. I feel for this Mary, 'tis all.'

'Well, she was also freed of the afterbirth, without the help of any other midwife, or any assisting woman present with her. This poor creature, leaning with her back against a wall, was quickly delivered and more easily than many have been by midwives in warm places.'

'Please God she goes well?' Lucie shook her head slowly as sadness washed over her for this pauper, at her time, shoeless in winter, bearing down against the cold walls of a privy, rather than the warmth of a friend's body.

'She and the child lived,' he replied bluntly, reaching over to place his cup on the table. 'It was reported that the child, a maid, lay naked upon the cold boards of the house of office more than a quarter of an hour.'

'I am indeed surprised she lived if that's so.'

'They were only found out by the child's crying, and some neighbours being called they took up the child and found the navel-string separated from the afterbirth, which came off itself afterward. I examined both the woman and infant and judged all they needed to thrive was warmth and nourishment. Your friend Midwife Wallis has taken her in and provided her with such items as a woman needs at this time.'

Lucie sighed as all the tension and sadness poured out of her. She clasped her hands.

'Oh now I am assured of a happy ending. Mistress Wallis will provide a warm bed under her roof and make sure this woman is not wanting necessaries fitting for a woman's relief. Although the parish will be keen for her to name the father so as not have to meet the costs of this Mary's care, I expect?'

'Naturally she will be expected to worry this intelligence from the mother, but as I told you it is my opinion the woman is a fool, and the midwife will get no sense from her. The child will have to go to nurse on the parish and the woman sent on her way when she is well.'

'The world is a cruel place, doctor. My son tells me they think upwards of fifty thousand folks were made homeless in the London fire.'

'I expect it will be a good deal higher in time when a true reckoning is made.' Somerton drank down the last of his wine. 'It is a good and fitting thing that every woman should have her midwife with her at the time of her delivery. But this demonstrates, does it not, that it is not absolutely necessary, for that many be delivered without the help of midwives.'

This again, thought Lucie, smoothing down her apron as she rose from her armchair. Her attempts to change the subject of their conversation had clearly failed. Warming to his topic, Dr Somerton began speaking again. 'It puts me in mind of a sorry case. Esther Bidway, I believe she was named. She slept with her sister, and on the night the unfortunate wretch sealed her fate, she rose up, and went into an outhouse, and there was delivered of a child. She returned quickly again into her bed. Her sister never heard a thing. Or so she swore. But being mistrusted by her neighbours, from whom she had not so successfully concealed her condition, some women upon suspicion being sent to search her, without any ado she confessed her wickedness, and showed them the place where the child was buried.'

Lucie turned her back, making a show of piling up the pewter plates and spoons, but the clatter did not deter the physician who droned on.

'She was asked by the coroner, why she had not a midwife to assist and help her in her labour. She answered that she needed no help, or assistance, and that she was well enough delivered without a midwife. Indeed, she was so well that she could have gone twenty miles the day following.'

'I expect I can guess the end to his wicked woman's tale,' Lucie said in a weary voice, a pile of tableware in her hands.

'She was sent to gaol, from thence she was conveyed to the place of execution, where she ended her sorrowful life with great repentance.'

Lucie went through to the scullery with the plates. He couldn't be saying this with poor Prudence in mind, could he?

'I realise you will not be swayed from this view,' Lucie said as she stepped back into the kitchen, 'but I will just say that had my last woman, Goodwife Hatch, not had two experienced midwives on hand, she and her son would be dead. We will have to agree to disagree, Doctor Somerton. I have spent my whole life being a midwife like my mother before me.' Lucie turned to open the door to the shop. 'I'll take a shilling and six pence for the balm; you may leave it on the counter if that is all.'

The metallic, bloody odour of flesh assailed Lucie as she drew near the butcher's shop. Sal Cordel, the butcher's brash wife, was leaning out the window through which she served her customers, black curls escaping her cap. Lucie knew her well, since she birthed every eighteen months like clockwork. She delivered with an ease that heifers – that she could cut through as easily as many a man – would envy. Still, Lucie felt a knot in her stomach each time she approached the shop. Like so many of the townswomen, Goodwife Cordel had been unwilling to speak in Lucie's defence at her trial last January, not because she had not received the best care possible from the midwife, but she preferred to stay out of it in case her business suffered. No matter that Lucie was exonerated, and the trial abandoned, the lack of support still hurt.

''E's in the cutting room if it's Joe you're after,' Sal said. 'He'll not rest no matter what you or anyone else says. I'm meant to be resting too, being this near my time,' she added with a snort. Lucie followed Goodwife Cordel inside, pulling her cloak tight. The room seemed colder than outside; the doors were open onto a courtyard where a pig rooted for scraps on the flagstones with no idea how near its end it was. A gulley down the middle of the yard ran with the blood of a recently slaughtered beast. Butcher Cordel was shouting instructions to his apprentices who were hacking at a cow, held high in the air with its back legs tied on two parallel wooden beams that ran across the room. On the block was a side of beef bigger than Lucie; the butcher saw her looking at it and laughed, 'about twelve stone of beef there Widow Smith, enough to keep you going for a few weeks, eh!'

'Indeed Goodman, indeed. Now could you kindly explain what you mean by hoisting that beast up like that when your wound is not healed?'

The butcher's cheeks coloured. 'Someone's got to keep this place going. This pair of lazy curs won't do a hand's turn if I am not watching over them.'

'There is not much you can tell me about raising apprentices, butcher, but you are not a well man.'

''E was one of the worst of that crew, your last. No offence, Widow Smith,' the butcher said with a rueful smile. After a few moments more setting things to rights, he declared it was now convenient for Lucie to examine him. They walked into the kitchen and he climbed on the table, loosening the cord that held up his breeches.

'Yon chirurgeon was here yesterday poking at me,' he grimaced at the memory.

'You've been keeping to a proper diet, I hope?' Lucie asked.

'Remind me again, Widow Smith, then I can say right enough if I have or no.'

'I told you to take heed you eat no cheese, butter, eggs, nor fish of the sea, nor fruit, but to only consume fine and light meats. Things like capons, chickens, rabbits and such.'

The butcher made a noise like he was sucking his teeth and scowled. Lucie washed her hands and dried them on a linen towel from her own bag.

'I can't say I have then. I like butter on my bread, and it wouldn't be natural for a butcher not to eat his own beef, would it? Ouch, have a care!' he yelled as Lucie untied his drawers to examine his wound.

'Very well. If you won't help yourself, I have but one more treatment to suggest,' she said, carefully touching the tender skin of Cordel's damaged scrotum. 'You will need to take the lungs of the next sheep you slaughter,' she paused, noting the puzzled look on the butcher's face. 'Its lights,' she said gently, using the colloquial name. 'While they're still hot, lay them upon the wound, and it is said that the flesh shall rise equal with the skin. Let's see how that works for you.'

It was already dark in the mid-afternoon as Lucie set out for the Three Doves. She had gone but a few yards when her heart started pounding like it was trying to get free of her. Her head dropped under the weight of her out-of-control thoughts. *Here I am at this late stage of my life trying to fill the breach my husband's death has left as the town's apothecary, and to keep delivering women, including those who would not aid me when I was in need of support at my trial last year, and to care for the Potton maids these past weeks.* Her thoughts continued to race. Lucie slumped against the wall of the nearest shop. 'Jasper,' the cry came out of her mouth before she could stop it, but it was muffled in her shawl and felt as though it went straight into her broken heart. Tears ran down her face and phlegm almost choked her. She slid down the shop wall to the floor. Allowed her heavy eyelids to fall. *How I wish to hear his counsel, to pray with him, to feel the weight of his body as he lay with me.* Her hands hugged her belly tightly, and she sat lost in her own world, until her breathing started to settle.

Taking a deep breath, she eventually clambered up. Across the road she could just make out the shape of a couple of townsfolk observing her. More fodder for the gossips. She bent wearily to pick up her hat and basket from the pavement.

'Don't trouble yourselves to assist me,' she called out. She pushed back her shoulders and set off once again, biting her lip with the effort of keeping going – one foot after the other – and the embarrassment she felt.

Chapter Seventeen

In the pitch dark, Lucie was confused as she was awoken by the sound of a maid screaming. The noise continued as she came round from her deep slumber and struggled to sit up.

'Don't concern yourself Widow Smith,' Mary was already on her feet, sliding them into her embroidered slippers. 'I expect she's having a nightmare after all the talk of them removing to Deptford. She is a nervous soul. I'll take her a cup of spiced wine, you go back to sleep.'

Lucie watched until Mary's candle bobbed out of sight, then lay back on her pillow. She must have dozed off, because the movement of her bed as Mary climbed back in roused her.

'Is she calm again, Mary?' Lucie asked.

'Yes. She had woken to find herself wet and panicked. She told Hester it was happening again. She was shaking and saying she had never lain with a man except that time the old man forced himself upon her and how could it be happening again.'

'The poor soul,' Lucie said with a shake of her head. 'Her courses had resumed, I take it?'

'Yes, that is all it was. Naturally, Pru was terrified and nothing Hester did would calm her. She's never had one in her life, has she, given that she caught so early? She settled when I put a burnt feather under her nose for a few moments. I have given her a double clout for the bleeding and told her this is naught but the benefit of nature. She's sleeping now. Curled up in her sister's arms.'

'I worry how she'll manage,' Lucie admitted. 'Removing to a strange household in a busy town. All she has known is country life. The same is true for Hester, of course. But that maid is more self-assured, more practical. Look at how she has settled in here.'

When the women woke again, the shutters in the chamber had been opened, the chamber pots emptied and cleaned, and two cups of beer were waiting on the table. Lucie rose and tucked her hair into a clean cap, and Mary laced her stays for her.

'We must persuade Martha to become the town midwife and to work with me. It is the only answer. I prayed on it long into the night,' Lucie said. She had written to Mary's father to plead for her to be allowed to stay in Tupingham, but his mind was set. His daughter was needed at home.

'Yes, it must be Martha,' Mary agreed. 'I wanted to propose this myself to her but apart from a hint some weeks ago, she's always seemed against any notion of becoming a midwife herself.'

'I did ask recently, and she said no again, but we agreed to each think on't and talk later. The way I see it is this, I never allow those I train to deliver a child until their third year, as you well know, and by that time they have assisted at dozens of births. Well, my Martha has assisted at many more. Mary, I lost count at forty-eight while I was sitting in bed waiting for you to join me last evening.'

Lucie tightened Mary's stays, and then fastened her own apron as Mary tidied their bed. As Mary walked with Lucie towards the door, the midwife turned to her former deputy.

'I'll go to Warley Lane immediately on closing the Three Doves at lunchtime.' On impulse she reached out and clasped Mary's face in both hands, looking directly in her eyes. 'Don't think for a moment this means we won't miss you, my dear. All my previous deputies left when their training ended, but I had allowed myself the comfort of thinking you would stay in the town.' She leaned in and kissed Mary on the forehead. 'I hope today sees Simon returned. The week is up, and we don't want a visit from Steward Friswell before we know if our charges have secured positions in Deptford.'

'You're not alone in proposing this, Widow Smith,' said Martha, pouring a small beer for Lucie. 'Tell her, Anthony. We have had quite the stream of visitors making the same request ever since the rumours about the physician began to circulate. That's even before they heard about Mary leaving. A few said the young lass needed an older woman like me for support, which is nonsense of course.'

'Aye, 'tis true,' said the weaver, not looking up from his loom. His nimble fingers threaded some wool. 'It's been like the market square in here with women streaming in and out. Mind, some came with gifts to woo our Marth, so it wasn't all bad.' He chuckled as, satisfied his thread was secure, he trod on the loom making it clack onto the next row. The light was fading rapidly on this December day and Goodman Higgs needed every available minute to make progress or there wouldn't be enough money coming in to feed the five of them. Lucie pulled her cloak tightly around herself. The cottage's window was unglazed, and even with Martha's fire roaring, the room was chilly. Martha pointed to the shelves at the side of the fire, and her faced flushed with embarrassment. It was true that they were more amply stocked than usual, with cheese, jars of pickles, and cakes.

'See how well regarded you are, Martha. What pray do you both say to this scheme?'

Before they could talk further little Jasper woke in his crib. Martha swung him out and placed him on the floor.

'Look how he goes; he slides on his belly almost crawling,' Martha's face lit in a smile as her son wriggled on the dirt floor. But not for long. Lucie scooped him up into a big hug, 'Oh my clever little man! How proud I am of you.'

George and Jemima came bursting through the door, their red noses glowing where the cold had nipped them. Both were ravenous and Lucie decided to leave their mother to see to their needs. She obtained the promise from Martha that she would at least keep thinking on Lucie's proposal and let her know her decision soon.

'Any sign of my son?' Lucie asked Hester, as she untied her cloak in the kitchen of the Three Doves half an hour later.

'Not yet, but a letter has arrived.'

Lucie immediately saw it was in her son's hand.

'Tonight's stewed beef will not be fit for at least an hour, Widow Smith,' Hester said. 'But shall I warm you some wine after that long walk?'

'I've just taken a message,' Prudence spoke up as she came into the kitchen from the shop, 'at the front door. The chirurgeon's sent for you on an urgent matter, Widow Smith. You are to bring some of the medicine a man called Old Tom takes for his nerves. Said you'd know what that means,' Prudence blushed.

'I do indeed, thank you for passing this message on. I think I'll sit and read Simon's letter and warm my bones before I set out again though. I will take that spiced wine, Hester, thank you. Mary is abroad?'

Prudence nodded. Lucie picked up one of the candles on the mantlepiece and leaning forward, took the opportunity to have a quick taste of the liquor in which the beef was bubbling away. 'Very tasty! I shall look forward to that when I return from the Collins house. We are having dumplings I hope?' The stodgy balls would provide comfort after yet another busy day pulled in all directions. She kept the candle in one hand as she shook open Simon's letter and read it quickly.

> *Dearest Mother,*
> *I hope this finds you well. I am delayed on business in London for an extra day or two, so am sending this to avoid you worrying.*

Mistress Scrawbrook runs a fine and Godly home. She is willing to engage both Potton maids. Her husband is a successful sea captain who is away much of the time, and she lacks company as well as help, just as Ned said. Her man conveyed this letter to you, as he has been charged with escorting the Pottons to Deptford. While it will be a change of condition for these maids, the Scrawbrook house is on the edge of town, and quite rural. They keep a cow, pigs, and hens so mayhap their skills as dairymaids will be called on. Ned was quite right that this is an opportunity beyond the ordinary. Mistress Scrawbrook, who was most hospitable to me, will be a fair and considerate mistress. The man is of middle years, sports an old-fashioned chin beard, and goes by the name of Bayham. He will carry a missive from his mistress to confirm the offer of a place in the Scrawbrook household. You may discharge the maids into his custody with an easy mind.

I have received intelligence as to the sale of some printing machinery from the estate of one of those master printers taken by the late plague and am keen to pursue this to see if I may acquire some items to help with my plans. I am told nearly one in five master printers was carried off by the pestilence, affirming my decision to repair to the countryside last summer. I will be home before father's memorial stone is commemorated in All Hallows. Of that you have my word.

Your affectionate son,

Sim. Smith

Folding the letter in her lap, Lucie took a swig of her wine. 'Well ladies, it seems you are to remove to Deptford presently.

We are to expect a gentleman to escort you to take up your new positions at any time.'

Hester flushed and smiled, but Lucie saw the flash of horror on Prudence's face, before the girl regained control of her passions.

'Why don't you accompany me to the barber-surgeon's house, Prudence? I should like company, and Hester can manage here, can't you? Let's hope Mary returns soon that we may eat all together one last time.' Lucie packed some of the calming waters that she knew Jasper mixed for Tom Mitchell on a regular basis, and also a sliver of soap and a new girdle for the itch as a precaution. Tom's addled mind, damaged on the battlefield, meant he neglected to care for himself.

Collins was just finishing trimming a beard when Lucie and Prudence arrived.

'Tom's up the first pair of stairs, Widow Smith,' he said without taking his eyes off his customer's face.

'Thank you, Mister Collins. We'll attend to him presently.'

'We?' Collins looked up. 'Oh, I was hoping to converse with you in private when you have attended to my patient. No matter, it'll keep,' he scowled in Prudence's direction.

'Pay no mind to him, Prudence,' Lucie said as the pair climbed the stairs. Her friend's irascibility was legendary, but he was a fine and kind-hearted fellow underneath his brusque exterior. 'Neither man would thank me for saying so, but in respect of their humours both he and my late husband are quite alike.'

Goodman Mitchell was in a highly agitated state, thrashing on the bed. He barely recognised Lucie.

'Here Tom, have a sip of this. I've mixed it just how Jasper did for you,' she said gently.

'I want t'pot'cary. Where is he? I don't want to stay here!'

'Jasper died, Tom, you remember. You're just to stay here until you're well again. Mister Collins tells me you're not too good at the moment. Drink this, and we'll see how it does you.'

She called to Prudence to seek out the housemaid to see if she could find a clean shift and shirt for the old soldier. While Collins was attentive to the medical needs of his in patients, he paid insufficient mind to their comfort, Lucie thought.

'Prudence, we'll take Goodman Mitchell's linen home and get it looking pristine again.'

The medicine began to take effect and Tom settled. By the time they took their leave the old man was sleeping peacefully in his bed, all clean in fresh linen.

'Let's hope the girdle kills whatever is nipping at him in short order. If those tiny sores don't dry up, they could become very nasty.' Lucie explained. She put her arm through Prudence's as they walked home. 'Did you know I grew up in Deptford? I hope to see the place again one day, and maybe visiting you girls will provide the excuse I need.'

'I miss my mother and the younger children so much, Widow Smith,' Prudence suddenly blurted out.

'I am sure you do my dear,' Lucie gave her charge's arm a squeeze. 'I will make sure to get word to your mother about your change of situation – the rector knows their new address, and perhaps in time the Lord will move your parents' heart to soften towards you.' Lucie wished she felt as confident as she sounded.

Chapter Eighteen

Urgent rapping on the front door woke Lucie from a fitful slumber. As she slowly roused, she heard the sounds of stones being thrown at her chamber window. With a jolt, she remembered she was quite alone in the house. Alone in a house overnight for the first time of her life, aged nearly sixty. She rose and pulled her shawl around herself.

Walking to the window she cried out, 'Who calls?'

'Begging your pardon, Widow Smith. It is Tim Smedley from Warley Lane, my wife Katherine is at her time and the women have sent me to fetch Midwife Thorne.'

Lucie slammed shut her window. She lit a candle from the fire and swiftly pulled a skirt over her night dress. There was no point attempting her stays by herself, so she would have to do as she was. She buttoned up her woollen jacket and sat on her bed to tie woollen stockings above her knees. Heading to the stairs, she found it easier on her aching knees to descend backwards these days. In the kitchen her single candle was no match for the inky air which surrounded her, the fire being down to but a few embers. *I must bank that back up*, she thought, but as she pulled open the bolt on the scullery door, Goodman Smedley was waiting anxiously, hopping from foot to foot, and all thoughts of the fire were forgotten.

'Mary is away visiting her family at present so you will have to accept my services,' Lucie told him brusquely. 'Can you manage this chair for me? If I had known your wife was near her time, arrangements would have been made for it to have been carried to your cottage in good time.'

'She's wanting of her time by a couple of weeks,' Smedley muttered. He picked up the bulky chair as if it was light as a feather. Small puffs of clouds appeared in front of Lucie on the frosty night as she negotiated the cobbles, struggling to keep up with the weaver who was carrying both the chair and a lantern. Conversation was impossible due to her panting.

As she was ushered into the cottage, Lucie let out a gasp. She felt her face, tingling from the cold air, draining of colour.

'Whatever is the matter, Widow Smith? You look like you have seen a ghost.' Martha rushed over from the alcove which was the only separation in the one roomed cottage between living and working space and the bed. Her hand flew to her mouth.

'Oh Widow Smith, I am truly sorry, come here.' Martha took Lucie in a tight hug. 'I neglected to tell you that the Smedleys had taken this cottage. Goodman Allen and his children left a few weeks ago to live with his mother. Here, drink this,' she released Lucie and handed her a cup of small beer that one of the other gossips passed over.

'I see.' The last time Lucie had been in this room was when she, Mary and Martha had cleaned it after the death of poor Anne Allen and her child. She shut her eyes in silent prayer.

'Widow Smith? Are you well enough to proceed?' asked Jane, one of the gossips. 'We heard about your indisposition in High Street several days ago.'

'Yes, Goodwife Croft, I am quite well. I delivered you and all your children without incident, did I not?'

'I mean no offense,' Jane reddened. 'I'm just worried about you, 'tis all.'

Fortunately, when Lucie approached the straw mattress, she found a robust young goodwife who was in no imminent danger.

'My dear, all appears well. I'll search you presently to see how matters are.'

As she rubbed oil of lilies all over her hands and forearms, Lucie felt a warm sensation pass through her as if her years of experience were fortifying her body. She bade the women join her in a prayer for the safe delivery of this young woman and then performed her examination. The head was crowning; she had arrived just in time.

'Come, Martha,' she beckoned her former housemaid. 'You should deliver this infant, it looks like to come very soon.'

Martha hesitated just a moment, looking at the other women. Jane Croft and Anne Jones exchanged glances, before Anne said, 'come cousin, leaving out Widow Smith, you are the most experienced woman here.'

'Very well,' said Martha. 'We are to help Katherine to the chair, Widow Smith?'

'Yes,' Lucie replied, busily padding the chair with clouts to make it more comfortable to sit in. 'When she is seated, you come and kneel before her, and I will guide you.'

Katherine let out a wail as the women helped her from the bed.

'The child comes! I feel it coming,' she panted.

'Come slowly, sit down here,' Martha spoke softly, guiding her into position. 'Jane, can you stroke Katherine's belly, please?'

Martha crouched so her eyes were level with the baby's crowning head.

'Slowly, slowly keep your hand on its head,' Lucie advised, 'and as the head comes move your hands like so.' She took Martha's hands and placed one on the top of the child's head and one underneath, under its chin. 'That's it. Now help the child ease out the first shoulder with the next of Katherine's pangs, we are almost there, you are both doing excellent work.'

Katherine's bright red face grimaced. 'It doesn't feel excellent from where I'm sitting,' she puffed.

Martha, hands full, looked up at Lucie and smiled. 'Like this?' she asked as Katherine let out a yell.

'Less shouting, my dear. Chin down and you shall have your baby on the next pain. If you use the strength you waste wailing to push, that is,' Lucie chided gently. She caught sight of Jane and Anne behind Katherine's back. Jane was poking her finger through a hole in one of the clouts being made ready to swaddle the child, rolling her eyes.

'Thank you, ladies. Those clouts warmed by the hearth will be needed very soon, if you please,' Lucie noted that the women had the grace to look embarrassed. She could not abide catty behaviour in her birthing chamber. Katherine followed Lucie's direction, obediently placing her chin to her chest, but gripped the handles on the chair with such force her knuckles went white. She did indeed push her son out whole on the next pang.

'Congratulations, my dear, you have a fine and lusty son.' Lucie inspected the slimy baby Martha handed to her. 'And you Martha, are on your way to being a midwife. You sit there and wait with Katherine. When the string finishes pulsing in a moment, I will cut it and you may tend to the infant while I guide the womb cake out.'

She had only been at the Smedley cottage for just over two hours by the time her duty was done. There was a glimmer of dawn in the sky, she noticed, as the door opened and the goodman came in to meet his son. It must have been later than she thought when she was woken. Perhaps just after five. But at least she could walk home by herself.

'Come to my house, Widow Smith, and break your fast with the children and us. You need some sustenance after our busy night.' Martha helped Lucie on with her cloak and said in a low voice so that Lucie alone might hear, 'I have not forgotten that today is the anniversary of Mister Smith's passing.'

Lucie's eyes filled. 'Do you mind if I decline, my dear? I wish to be alone today, to spend the day in prayer and contemplation. Give my dear little ones a kiss from me. Oh, and Martha, you should keep the fee for today's delivery. It is just three shillings, the usual reduced rate for the women of Warley Lane, but see you collect it and keep it, you did the work.'

'I'll say a prayer for Mister Smith this day too. Send for me if you find you would like company later this day. Anthony will understand.'

'Thank you. Have one of the men return the chair. There is no urgency. I'll see you at the baptism in a day or two, ladies. Good day.' Lucie felt a smile stretching her lips as she stepped out into the cold morning. Perhaps Jasper was watching over her, and the lusty boy child born this day could lay the ghost of the melancholy she had felt ever since she lost Anne and her son in that very room. She shuddered and lost the smile as her nose filled with the memory of the metallic tang that marked that bloody day.

Unpacking the soiled clouts in the scullery, Lucie was already missing the Pottons. They would have spirited this laundry off and had it soaking in urine and soap in a heartbeat. She ran her eyes over the remaining contents of her bag, noting what was in need of replenishment.

'The fire,' her hand rushed to her forehead. 'I neglected to bank it.'

She quickly walked through to the kitchen. 'Dead. Oh, Lucie you must have a care.' Her stomach rumbled loudly, echoing in the empty room. I should attend to the fire, just fetch a few coals from upstairs, she thought, but the continuing rumbling of her stomach forced her to acknowledge her weakness from want of sustenance.

'This is but a miserable meal,' she said aloud to the empty room, frowning and pulling her shawl close. She picked at a hunk of cheese and some bread where she stood in front of the dresser. The watery morning sun barely made an impression on the gloom, and it suited her dark mood perfectly. 'That's quite enough to quieten you,' she told her stomach after a few bites, 'we've a fire to make.'

To her relief, the fire in her chamber was still alight, even if it had only had the barest of glows from a few dying embers. She eased herself to her knees, gripping the mantel shelf. She could hear her mother's voice ringing in her ears, 'Any housewife worth the name knows never to let all the fires in a house die, Lucie.'

I don't think I can go back downstairs to search out rags, she thought wearily. Instead, she shuffled to the wooden box in which she kept her papers and tore some strips from a sheet. The papers took time to catch as she dandled them in the embers, but at length flames appeared and she was able to light the kindling wood that she had placed under coals.

'Thank goodness,' she gripped the mantle shelf again to pull herself up. Gratefully she climbed into her bed and drew up the covers.

But after ten minutes spent tossing and turning, she was out of bed again and pacing her chamber. Her breathing became erratic. Thoughts she did not recognise flooded her mind. *How could Jasper have been so lacking in care as to ride to London in the middle of winter, knowing he'd meet the plague?* Back and forth she walked. *Did he think I'd not known grief enough?* Suddenly she became aware of a strange noise, a howl of pain. She looked around in alarm, before it dawned on her that the sound was coming from her own body. It matters not, for I'm quite alone, Lucie thought. Aye that's my life now. Three children in yon graveyard and a husband buried goodness knows where in the middle of London, under a pile of rubble from the fire. And Simon, where's he? He promised to be back before today. By and by her breathing settled, and the room slowly warmed.

Time to build a fire in the kitchen. Imagine if Martha or Mary visit and find the fire out. The shame will be more than I can bear.

Carrying a shovel filled with glowing coals, Lucie made hard work of crawling down the stairs. She winced as her sore joints struggled with carrying the heavy shovel and her weary body down the steps. As she rose to her feet at the bottom of the pair of stairs, Lucie's eye was distracted by Simon's painting on the kitchen wall. The image transfixed her, and she could not turn her gaze from it.

'That life is over,' she said to herself in a low growl. 'Finished, and you need not taunt me so.'

The shovel crashed to the flagstones, and coals spilled hither and thither. Still, she stared at the painting as if in a trance. Then, without being aware of what she was doing, Lucie climbed first onto the bench and next up onto the kitchen table, knocking off the butter dish and bowl of salt. The sand box was tucked at the end of the table and Lucie took a palmful and rubbed the wall with her bare hands. Slowly at first, then faster and faster. She pulled up her apron, spitting on it to dampen it, and rubbed at the wall with it. The picture of the Three Doves slowly disappeared, leaving a large dirty smear. Her hair fell from her cap, and blood ran down her fingers as her skin tore on the rough limed walls, but she didn't notice. Neither did she notice the wisps of smoke rising up as the coals smouldered on the reed mat on the kitchen floor.

Chapter Nineteen

Lucie's nose twitched, there was a smoky smell in her nostrils. She couldn't place it. Perhaps her nose was playing tricks on her. Slowly her eyelids fluttered open, and she winced as light entered her eyes for the first time in many days. The fire was roaring; the shutters were closed, and a pair of candles provided weak light. Something isn't right, she thought. She tried to move, only to cry out as a pain shot through her arm and shoulder.

'Ah you've come back to us midwife Smith. I knew you would once my remedies had worked their magic.'

'Ag. . . ,' Lucie tried to speak but her body spasmed as a cough broke her attempt.

'Mother, you're awake. God be praised,' Simon rushed to his mother's side from his seat at her desk. 'What are you trying to say? Pray try again.'

'Leave her Simon Smith, she is saying my name. Agnes, it is. She's doubtless surprised to see me here,' Mother Henshaw turned to Lucie. 'You have caused a lot of folk worry. No, don't try to talk. Let me call your deputy, she has been a most diligent attendant at your bedside.'

Lucie fell back into a doze on her pillow. When she awoke a second time her bedchamber was more crowded. Screwing her eyes, she tried to focus on the figures in front of her. Mother Henshaw was snoozing upright on a chair in the corner, Mary was sitting on the edge of the bed and Timothy Collins the chirurgeon was locked in what appeared to be animated discourse with Dr Somerton, waving his arms in annoyance.

'Beer please,' Lucie croaked.

'The danger is over, just as I predicted. Much good you two were,' Mother Henshaw scoffed at the medical men, rousing as if she had a sixth sense alerting her to Lucie's wakening.

Lucie couldn't make out the discussion between the chirurgeon and physician which was still ongoing. Moving her arm, she winced.

'I'll not be bled again,' she whispered, guessing that was what they must be talking about. She turned her head slowly to Mary and implored her by flicking her eyes over to the men.

'Ah yes. I understand,' Mary rose from the bed and headed not to the men but out the door. Lucie let out a groan and closed her eyes, as Mary's receding footsteps sounded on the staircase. Moments later Mary returned with Simon.

'Mother, you're awake again,' he said with a crack in his voice as he leaned over to kiss her cheek. 'How pleased I am to bid you a merry Christmas. Yes, it is Christmas morn, Mother. Now come gentlemen, join me downstairs in a toast to my mother's return to us. We had a large mince pie left on our threshold this day by some kind soul and I hope you'll both take a slice with me?'

'Thank you, Mary,' Lucie's mouth turned up in a weak smile. Mary helped Lucie take some sips of beer.

'Now will one of you two please tell me what the occasion of all these visitors to my chamber might be?'

Mary sat back on the edge of Lucie's bed. 'What a fright you have given us, Widow Smith.' She dabbed the corner of Lucie's lips with a linen clout. 'When Simon returned from London he found you lying on the cold flags of the kitchen. God alone knows how long you must have been lying there for the fire was stone cold.'

Lucie felt her eyes widening.

'The reed matting was scorched, but it was too damp to catch, thank God.'

'Amen,' Lucie mouthed.

'The constable is of the opinion you were assaulted, Widow Smith. Simon thought you dead.'

Lucie pulled the coverlet higher.

'Simon covered you in his coat, and went outside to raise a hue and cry, sending for the chirurgeon and the constable. He's not left the Three Doves since his return. Widow Smith, he has attended you day and night, laying with you in the hope his warmth would aid your recovery.'

'Those men haven't half messed about with you Lucie,' the ancient hand woman chimed in. 'They've bloodied you with leeches behind your ears and by opening a vein in your arm.'

'They only did what was best,' Mary gave the hand woman a warning look. 'One of the Wadeston youths from the smithy rode to my parents and fetched me.'

'Oh my poor son. I must have given him a sore fright. And you my dear, I'm so sorry,' Slowly, more memories of what happened that day came back, and Lucie rubbed her pounding head.

'Do you have a headache? Shall I prepare a cooling frontlet for you?'

'No, thank you, dear. It is not bad.'

Lucie tried to sit up but cried out as a pain shot across her shoulder.

'Please don't move, you have a broken collarbone that'll take some healing,' Mary said.

'It's a crying shame what happened to that simple lad,' Mother Henshaw blurted from her chair near the fire.

Lucie groaned. 'Whatever are you talking about, Agnes?'

'Dick Cobb,' Mary answered. 'The constable will want to talk to you as soon as he knows you are sensible. I had hoped to break this to you a bit more gently,' Mary shifted to be closer to Lucie. 'The thing is, once you were in bed, and the fires were lit, Simon went out to the privy and found Dick inside rocking back and to on the seat. The lad was half frozen but well in his body, because he had that enormous mutt from the inn in there with him.'

'Oh no, poor Dick,' her brow furrowed. What did Dick and Lad have to do with her being ill?

'Simon dealt with him gently and brought him inside for some warm wine. The constable returned with some further questions, and he demanded the boy account for his movements that afternoon thinking he was the one who assaulted you. Of course, Dick could not explain, and put his hands across his ears and cried and cried, Simon said. The constable arrested him and dragged him away.'

'The constable said just because the lad's a wantwit, it didn't mean he wasn't a bad 'un,' Mother Henshaw said. 'Disgusting.'

'Dick would never hurt me.' Lucie wriggled her arm free from the coverlet.

'Biske and Dick's mother went to the constable's house to demand he be released into their custody.' Mary's lip trembled.

'I remember now. Dick bursting into the kitchen when I was scrubbing the wall. His dog . . . Lad, pushed past him and knocked him over. I do remember that . . . I turned to climb off the table and help Dick. That must have been when I fell.'

'See,' Mother Henshaw rose from her seat. 'What have I been saying? That lad's as soft as anything, but he'd not hurt a fly.'

Lucie's faculties might be fuddled, but there was no mistaking a strong musty odour coming off the hand woman whenever she moved, not even the smoke from her pipe concealed it.

'I wonder at him not running to his mother for help after I fell. Think how he found Prudence and insisted I follow him to save her.' Lucie discreetly pressed the back of her hand to her nose.

'He did run for Joyce,' the old woman answered. 'Seems he'd been driving her to distraction dragging her out to lock at the building works for the Town Hall two, three, four or more times a day. So, when he ran into the Boar yet again, she thought he was tugging at her arm to go see another row of stones being laid or some such and bade him leave her be.'

Mary nodded. 'It's true, and poor Joyce Cobb has been beside herself with sorrow ever since that day.'

'Dick does not remain in custody, please God. Tell me he was released?'

'Oh Widow Smith, wait until you hear this part,' Mary managed a smile, shaking her head. 'The women gathered outside the constable's house. They banged on pans with wooden spoons and raised a clamour for the boy's freedom. At first the constable was unmoved; you know how he is.'

'A ninnyhammer.'

'Agnes,' scolded Lucie.

The corners of Mary's mouth twitched. 'When Mister Biske threatened to close the inn until the boy was home, Widow Bridges, who runs Hearne's Coffee House, joined in and said she'd not close but neither the constable nor any of the aldermen or parish officials had any chance of being served while the lad was under lock and key. Cordel's wife shouted out of their shop window that they'd all be looking for their meat somewhere else too.'

'It sounds like it was quite a scene,' Lucie said, arching her eyebrows.

'That's when I arrived back in Tupingham. Alewife Dill had come from the Bull with her maids and was selling ale from large pitchers.'

'Good old Peggy,' Lucie's lips stretched in a thin smile. 'I'd be worried if she missed a chance to make a few pennies.'

'That's when I decided to walk into town,' the hand woman said. 'I could hear the commotion from my cottage.'

'I reckon Alderman Robbins sensed that there could be trouble if matters were not resolved. He went inside and was back with Dick in under ten minutes.'

Lucie let out a deep sigh, her eyes watery. 'The poor boy, he won't have understood what was happening.'

'If only the townswomen had risen up in the like kind when you were falsely accused,' Mary's eyes flashed with anger.

'Nay, do not think that way, Mary.' But for a brief moment their eyes met showing they were of a mind. 'Fetch the constable, if you please, and we can clear Dick's good name.'

'He'll not come on Christmas Day. He'll be in his cups by this late hour. Anyway, you have had enough excitement for one day. It'll wait until the morrow.' Mary rose and straightened the bed covers. 'You should rest now.'

'I will but first I wish to discourse with Agnes. I believe I should thank you for some remedies which have occasioned my recovery?'

'That too can wait. I have been here the past two nights and one more won't hurt. We'll speak in the morning. Perhaps that son of yours will be so good as to send some Christmas fare up for Mary and me?'

As Mary left to run downstairs to find some food and drink, Mother Henshaw whispered to Lucie, 'We've not seen eye-to-eye many times over the last years, but it was as well I arrived when I did. Those men,' she hissed out the names of the chirurgeon and physician, 'would've seen you in your grave with their bungling.'

Chapter Twenty

'What are you writing, son?' Lucie had awoken from a nap to the sounds of Simon's pen scratching. The morning looked crisp and bright, winter sun streaming through the cross-leaded windowpanes.

'I'm just sketching out ideas for your new house, Mother. See I have drawn some different styles for you to choose between,' Simon quickly sanded his work dry before getting up from Lucie's writing desk. Talking her through his drawings, he explained how her indisposition had convinced him they should think again about the land his father had bequeathed. 'We could build a home for you on one level without the stairs which trouble you so.'

Lucie studied the plans. The final one was for a building almost twice the size of the other designs on the ground floor.

'What is this?' Lucie asked. Simon avoided her eye.

'Just an idea, nothing really. I was just toying with some notions.'

'Come on, out with it,' she prompted him with a smile.

'Well, how would it be if I set up a printing house in Tupingham? The builder offered us a good price for a basic house when we spoke a couple of months ago and reckons this bigger one would add but a few pounds more, if it were all done at once.'

Lucie's brow furrowed.

'I think you might pass me a cup of wine and sit down,' she patted the bed. 'It's past time you told me all that happened on your recent trip to London, I fancy then I shall better understand what you're about.'

Simon explained that the premises in London had been entirely unsuited to a print house, and in an inconvenient location. 'London is unrecognisable, Mother. An acrid air hangs over the city, clogging your lungs. It's a shadow of the place it was. Some of those made homeless have returned and are squashed into premises like fish in barrels,' he took a sip of his wine. 'And if I did wish to trade there, the price of a lease has risen beyond anything I could run to.'

Lucie nodded, 'I am beginning to see, I think. With your company gone, your business partner removed . . . '

'Mother, throughout the country presses are springing up,' Simon's eyes shone. 'I don't need the city now. I'd been minded to look for property in Grantby, but then I had a moment of clarity as I sat by your bedside. If I met the difference between your house and one with a printworks attached, I could remain in Tupingham.' He squeezed Lucie's hand, 'Well, what say you?'

'I don't know. This is a surprise. What about all the machinery you would be in need of?'

'I met with the contact I wrote to you of, in London. The widow selling off her late husband's inventory. We dealt upon a fair price. So, I own everything I need to begin a new business. It's in store in London at one of Mister Wallis's warehouses.'

'And that was what kept you in London longer than you planned? Stop picking at that whitlow, you'll make it sore.' Simon had always worried at his fingers when he was distressed, his father had had to make poultices to draw out the bad humours. He stood up and paced, tucking his hands into the pocket of his breeches.

'Yes, I had to oversee the removal of the press and tools.'

'You don't seem very happy about it, Simon. I thought you'd be delighted to have secured such items as you need.'

'They made me late home. I should have returned as

planned and you wouldn't have fallen, Mother. Will you ever forgive me?'

'Son, there is no blame to you,' Lucie said. 'What more news do you have for me from your trip. Did you visit Sir Robert?'

'Sir Robert has left for the Continent.' Lucie caught a catch in his voice. 'The footman at Calstone House handed me a letter but would not admit me.'

'Have you the letter to show me, son?'

'It is burnt,' Simon stared intently at the floorboard.

'Why would you do that?' Lucie made to rise from her bed but gasped at the sharp pain in her shoulder. 'Is it not usual for young men of his rank to tour the Continent?'

Simon made a groaning noise. Lucie, alarmed, shuffled over to him. She leaned in close, wincing as she moved. 'Son?'

'Forgive me, Mother. I forgot myself momentarily,' he dropped a kiss onto his mother's head. 'He was my companion, my friend. For him to leave without my having the least intelligence, to likely be in Italy before I had a notion of his intentions, that felt like a betrayal.'

'It was poor manners, yes, after all you did for him after the fire. I see now why you were so vexed,' Lucie attempted to keep her voice level. 'Did the letter contain any further information?'

Simon smiled at that, and his eyes met Lucie's. 'Indeed. If you feel up to rising for a while, we can set you in the chair by the fire, and I'll tell you all.' He helped Lucie walk the few paces and tucked a blanket over her knees, placing a shawl around her shoulders. Sir Robert was well healed, he said, and had decided his livid scar made him look rather dashing, as if he had been the hero of some voyage to exotic lands.

'That young man is incorrigible,' Lucie chuckled, holding her collar bone.

'Do you remember the letter some months ago that told us his new daughter was named Barbara? It seems that the name went down badly at Court. Lord Calstone is banished.'

'Banished over a name? Surely there is more to the story than that?'

'The King had thought it a great jest when he heard that Sir Robert had now a Barbara along with his Charles. The Queen took it very ill. She decreed that Lady Eleanor would not be received back as a lady of the bedchamber upon her recovery from childbed.'

'Anyone with an ounce of sense would have anticipated her reaction, if what you said about this Lady Castlemaine being the King's mistress is true,' Lucie said.

'I wish I had the letter to show you. That old goat has been banished and forbidden to return to Court until next summer at the earliest, if you please, on occasion of events he was not party to. It is exquisite.'

The pair chatted merrily for a while when Lucie felt her lips purse at a sudden thought. 'I wonder what Calstone's banishment will mean for Tupingham?'

'Sir Robert wrote something about his father having a tame alderman from Tupingham whom he means to make Member of Parliament, to represent his affairs in the House.'

'Robbins, without a doubt,' Lucie said, rising stiffly. An hour out of bed had been pleasant but she was wearied now. 'I might venture downstairs tomorrow and sit in the kitchen a while.'

'God be praised. In that case I will leave you to rest and I will repair to Hearne's for an hour. But before I go, the plans? You will consider them at least?'

'I'll need a while to think on't son. Could you take the pot down with you and ask Mary to empty it? Thank you, my dear.' She climbed back into bed, one hand over the tender, healing collar bone.

As she sat in bed looking over the drawings, Lucie found she was biting her lip. Commissioning a property was such a big step. Although a chamber on the ground floor was pleasing. The idea of a print house trading from her new home needed thought too, but it would be good to have her boy home for good.

She must have dozed for it was dusk when a rapping on the door woke her.

'Mister Collins is in the kitchen, requesting permission to examine his patient,' Mary said.

'That is good of him, but please give my apologies. I mean no insult to his ministrations but would be left alone at present.'

Evidently Lucie's wishes carried no weight with the chirurgeon, for she heard his heavy footsteps on her stairs shortly afterwards.

'Widow Smith, please forgive the intrusion, but I must discourse with you on a matter of some urgency,' the chirurgeon removed his hat.

'Are you about to take a trip, Mister Collins? You are dressed in your best attire, not your workaday breeches,' Lucie grimaced as she pulled herself more upright and tucked the coverlet in tightly.

Collins cleared his throat by way of an answer. He was then silent a moment, as if summoning the courage to continue. Lucie's stomach twisted a little.

'Widow Smith, I wanted to tell you in person that I have taken the lease for the Three Doves, beginning next Lady Day,' he shifted from foot to foot.

'Is that so?' Lucie found herself smiling. 'I am delighted for you.'

Collins looked bemused for a moment, then cleared his throat.

'It is my contention that your hysterical fever was occasioned by your unease about leaving your abode. You were in passion when you fell from the table, and it is my opinion that this has been building for some weeks, perhaps since word of my plans to take the Three Doves reached your ear,' he held himself tall and puffed out his chest.

‘No, no. I was in a passion that day I admit, but who would not be the same? It was the anniversary of my dear husband’s passing, and Simon had not yet returned.’

‘That’s not sufficient to make a full explanation of your symptoms, Widow Smith. Come now, we have been friends for many years, you can speak true to me. Your lad’s perplexed at you scrubbing his drawing from the wall. You and Jasper always took such delight in that childish picture.’

Lucie flushed, fussing with her coverlet a moment.

‘I was merely spring cleaning. The new occupiers of the Three Doves will want a fresh home, will they not?’

‘Spring cleaning? In mid-winter, and on your own, and on the anniversary of your bereavement?’ Collins raised his eyebrows.

‘I’ll speak to Simon, I didn’t know he was upset, he has not made mention of it.’

Collins cleared his throat. ‘A year has now passed since the departure of our much lamented and much esteemed apothecary. I was waiting until that sad anniversary was passed to speak with you about my taking over the lease of these premises.’

Lucie frowned. ‘I do not follow, Mister Collins. I always knew I would have to vacate the Three Doves after my poor husband’s untimely death, and indeed have come to think it would have been beneficial to my health to have removed long since. When the physician told me of your plans some weeks ago, I informed him you would have my blessing.’

The chirurgeon shook his head, raising his hand. ‘No need to put a brave face on the matter, Widow Smith, for I have a resolution to propose, which will be to both our advantages. Widow Smith, Lucie, will you agree to become my wife?’

‘Mister Collins!’

‘Please call me Timothy. It has been many long years since my dear wife died. You performed her last offices for which I will always be in your debt. But now we both find ourselves in a widowed condition and are practitioners of the healing arts.

You must agree it makes good sense for us to wed. You will have no more occasion for hysterical indisposition, with me to care for you.'

It seemed the chirurgeon had got matters quite upside down. How to tell him so gently? Luckily, Collins saved her from making an immediate answer.

'I'll say just one thing more, Lucie. I know Mister Smith left you well provided for, but I am comfortable too in that regard and do not seek to meddle with that which your son has a right to expect in turn. I seek only comfort and companionship in my older years and would never solicit notions of greater affection than your heart was moved to supply. It will be good for the townsfolk too.' It was Mister Collins whose face flushed now, and he looked to the floor. 'I can see this has been a shock to you. Not an unpleasant one I hope; I'd half a hope that a match with me had been in your thoughts too. Pray think on't and I'll call in again in a few days. Until then, farewell,' he turned on his heels and hastily departed, leaving Lucie rubbing her aching collarbone.

Chapter Twenty-one

Lucie watched Martha sanding the kitchen table. 'The place is gleaming, Martha, thank you so much. You've whitewashed the wall I damaged, too, for which I am grateful.'

Martha looked up from her work, 'Well we can't have standards slipping while you're convalescing, can we? There was some powder left from when the Pottons tidied up Mister Smith's room. It was the work of a few minutes to mix the wash. Anthony helped me.'

'I must pay him. Pray pass on my gratitude, I shouldn't have done it, I don't know what came over me.'

'Anthony'll not accept money. You do so much for our family,' Martha's smile lit up her face and Lucie thought once again how much more content her friend seemed these days. 'Those Potton girls kept everywhere so well. Do you miss their company?'

'I must confess to paying them but little mind. I hope they go well in their new home,' Lucie said. 'It was fortunate indeed that Ned returned when he did. I just hope he and Hester behave properly.'

'Youngsters,' Martha rolled her eyes. 'Not that I am in a position to judge. Anyway, that's my work done. I'll stay and sit with you a while and then better get back home.'

'Let me give you some coins, Martha.'

'Indeed, you will not, Widow Smith. Think of it as a New Year's gift.' Sitting down in the chair opposite Lucie, Martha grasped her former mistress's hand.

'I have some news which I've been excited to tell you. After that day at Goodwife Smedley's birthing, and after your sickness, I set to thinking. Well more than thinking, I've attended two further deliveries with Mary. I now have three goodwives who would be able to testify to my skills.'

Lucie patted Martha's hand. 'This calls for a celebration. Let's warm some of that spiced wine. I think there is some minced pie somewhere too.'

'I'll need your help to gain more practise, but I am excited by this turn. Until I had baby Jasper, I never thought of following in your footsteps, as you know, but his arrival and this moment of necessity seems it is meant to be. What do you think Mother Henshaw will say when she hears of this? Simon told me she came here and nursed you. I was amazed at that.'

'I am grateful to her for her trouble, but who is Tupingham's midwife is no concern of hers. Oh Martha, can you imagine how Mister Smith would have reacted at the thought of Mother Henshaw rifling through his wares? But it cannot be denied that whatever she mixed for me did me much good.'

Both women sat with their thoughts in companiable silence.

'I feel terrible now,' Martha blurted out, suddenly serious.

'Whatever for?'

'You'll be cross when I tell you,' Martha rubbed her mouth as if trying to suppress the words she needed to get out. 'Last winter we had talked about how your luck was so bad it was like Mother Henshaw had cursed you, you remember?'

'Oh yes, but that was just idle talk. We don't believe in that nonsense.'

'The thing is,' Martha looked down at her hands. 'I buried a bottle in your garden as a counter curse on the ancient woman. I wanted to help. I used bent pins . . .'

Lucie burst out laughing. 'I found that months ago and slung it on the rubbish heap. Seriously though Martha, you should not be engaging in such arts. It is not fitting, and certainly not for a deputy midwife.'

'You don't think it harmed Mother Henshaw? My mother swore by it.'

'No, I do not. And would thank you not to mention it again,' Lucie spoke sternly but she felt the twinkling in her eyes. Martha sighed with relief, and after some moments began gathering her belongings to return home.

'Mary has sewn a new cap for each of the children as New Year presents. They are on the dresser, don't forget them or she'll be upset.' Lucie gathered three pennies from the mantel shelf. 'Here take these from me too. A penny for each child as my New Year's gift. Next time you visit, you can tell me who you delivered and how our Mary did as a teacher. I look forward to hearing all the details.'

An hour later Lucie was considering cutting a slice of bread when Simon arrived home. He was red in the face and somewhat out of breath.

'Are you ailing, Simon?' his worried mother asked.

'No, indeed. It's freezing outside but I am hot from exertion, 'tis all. Here Mother, Dr Archer's wife sent us some powdered goose as a New Year gift. We'll dine like the Court on this,' he placed an earthenware dish on Martha's newly-scrubbed table. His eyes beamed against his frost-bitten face.

'Simon, please don't speak in riddles. What have you been doing to get so overheated?'

'Scything, mother, scything. I have been cutting down all the growth on your land. It was quite the wilderness, but I have been at it for several days since you began to recover and am making good progress. Young Dick has been helping me.'

'Really? How does he go? I'm so distressed whenever I think about that poor simple soul being hauled off by the constable.'

'Well, and Joyce Cobb lays none of the blame at your door, Mother. Quite the contrary. She's fearful to visit you, lest you are in a bad humour with her. She was pleased to let Dick work the land with me though.'

'What made you start clearing the land? We have not yet agreed a plan nor bargained with the builder.'

'It will be easier to pace out when it is clear, and you and the builder might have a better view of what manner of house will suit the land. Mother, pay no mind to my sketches if they please you not. You must say what you wish to commission. But if the scheme for a print house displeases you, please inform me as soon as you reach a firm decision as I'll need to see what is available to lease.'

They both turned as Mary came through the scullery, looking tired but content. She went straight to the fire to warm her hands.

'The Robbins have a new son,' she stamped her feet in front of the flames. 'Mistress Robbins is resting. They have engaged a nurse from Grantby to suckle the infant and she has been sent for. I gave him some sugared water and he is sleeping contentedly enough.'

'You did not take your new deputy with you?' Simon teased Mary.

'There was no time to send for Martha. Alderman Robbins' man found me at the last moment when I was on the High Street running errands. They had been awaiting Dr Somerton's arrival, but matters outpaced even his horse.' Mary glanced around the kitchen. 'It does mean you should expect a visit from the physician this day Widow Smith, while he is in town. Since Martha has worked her magic on the house, he'll think we've made a special effort on his behalf.'

Simon roared with laughter, 'Well he might think so, but he is having not so much as a taste of this powdered goose. This is all for us. Come ladies, let's eat.'

After her meal, Lucie asked to be helped back up the stairs to sit in her bed. It had been her first trip down to the kitchen in three weeks.

'Pray tell Dr Somerton I am not to be disturbed if he does

call, Mary,' Lucie said as Mary put more coal on the fire, checking Lucie had all she needed to hand.

'Very well, but just call if there's aught you require. I shall be in the scullery soaking the clouts from this morning's birthing.' Just then both women heard Dr Somerton talking to Simon downstairs. Lucie sighed.

'It appears to be too late to stall the physician. If he wishes to converse with me, pray have him come up presently, that I might rest soon,' Lucie felt her weariness in her weak voice.

'Good afternoon, Widow Smith. I am delighted to see you much recovered. I am given to understand you sat a while down the stairs and took some meat? That is good news indeed.'

The physician was normally immaculately attired, but this afternoon had mud on his boots and breeches and what looked very much like blood on his shirt. Herbert Somerton had the look of a man who'd had quite a day of it.

'Did my family offer you some refreshment? A cup of wine, something to eat, doctor?'

'No indeed, I had food and drink aplenty at the Robbins gossiping. Mistress Robbins and her infant son are doing splendidly. I must say, thy young deputy is highly esteemed by the couple.'

'Mary Thorne is fully trained and no longer deputy to anyone. She's a very skilful midwife, and the Robbins were fuddled to think of asking anyone else to deliver their child,' Lucie's nostrils flared ever so slightly.

Dr Somerton raised an eyebrow and looked amused. 'Forgive my appearance. I have been around women all this day and ridden hard to get from my patient in Grantby to the Robbins' house.'

The physician lowered himself into the chair beside Lucie's bed without waiting to be invited.

'I attended a woman this morning who had a long, sore time. She'd been attended by an unskilful woman – no not Mistress Wallis, there are at least three midwives working in Grantby, Madam,' Somerton raised a hand to stop the interjection he could evidently see Lucie was about to make. 'The woman had much hauled and pulled her about, and her privities were terribly swollen and discoloured.'

Lucie's eyes were closing, she was not in the mood for another of Dr Somerton's tall tales.

'The ridiculous creature, her midwife, told me she supposed the swellings were part of the afterbirth, and so had thrust her fingers into them.'

Lucie's eyes shot open. 'Surely not!'

'Indeed. Naturally, blood spurted out of the mother, a Goodwife by the name of Frith, and onto the midwife's face, which then dripped onto her gorget. That was the moment I entered the chamber and the blood fell on my shirt, too.'

'Oh, that poor woman,' Lucie said. 'Was she looking ill when you left her?'

'I expect she'll live, but will need a long recovery. Her woman's month may extend well past Candlemas, which is the day I recommended Mistress Robbins rise.'

Lucie nodded. 'If you'd excuse me now, Sir. I need to rest.'

'Widow Smith, I am in negotiations for the lease on the Chestnut House.'

'I had no idea the Hills were vacating their property, so you have the advantage over me there Dr Somerton,' Lucie's eyes felt irresistibly heavy.

'It is an attractive house which will suit my purpose very well. You'd be happy there, I think. Widow Smith, will you do me the honour of becoming my wife?'

Lucie's body shuddered with a sudden coughing fit. She put up her hand to stop the physician, but after passing her a wine cup, he continued speaking,

'There is no occasion for taking on so, Widow Smith. Doubtless this honour is a surprise. And it is true that my rank is beyond that which you have a right to expect as a simple country midwife, late in years, but I pay no mind to such things. Especially as your widow's portion when added to my own worth will see us most comfortably prepared for our old age. You accept, I take it?'

Lucie went into another coughing spasm, before managing to speak. 'Indeed, I do not, Doctor Somerton. Please leave me now, I need to rest.'

'The shock speaking, I am sure. When you've had a chance to accustom yourself to the generosity of my offer, and have taken your son's counsel, I'm quite sure your view will be altered, madam. I will call again in due course to receive your formal acceptance of my proposal.'

As the sound of his steps receded, Lucie wondered where Somerton had learned of the value of her inheritance. This was not the first time he had made mention of it. How would he know that Jasper had left her relatively well to do when compared to many in her situation? Her eyelids closed but as she drifted towards sleep the answer came. Friswell. I'll wager he tricked Sir Robert into revealing something of my personal circumstances looking for something to hold over me. He'd know as well as anyone Simon would have taken his friend into his confidence.

Chapter Twenty-two

Dr Archer recited the words from Corinthians, 'O Lord our God, all this store that we have prepared to build thee an house for thine holy name cometh of thine hand, and is all thine own.' This was the dedication of the newly installed memorial plaque for Apothecary Smith. Those members of the congregation who had stayed for the ceremony in the chancel were gathered around the rector. Lucie watched from a chair, this being her first time abroad since her fall, with her son standing beside her.

'I know also, my God, that thou triest the heart, and hast pleasure in uprightness. As for me, in the uprightness of mine heart I have willingly offered all these things,' the rector continued.

Lucie and Simon caught each other's eyes. Lucie recognised her late husband in those words. His heart, like hers, had been sorely tried over the years, but for Jasper, every trial had deepened his faith, not challenged it.

'Are you sure you're up to eating at the rectory, Mother?'

'I am looking forward to it, pray help me up,' she smiled at her son as he assisted her. 'The plaque is fitting, isn't it? You made a splendid choice.'

'It's a little more robust than a child's painting.' Simon glanced over at the marble, mounted on the wall of All Hallows' chancel.

'Son, I've been remiss in not speaking with you about that. Come help me down the aisle,' she slipped her arm through her tall son's and leaned on him. 'The truth, as the Lord knows, is the picture from happier times was too painful a reminder of all we've lost, Simon, just in that moment. I'm sorry you had to find me like that, you must have thought I'd lost my mind. In truth, in my grief, I fear I had.'

Simon bent and kissed his mother's cheek.

'I was teasing about the picture; I've always been amazed you and father liked it so. If I'd known it was distressing you for a second, I'd have painted it out myself long since,' he held his face to hers for a moment.

Mrs Archer had prepared a haunch of venison for the party who had gathered in the rectory after the morning service.

'It has been a long week,' observed Dr Archer. 'But this company and the fine meat my wife has prepared for us is the tonic I was in sore need of. It is so good to see you up and about again my dear Widow Smith, the Lord deserves all our praise.'

'Thank you, Rector. It does indeed seem scarcely believable that it's just a week since Twelfth Night. It is not a Christmas season I shall remember with any fondness. Although the one before was surely worse.'

The table fell to silence as Simon, Mary, Lucie and Dr and Mistress Archer remembered that Christmas meal around the table of the Three Doves, mourning Jasper's recent death and knowing Lucie's trial before the Bishop was imminent. To change the subject, the rector turned to Simon,

'I hear you are not minded to return to London to establish yourself as a master printer there once again. This surprised me a little. I understood you to be settled in that city.'

Simon swallowed the piece of meat he had been chewing. He seemed to be struggling to find words to explain the disenchantment Lucie knew he now felt for the city that had been his home since he was a smooth-faced boy of fourteen.

'I think Rector, that London has left me, more than I have left it. Of my home and business, nothing but ash remains. My friends are dispersed. When I accompanied Ned Brock to

London last month, I found I had not my customary affinity with the place.' Simon took a swig of his wine. Lucie chewed her meat and concentrated on her plate. She wished the rector wouldn't press Simon so.

'But surely in time the city will recover and be rebuilt. You are yet a young man, Simon, with your life ahead of you.'

'Rector, I find myself quite unable to rightly express it . . . The area around Paul's is lost to fire, almost as if it never was, but in the places the fire spared, well, life carries on as it ever did. It is as if the fire is of no consequence – except if they can profit by raising rents and such like – and there are now tens of hundreds of displaced souls camping beyond the walls.'

'Thank you for a delicious meal, Mistress Archer. The meat was beautifully tender,' Lucie spoke into the following pause.

Simon looked over at her gratefully. 'Shall we raise a glass to Midwife Thorne?'

The servant filled everyone's cups on Dr Archer's signal.

'You are leaving us tomorrow, I understand?' he said to Mary. 'You are a credit to your years in Tupingham, and the town's women will miss you. Your very good health, my dear.'

'To Mary's good health.'

Simon, Lucie, Mary and Mistress Archer clinked cups with the rector.

Lucie was tucked up in bed by late afternoon. Mary pottered about Lucie's chamber, hanging up her dress and brushing it down.

'Mary, leave all that be, come sit down,' Lucie patted the side of the bed. 'Actually, before you do I need you to look under the bed. I have a parting gift for you which fortunately I commissioned from the carpenter before my indisposition.'

Mary put her candle on the floor and knelt down. Feeling around under the bed, she pulled out a leather bag with what appeared to be some sticks of wood within.

'There you go, Mary my dear. My present to you. Could you lay out the contents on the bed?'

Mary pulled out three ten-inch sticks, each with a screw thread carved in the top. There was also a thick plank of wood which curved up at either end, with oval holes cut into the curves. Finally, the bag contained a longer piece, rounded at one end and with a brass screw at the bottom. This piece had a beautiful carving of three small doves, one atop the other, along the thickest part. It was finished with a brown stain, making it gleam.

'Let me show you, Mary,' Lucie shuffled into a more upright position, pulling the different pieces closer. 'See, this part screws in here like so. You'll have to do it Mary, my shoulder is sore this evening.'

With Lucie guiding her, Mary deftly screwed each of the legs into the curved-ended wood to form a small stool. Next, she attached the largest piece of the puzzle, which formed a backrest. On the red coverlet stood a beautiful, small birthing stool with what could now be identified as hand holes for the labouring mother to grip onto.

'See how easy that is to put together, Mary, and so much more portable than my cumbersome chair. I had it made so that if you take the chair apart, place the seat on the back rest and the three legs atop that, it will all fit into its bag as you saw. It takes next-to-no room up on the back of your horse. My mother had one the very same. No, no crying my dear, I forbid it.' Lucie beckoned her former deputy towards her. Ignoring the nagging pain in her shoulder, she hugged her close.

'The little doves are so you don't forget us.'

'As if I ever could, my dearest Widow Smith. Thank you so much for everything you have done for me, and for this chair. I will treasure it always.'

Simon tapped at the door.

'Simon, see what a beautiful gift Widow Smith has made me,' Mary said.

'It is from us both, Mary. Simon walked over to collect it for me a few days ago.'

'Thank you, Simon,' Mary reached up and hugged him tightly. Lucie sensed that neither of them wanted to let go.

'I came up the stairs to tell you your father is outside, Mary,' Simon said at last.

'He isn't due until the morning!' Mary wiped her eyes with the back of her hand.

'I know, but he is here with a wagon and a lantern. He means to take you now.'

Lucie remained in her bed, listening to the bustle as Simon helped Mary carry her belongings down to the kitchen. Minutes later she heard the door bang, followed by the sounds of a horse's hooves and wagon wheels trundling on the cobbles. Leaning back on her bolster, Lucie took a pillow and hugged it close.

'Just me and you now, Mother,' Simon said as he checked in on Lucie later. 'Would you like some supper? A drink perhaps?'

'Son, could you just sit with me a moment? I have some intelligence of my own to impart. You will think I have lost my mind entirely when I tell you.'

''Ods blood, what now Mother?' Simon teased. Lucie let the curse go by with only a raised eyebrow.

'My turn to surprise you, I fear.' She coughed. 'In the last few days I have been made not one but two offers of marriage.' She waited, studying his face.

'I thought the chirurgeon was looking at you strangely at the service this morning. Good for him not troubling you at that solemn occasion though, Mother. He is one of your suitors, I'll warrant.'

'Indeed. He thinks it fitting since we could remain living here and conduct the healing arts together.'

'Logical as ever, our Mister Collins, but not the most romantic of proposals,' Simon laughed. 'Come tell who made the other offer? I can't begin to guess.'

Lucie smiled, shaking her head. 'He's a good man, Timothy Collins, and just looking for a practical answer as is his way. However, the other hand was offered by Dr Somerton.'

Simon's mouth fell open. 'The fashionable physician. Well I never.'

'I am sure he's a good man too, Simon. But your attire and fancy periwigs are enough for one household without introducing another of the like kind.' The edges of Lucie's mouth twitched.

'But you'd be quite the fine lady living at the Hills' house, wanting for nothing as a physician's wife,' Simon teased in turn. He took his mother's hand, 'In all earnestness Mother, I want you to be content. And if you should have an inclination to remarry, you have my blessing, whichever suitor you choose.'

'I will take neither, son. Now why don't you go down the stairs and find some bread and cheese to make a supper?'

As he clattered down the stairs, Lucie got out of bed, still holding her sore collar, and slipped her feet into her embroidered slippers. She shuffled over to her writing desk, one hand nursing her collarbone and one holding her candle, to look for a particular sheet of paper. When Simon came back moments later carrying a laden tray, Lucie showed him a plan she had sketched of a design for her new home. It included a separate building to the right-hand side, attached to the main house but with its own entrance.

'Truly, Mother? This is your wish?' Simon placed the tray down on the end of the bed. Her son's eyes shone.

'Yes, son. This is what I want. Not to remarry, but to build my house. Our house. With room to establish your print house alongside. Come study my plan. How do you like it?'

Chapter Twenty-three

'Mother, do you feel well enough to attend one of your women?' Simon called through to Lucie who was back working in the apothecary shop. 'She is at her time. I have already sent the butcher's boy to fetch Martha.'

'It is Goodwife Cordel who is at her time, Simon?'

'Yes, the boy said it was his mistress and that the butcher has taken a turn for the worse, too.'

'I thought he'd recovered from his unfortunate accident. You'd better fetch Mister Collins, son. I'll be busy with the goodwife until Martha arrives at least, and he will have to attend to the husband. I hope Martha comes hastily for I fear I cannot receive a child in my arms yet. Can you carry the chair to the butcher's shop for me, and then run on to the chirurgeon's?' Lucie hurried over to lock the shop door as she spoke. 'I am sorry to have to send you on all these errands, but at least the butcher's is on your way to the barber-surgeon's.'

Arriving at the butcher's, Lucie found Martha already there. Standing in the doorway of the bed chamber she watched as her former housemaid crouched in front of the labouring mother, stroking her belly and speaking in a low reassuring tone. Unable to stop herself smiling, she took a step into the room. Martha glanced behind her at the sound of a creaking floorboard.

'No, don't get up Martha. I am content to sit in this chair and watch you at your work. I will be right here if I am needed but otherwise you carry on.'

Time passed in the chamber with the women idly chatting and exchanging stories.

'Take a slice of this groaning cake, Widow Smith,' Sal Cordel called over as she paced the room between pangs. 'My mother has sent it over; she is watching the younger ones so won't be here for this one's arrival.' Sal pointed at her large belly. Sal was an old hand at birthing, this being her eleventh, and so she was calm and happy for nature to take its course. After three hours, Sal let out a loud grunt and clutched her belly. Rising from the chair where she had been resting, Lucie smiled.

'The time has come, I think, Martha. Do you agree?'

'Come sit on the chair and let me search you, Goodwife Cordel,' Martha said. On lifting the woman's skirts, she found herself greeted by a tiny hand. 'Widow Smith, could you come over here?' she said. Lucie knew Martha well enough to hear the slight panic in her tone that the other women would not detect.

'Is all well?' Sal Cordel asked between pangs, now coming thick and fast. Sweat beaded on her brow. 'Ooooh. I need to bear down.'

Lucie crouched in front of the birthing chair, her knees creaking.

'All in good time, Sal, all in good time.'

In response the butcher's wife let out another loud grunt, and the pressure caused her bowels to empty.

''Ods Blood,' Sal called. 'Help me, please.'

A noisome smell filled the small room but luckily all the matter was fallen on the clouts Martha had arranged around the chair. A gossip scooped the linen up and dealt with it without need of direction. The strain had, though, brought forth more of the child's arm.

'Come Martha,' Lucie instructed, discretely cleaning Sal up. 'We need to help Goodwife Cordel off the chair and into a kneeling position. Put the bolster on the floor. Come Sal, let's have you kneeling against the side of your bed. Bess, you sit in front of Sal here, on the edge of the bed. Good.'

Having arranged Sal with her head in her gossip's lap, and her body sloping away from the bed, she beckoned Martha over.

'Oil your hand and arm very well, Martha,' she instructed.

'Hurry please. I cannot endure it,' Sal groaned.

'Now slide your hand in alongside this little one's arm. Tuck the arm back. That's right, all the way inside. Do you feel the feet? They are normally tucked alongside its belly.'

The atmosphere in the room became heavy with anxiety.

'All is well, women. Let Martha and me do our work, try to loose your body, Sal,' Lucie's voice was calming, and she saw the gathered women's faces relax a little. 'Right Martha, you'll know the back of the child from the front. The back is hard, you'll feel the ridge of its spine. That's good.'

'I have them,' Martha said. 'I have the feet.'

'Place one foot between your forefinger and the middle one, and hold it with your thumb,' Lucie talked Martha through the actions.'Now this will be sore, Goodwife, but your child lives, and we need to help it out carefully.' Lucie swallowed hard, pushing down an urge to take over the operation. 'I need you to draw down the foot, Martha, leisurely and gently, that's right,' Lucie watched closely as Martha's face flushed in concentration. The younger woman let out her held breath as a tiny foot appeared to view. 'Good, Martha,' Lucie patted her on the back.

'Pass me a warm clout,' Lucie reached out to take the linen cloth, then wrapped the little foot with it. 'Now do the like with the next foot, Martha.'

Sal screamed as Martha inserted her hand into her womb a second time.

'I'm sorry, Goodwife. I am trying to be gentle,' Martha said in a strained voice.

'You are doing well. Carry on,' Lucie reassured her. 'Not long now, Sal, you too are doing very well, but I need you now to change position.'

'I cannot,' groaned the goodwife, her voice muffled in Bess's lap. Martha crawled nearer to Sal and spoke soothingly. Gently she helped Sal to stretch up, hooking her arms around Bess's neck. Sal sobbed, fat tears falling freely off her chin.

'You can and will, my dear, just as women through the ages have,' Lucie reassured her.

As Sal grunted out another pang, Martha helped the baby be born as far as its bottom.

'The child faces forwards, Widow Smith,' Martha said, her hand still inside Sal's vagina.

'So we need to turn him around gently, hold him like this,' Lucie showed Martha how to move her hands. Sal's groan was like that of a wounded animal as she hung from her friend's neck. Lucie took some powders from her bag and asked that they be dissolved into wine to help ease the mother's pains.

'Here take a little sip, Sal,' Lucie had been helped to her feet by a gossip, and offered up the drink to Goodwife Cordel herself. After Sal had taken some sips, Martha eased the baby out to its neck.

'Last part now Sal. Your ordeal is almost over,' Lucie glanced down to check on Martha's actions.

With her next pain, Sal and Martha worked together until the head was born. The baby was silent, and Sal slumped from Bess's neck into a kneeling position on the floor.

'He lives? Widow Smith tell me my child lives!' Lucie was busy drawing some filth from the child's nose. She then rubbed his chest a little, at which he let out an indignant howl.

'He does. He is most hale and hearty. I suspect you will have your work cut out with this young man from the awkward manner of his arrival. Now back up you go, onto your knees so that your after burden can be delivered and we can set you to rights.' Lucie passed the baby to one of the women to swaddle.

In an hour, Martha and Lucie had mother and son cleanly tucked up in bed together and were ready to leave.

'Please will you see how my husband goes before you leave, Widow Smith? I am afeared for him. Mister Collins attended this afternoon, I know, but I should like to know what was decided upon.'

Lucie readily agreed and made her way cautiously down the pair of stairs while Martha packed away the last of the clouts and washed the birthing chair. As she crawled down the steps, an acrid smell hit Lucie's nose. Joseph Cordel lay on the kitchen table with a stick across his slack mouth. Mister Collins was finishing stitching a wound. A pile of putrefied flesh sat in a bucket at his feet.

'Widow Smith, have you any laudanum in your bag? The butcher here would welcome a draft. He has been most brave, not wishing to disturb his wife in her travail, but he has now fainted away. He'll be in a great deal of pain when he awakes, I fear.'

Lucie examined the wound and saw it was clean and neat. 'You removed all the gangrene, Mister Collins?'

'Aye, its all removed. I am joining healthy flesh together now. He is like to do well but has fathered his last child. I've had to geld him to remove the rot.'

'Just as well he has a fine lusty son upstairs then. It is for the best that Goodwife Cordel will not face that tribulation again, her body has been through more than sufficient travail.'

The pair worked together to revive the patient and offered him the medicament to ease his suffering. The older children were dispatched to fetch a truckle bed from their attic room and set it up in the kitchen for their father to recuperate on. The oldest apprentice butcher was given instructions how to tend to his master, and the oldest daughter was charged with running the house with both parents now indisposed. The lass was barely twelve, but capable enough.

'May I walk you home now we have both discharged our duties, Widow Smith?' Collins asked.

They stepped out together into the crisp, frosty January evening. They walked in silence a little while, their breath forming clouds in front of them. At length, Mister Collins spoke up, 'You'll have had chance to reflect upon my offer of marriage, Widow Smith. Have you an answer for me?'

'I should like to discourse with you on this matter, but not in the street Mister Collins. Will your servant have made your meat, or would you care to join me? My son sent word while I was attending Goodwife Cordel to inform me he was leaving for Grantby to meet with our architect, but that he had bought a pigeon pie for my supper.'

'That would be most welcome,' the chirurgeon replied. His lips curved at their corners.

After a convivial supper, Lucie stood up to clear the table.

'We manage quite well without help, Mister Collins, but should you hear of anyone looking for such work, pray inform me. It is too much to keep this big house and also keep trading.'

'Leave that, surely it can wait. We should talk.'

Lucie sat back down, grabbing at the table as she stumbled a little.

'I fear I am wearied from this long day,' she said. 'You are very dear to me Mister Collins. If I were minded to change my situation, I would accept your kind offer without reservation.'

'You are not so minded then, Widow Smith?' Timothy looked crestfallen. 'I should leave.'

'No, stay,' Lucie touched his arm. 'It is not simply that I am not considering remarrying, though I confess I am not at present. I cannot consent to remain at the Three Doves, and you are contracted to lease these buildings from Lady Day.'

'I signed that contract for you, Widow Smith. When you were ailing, I was so very worried, and I was certain it was the prospect of removing that had brought about your distemper.'

'Oh, Timothy. I am so very sorry to have put you to this inconvenience. I'm afraid that was an assumption too far. I cannot remain here, not for anything. This place has memories which sometimes threaten to overwhelm me.'

'This is to do with that fancy physician, I fear,' Mister Collins spoke through gritted teeth.

'Indeed it is not, Mister Collins. Why do you say that?'

'I heard he has been negotiating the lease on Chestnut House. He is in a widowed condition as are we. I know he thinks highly of you . . . '

Lucie's smile for the chirurgeon was tender. She could see he was sincere, whereas she knew Somerton thought more highly of her purse than herself. 'You miss nothing, Timothy. And your suspicion is true. When I was lately indisposed, he too offered his hand.'

'I knew it! The scoundrel,' Collins let out a huff of breath.

Lucie found herself laughing. 'Oh look at us, Timothy. I am nearing sixty and have had two marriage proposals. Who would have thought it?'

'I do not find anything to laugh at, you mock me madam.' Colour flushed in the chirurgeon's face.

'You think so little of the woman you meant so recently to make your wife? I did not accept Dr Somerton's hand. Nor did I consider his suit for a second,' Lucie rose from her chair. She reached up to hold her aching shoulder. 'Come, it is late. I must retire to my bed. Thank you for a lovely evening. We have much to be proud of in our joint labours this day. Allow me to see you out.'

Chapter Twenty-Four

'Simon, could you take over serving in the shop please? I am required at the chirurgeon's house. Old Tom Mitchell is approaching his end, and I would sit with him and pray. I will then perform the last offices for him.' Lucie came through to the kitchen from the counter of the Three Doves apothecary shop. 'You know where most things are, and you can take down messages for anything you are unsure about.'

The sun was high in the sky although the day was bitterly cold. The weather had been unseasonably warm over the past several days but as January drew to a close it had taken a freezing turn. Lucie knew Goodman Mitchell was taking of his last several breaths as soon as she stepped into his chamber. His breathing was erratic, and he had lost a lot of weight even since she saw him last before Christmas. Lucie sat on the edge of the bed and took the old man's hand.

'Good morning, Goodman. This is the apothecary's widow. I've come to sit with you a little while, if you'll permit me.'

The old man responded with a weak squeeze of her hand. Lucie settled on a chair next to the bed, and started to tell the old soldier the stories Jasper had told her about when he was a boy. One such was how Tom had taught her husband to fish in the river that ran through the market town.

'You were a hero to Jasper, Goodman Mitchell – Tom,' Lucie told the dying man. 'Like a big brother to him. We were both so afraid when you went off to the late wars, but nothing would stay you, would it? Not many volunteers were in their sixth decade.'

He had no wife or children, a man happy enough in his own company he'd always said. After his return from the battlefield he was a changed man, often deeply melancholic, muttering incoherent phrases over and over, and sometimes flying into a rage, before becoming silent again for days at a time. He chose only the company of fellow veterans, men who had seen battle and perhaps understood him better. Tom made a noise like a low growl.

'I've got some of the soothing waters Jasper used to mix for you. Will you take a sip?' Lucie stood and dripped some of the medicated water off the end of her fingers onto Tom's lips. 'Jasper considered it an honour making this for you, his friend and a true servant of parliament's cause.'

The old man's eyes fluttered open. 'Agnes Henshaw?' he croaked.

'No, it's Widow Smith here. Tom?'

Goodman Mitchell's eyes flashed faintly. 'I know who you are, woman.'

'Hush now, help me understand. Were you hoping to see Mother Henshaw?' Lucie stroked his hand.

'Agnes is a good woman,' he replied, his eyes closing again. The pair sat in silence for a while. It was just past four of the clock and Lucie went to light another candle. The nights were drawing out now, but darkness encircled the small chamber above the barber-surgeon's.

'I used to visit her sometimes ... she had draughts, like yon 'pot'cary ... an' she'd be happy to mix 'em in exchange for the odd job of work ... repairs and the like. Always damp her place ... battle to keep the rain out.'

While Tom drifted back into sleep, Lucie got up and closed the shutters. That'll be why she always smells so musty, Lucie thought with a sigh, living in an unfit cottage. She went down the stairs to seek a cup of beer and use the privy.

'How goes he?' asked Mister Collins when he saw Lucie pouring her beer.

'He was surprisingly lucid just now. He said he would visit the old hand woman, Mother Henshaw, betimes. I suppose they would be of an age. Can I pour you one?'

Collins shook his head and headed back into his shop. As she climbed back upstairs, she could hear Goodman Mitchell making a ruttling sound in his throat. Taking one of the pillows off the bed, Lucie placed it on the floor beside and slowly knelt.

She was glad to hold his hand as he passed to the next world.

'First earth he was, now earth he is. And him the earth must have. Amen,' Lucie whispered as Tom's breath stayed, and then he was gone. She looked up and saw Mister Collins standing in the doorway. She hadn't heard him come up the stairs. She nodded and he returned the gesture. Collins walked to the bed and felt for a pulse in Tom's wrist.

'I'll have some warm water and soap sent up, Widow Smith, that you may go about your work presently,' he said. 'Rest in peace old man.'

'Amen.'

Chapter Twenty-Five

'Matty has still not passed water, Widow Smith. The medicine you supplied yesterday has not worked. He wails so, please come.' A distraught Jane Croft had burst into the kitchen of the Three Doves. Her cap had fallen down her back and her hair hung loose around her face. Lucie could see the poor woman had not slept in days.

'You go home, and I will be along presently, Goodwife Croft. Try not to worry so.'

Lucie had no help, and Simon was yet again away in Grantby. She was utterly weary.

'At least I have kept all the fires burning this time,' she said aloud as she crawled up the stairs to her chamber. She'd only closed the shop a quarter part of an hour before Jane Croft's dramatic arrival.

As she sat down at her desk, running her finger down the index of Jasper's receipt book, a movement caught her eye.

'Peter, is that you?' a young male figure stood in the shadows. 'Your football should not be upstairs.' Lucie's head dropped forward. Her eyes sprang open, and she shook herself properly awake.

'Now where is that recipe?' she needed to remind herself of medication she'd mixed up for the child. It might only have been a day earlier but with the bustle of the days, Lucie was not confident she'd remember rightly, it was a complicated recipe. 'Ah here we are.' Stone parsley, marshmallow, fennel, *sal prunella*, bean stalks and some little red crab-eyes seeds.

The stone parsley had given off the most obnoxious smell as she'd crushed it, and crab-eyes were marked by Jasper as being very poisonous. 'We won't give him yet more of this,' she said to herself, closing the book.

She crawled backwards down the stairs and pulled on her cloak. Pausing to wrap some biscuits in paper for the children in Warley Lane, and double checking the fire was well banked, Lucie stepped out on another cold and frosty afternoon.

'Hey Lad, where's your friend this day?' she called to the wolfhound from the Boar who was rooting in the waste gully and chewing something unwholesome. It would have been nice to have Dick's company on the walk, and the pair were normally inseparable. It was cold but bright at least and so the half an hour walk to the row of weavers' cottages was pleasant enough.

In Jane Croft's small cottage, Lucie was pleased to find Martha amongst those gathered tending to the ailing toddler. He was now running a fever and clutching his swollen belly, as he lay on his parents' bed.

'Jane, I need you to listen carefully. If we work together we can have this little man set to rights in no time.' Lucie had examined the boy's belly, yard and cods. 'Now, I need you to apply your mouth to Matty's yard, and suck as hard as you can. There is a stone lodged in his pipes and only his mother can remove it.'

Jane looked uncertain but nodded. Lucie noticed her glance over to where her husband was standing by his loom and saw the goodman nod, as if giving permission.

'I felt something move, Widow Smith,' Jane announced moments later.

'Success,' Lucie said after re-examining the boy. 'I can feel the stone at the top of his pipe. Martha pass me the smallest hook in my bag and we'll have it out in trice.' Immediately Lucie had freed the stone, a torrent of piss spilled forth, covering her arm, apron, and soaking the bed. The toddler wailed, confused by the sudden relief. A ripple went around the crowded room as Matthew jumped up.

'There is a biscuit for you in my bag, young man. All boys as brave as you've been deserve a treat. I'll leave these biscuits on the table for any that wants one, and bid you good day. There's no charge Goodman Croft, I am only sorry the medication I mixed yesterday did not provide a cure, and the little lad had to suffer a day longer. Good day to you all.'

'Widow Smith?' Martha called as Lucie was tying her cloak. 'Are you well? You look pale.'

'I'm just tired Martha. Give the little ones my love, and pray bring them to see me soon.'

On her way back to the Three Doves Lucie walked in the direction of the new Town Hall, having a notion she might find young Dick Cobb there. The exterior was now built, and the stone building towered above the rest of Market Square.

'Alderman Robbins, your hall does you credit. It is a fine addition to the town. Congratulations, too, on the birth of your new son. He goes well?'

'Widow Smith, it is good to see you out and about. I had heard of your long indisposition this winter. The Town Hall is very fine. Future generations will look on't as a sign of Tupingham's ambition and foresight. Come let me walk you around it,' Mister Robbins offered his arm to Lucie.

'I'm sure you'll have heard that we named the boy for Lord Calstone. Adrian Robert Robbins. My Lord agreed to stand godfather for my son. My wife goes well too.' The alderman's smile faded as if something unpleasant had just crossed his mind.

'Something's amiss, Alderman?' Lucie asked.

Without replying, the alderman took an iron key from his coat pocket and unlocked the large doors. 'Come let me show you the inside. It is unfinished, so we must take care, but the views from the windows over the town are worth the inconvenience.' Lucie was a little hesitant to climb the stairs facing the door, for she was so very tired, and worried she might struggle to get back down. She would not like to seem frail in front of the alderman. Out of the corner of her eye she caught sight of the figure she'd hoped to find.

'Dick, my dear. I've been looking for you; I was a little worried when Lad was out without you earlier. Alderman, is it permissible for this young man to come inside too?' Lucie knew Dick would be curious to see the interior of the structure. He had been so entranced watching it take shape in front of his eyes these past months.

'Of course, please come inside Widow Smith. You too, boy.' The alderman opened the door and showed the pair in.

'I'm glad to have the opportunity to speak with you Widow Smith. It's been brought to my attention that the rector might have led you to believe the main chamber would be named for Apothecary Smith. He should not have, as it will not be possible, I am afraid.'

Lucie frowned. She hadn't been in favour of the scheme when it was first relayed to her but had been given to understand it was a settled matter.

'How so?'

'My Lord Calstone is the major financier for this building, and it is contrary to his wish,' the alderman said bluntly.

'It was not my wish either,' Lucie said. 'Which you would have known had I been consulted.' Lucie felt her lips thin. 'There is no denying this is a very impressive room, however. It is very well done.'

With tall, glazed windows on every aspect, the views of the whole town were every bit as wonderful as the alderman had suggested. Over the tops of the shops and dwellings, Lucie could see all the way to All Hallows on her left, and miles over green fields to the right. The clear afternoon meant the view was unrestricted. Through the window facing High Street, Lucie could just about make out a figure of a man on a horse which looked just like Dapple.

'Look Dick. Do you think that could be Simon? Right down the end of High Street. Do you see?'

'The boy is well, after the unpleasantness last month?' Alderman Robbins asked as he showed them out. Lucie leaned heavily on Dick's arm and slowly climbed down the stairs.

'Yes, I am grateful to you for intervening to secure his release. Of course, he shouldn't have been detained on any occasion.'

'Good day to you Widow Smith,' the alderman turned his back to lock the door.

'Good day to you, Sir, and thank you for showing us the progress. Dick, you get off back to the Boar now before your mother misses you.' It was too cold to be wandering around for long. 'Oh, one thing more, Alderman. The late funeral was well done. Thank you for allowing sufficient funds to provide a burial for Old Tom. He served this town and country well.' The alderman's face flushed. Like all in Tupingham, Robbins had been on the side of parliament, but his loyalties had shifted with the Restoration, and he was now very much currying favour with the Calstones in order to seek advancement for himself and the town.

'It was my pleasure, Widow Smith.'

'Mistress Archer saw to it that we all did eat very well of pasties made with hares, cheesecakes, and the like.' The criticism in Lucie's tone was impossible to miss. The Alderman should have attended the funeral, but he had become too puffed up of late to pay his respects to one of the town's oldest residents.

'Now you have this fine hall, I should be pleased to learn the next building works planned by the council were to be some alms-houses. Goodman Mitchell deserved more than lodging in a single room, eking out his pension. Mother Henshaw too, Goodman Mitchell told me she resides in a damp hovel in yonder woods.' Lucie turned and walked off briskly.

Simon arrived back at the Three Doves a few minutes after Lucie.

'Simon, how pleased I am to see you returned. I expected you to be gone but the one night not two, though I know the roads are unpredictable at this time of year. Whatever has happened to your eye?' She took hold of her son's chin and turned it towards the candle.

''Tis nothing Mother. I was set upon by a rogue in Grantby after my purse, but am well otherwise,' Simon's eyes flicked away as he spoke, and Lucie's brows knitted. She busied herself looking for a goose quill and broke some sugar into a mortar to grind to a fine powder while Simon took off his riding boots and heavy coat.

'You have the plans properly drawn from the architect, son?' she asked while she worked.

'I have. They look splendid too. The alterations you drew on my rough sketch have been drawn in their proper proportions and I am excited to reveal them to you.' He took a scroll tied with a string from a pocket inside his coat. 'The builder said he is ready to begin work in a sennight and it will take three months. It should be ready for you to remove to by the end of May at the latest.'

'Come sit in this chair.' Lucie filled the goose quill with the powdered sugar. 'We'll need to find temporary accommodation when we quit here on Lady Day but the rector has offered us the hospitality of his home, of course. Now look towards me and keep your head still.' She blew the powder into Simon's eye, and he flinched. 'That's a ready cure son, just sit a few moments.'

Lucie unrolled the plans on the kitchen table. She eased her heavy mortar to hold down one end of the paper, and a tankard the other. She stared at the drawings. To the front of the cottage was a porch, with screens on the inside of the house to keep out draughts from the front door. The ground floor was to be built with bricks, and there would be a timber framed upper floor.

'The builder has all the trusses on order. They will arrive as soon as the ground floor is ready and he says we will marvel at how quickly the house takes its finished form from that point.' Simon explained that some changes had been unavoidable because of certain requirements Tupingham council had insisted upon. 'The thatched roof you had set upon must be tiled, I'm afraid, Mother. See here on the plan. A consequence of the recent fire in London, the architect reckons. There's all manner of rules we had no notion of when we were idly drawing up our sketches. Here is the note from the architect: "The Chimney shall be set upon a truss two foot six inches from the upside of the truss to the upside of the floor." This just means the chimneys are in a slightly different situation to the ones we drew.'

Lucie studied the plans, using her candle to light a second one so she could see all parts at once. Through the porch, one entered a passage that ran the length of the house, and off this to the left was the main hall. Also to the left of the passage was the kitchen, and a small scullery led off that. Unlike the Three Doves, the back door was at the end of the passage and not in the scullery. The room to the right of the passage, which was to be Lucie's chamber, had a small room off it which was to be her private closet. There she would be able to read and write and pray.

The kitchen was to be of double height, and there would be three further chambers on the second floor. The largest matched the size of the main hall. The two smaller chambers were both accessed through the main one. Outside, there were to be several smaller brick buildings. One of these was the privy, Lucie could see. A pigsty and a store had also been added to the drawings.

'We can keep Dapple at home, as the store will be sufficiently large to accommodate her needs,' Simon said.

'I think Dapple does well where she is, and there she has

the company of others of her kind,' Lucie said. 'The blacksmith has always charged me fairly for her stabling. But we will have a pigsty and room for many more chickens than we are accustomed to keeping. We'll be able to eat well from our own produce.'

Lucie familiarised herself with the plans a little longer. 'Simon, son, where is the print house? It does not appear on this plan. Take it back to the architect. He has drawn it incorrectly.'

'No, look at this additional sheet,' said Simon, pulling a smaller drawing from his inside pocket. 'See how we now have the provision to build in stages? This first building, our home, will cost you a good bit more than the sum we were quoted earlier. So much timber is reserved at a premium for the rebuilding of London. The extra buildings and tiled roof add up too. The architect and builder have settled upon this as a firm price.' Simon indicated the figure in the corner of the main plans.

'That is more than we planned, but it is justified by the changes. But I understood we had a better deal by building both at once?'

'I have a contract here which I must return signed by you tomorrow if the building is to commence in a sennight. The builder requires a quarter part payment in advance, with the rest in stages as the work progresses. There is also a bond we must lodge with the council to promise to keep to their rules. When the property is completed and passes inspection, the bond will be returned to you.'

'You are not making sense about the print house, son.'

'With the rising costs, I took the liberty of asking the architect to design the print house as an additional endeavour for a later date,' Simon said.

Lucie frowned, she could always tell when one of her children was being untruthful and she knew Simon was not telling her all in this moment. She lowered herself into her armchair and took a long swig from her spiced wine. There was a lot to think on, but she did feel a rising excitement in her belly.

'Simon, as you know I have never signed a contract for such a large sum of money. I need you to speak true. Is there anything material to this scheme which you are keeping from me that would affect the wisdom of my signing this contract?'

'Nothing at all Mother. It will be a fine place for your retirement years. I simply think we should be mindful of the cost of an additional building, and that you should wait until you have a sense of the place before committing to having the noise, the clanking, the bustle of a print-house on your threshold.'

'Very well. Fetch me my quill and inkhorn, son, would you?' She was resolved, and she couldn't help smiling.

The contract signed and sealed, Simon offered to go to the tavern and fetch a hot plate of food for each of them and a jug of ale to celebrate this auspicious day.

Chapter Twenty-six

Lucie and Martha walked arm-in-arm back to the Three Doves. Martha had just delivered Barbara Bennet of a maid, and Lucie had not been required to help at all. It was unseasonably mild out, so the walk was a pleasant one, and Lucie tipped her face towards the sky as she walked, pleased to feel the sun's weak February warmth on her skin.

'I cannot deny feeling relieved there was not a second child for Goodwife Bennet today,' Martha said.

'I think all those present were too,' Lucie replied. 'This little maid was a good size and lusty, not like the twins.'

Although little Bartholomew Bennet had not lived many weeks, Benjamin was now a rotund, ruddy faced toddler. Lucie was minded to have a quiet word once Goodwife Bennet had completed lying in, to advise against over indulging the little lad.

In the kitchen Lucie and Martha worked together to sort through the dirty clouts and make sure Lucie's midwifery bag was replenished of the powders, ointments, and other remedies she liked to carry.

'Martha, we must furnish you with your own midwifery bag. You may use mine, but I will speak to the tanner immediately and purchase some good, strong leather. I will have you a bag made that will last you a lifetime, as mine has. It will be my gift to you.'

Lucie had turned too quickly, and her head began to swim. The room went dark. She awoke to a stink under her nose.

Martha was holding a burnt feather to her face. She found that she was sitting in her own armchair.

'Mother, you have been doing too much. It is but a few weeks since you rose from your sick bed and you have been labouring each day since, nursing the sick, attending to your women, and serving in the shop.' Simon was crouching next to Lucie's chair.

'I'll drink this and then go up to bed.' Lucie accepted a cup of warmed wine from Martha.

When she was tucked up in her bed and Martha had made her farewells, Simon came up and sat on the edge of his mother's bed.

'You look better, Mother. Martha has made a good fire,' he squeezed her hand.

Lucie leaned close. 'I thought I saw your brother in the corner the other day. He had a pig's bladder blown up to play football with and I chided him for bringing it up the stairs.' She had expected Simon to be shocked, but instead he smiled.

'I think I can explain that.' He brought Jasper's recipe book over for her to see. 'Ned showed me this when he was copying out receipts.' Simon pointed to a tiny drawing in the margins of a page. 'Look, see, a poor drawing of a boy and a ball. I was soundly reprimanded by Father for touching his book, I remember. I'd wager anything you saw this when looking up a recipe and your mind played tricks on you in your weariness.' He closed the book and put it down on the bed. 'We cannot continue like this, can we? While Martha was attending to you, I called on Baker Healey and reengaged Deb. She will come back to the Three Doves for a few hours in the mornings at least, with her mother's blessing.'

Lucie had seen the concern in Simon's face. 'Truly, I do not think this is a return of my previous indisposition, Simon.'

Two days later and Lucie was well enough to come down the stairs. The weather had taken a cold turn and the chickens' water was frozen solid when she went to tend them. As she walked back into the kitchen, stamping her cold feet, Simon proposed that when the shop was closed later that day, and the temperature had risen, they take a walk across town to see how the building works had progressed.

A group of half a dozen men were busy on Lucie's plot. Good progress had been made in the mild early days of the month and now the footings were all filled with gravel it was possible to see the exact shape of her future home.

'Come let me give you a tour,' said the oldest builder, introducing himself as the foreman. 'See all the foundations here are set out true.'

'I must confess it does not look as large as I envisaged,' Lucie said as they walked across the land.

'Trust me,' the foreman said, his weather-beaten face wrinkling into a smile. 'The times I've heard that. You'll feel differently when the walls go up.' It was too cold to lay the bricks that had just arrived, so the men were unloading the waiting cart and stacking them in squares then covering them in hessian.

'It'll not take us long to get them laid once the weather warms up a touch, Misses,' one of the men called out to Lucie.

'I think we have perhaps seen enough, Mother,' Simon took her arm. 'Let's get you home and in the warm.'

'And I think I should like to call into the seamstress's house on the way back. If I am to take a trip, I shall need an additional suit of clothes.'

Simon squeezed his mother's arm. 'You are doing the right thing. I'll keep this crew in my sights.'

While laid in her bed, Lucie had planned how she would travel to Grantby for a trip to see Alice Wallis in a few weeks' time. A change was a good as a rest, and there she might pick out some linen for her new home. She would spend three or four nights with Alice and she knew she'd have a warm welcome. She'd sent Deb to the postmaster's with a short note for Alice the previous day.

‘It would be my pleasure to escort you to Grantby, Mother,’ Simon assured her as they walked. ‘I can take one of the blacksmith’s other horses and lead Dapple back.’

Chapter Twenty-seven

The bitter chill had obliged Lucie and Simon to wrap their scarves tightly around their faces as they rode to Grantby. It was a lengthier journey than Lucie had made on horseback for a very long time, but despite her stiffness on finally dismounting Dapple, she felt more joyful than she had in many a month. Alice's merchant husband was waiting for them at the Silver Lion, the coaching inn where Simon would stay overnight while the horses rested.

'It's good to see you Widow Smith, and you Simon, looking far better than when we last saw you,' Michael Wallis slapped Simon on the back. Lucie shot the pair a look.

'Mister Wallis kindly provided assistance to me the night I was robbed, Mother.' Simon did not quite meet Lucie's eye.

'I thought you meant to return with the signed contracts?' Mister Wallis asked.

'By happy chance a fellow I trust in Hearne's made mention he was setting out for the city, and he was happy to carry our papers and money, which saved me a good deal of inconvenience,' Simon replied. 'Building work is well underway.'

'I see,' said Mister Wallis. He turned back to Lucie. 'Come, let's go inside. I have my instructions from my good lady wife. I am to warm you through with a dish of the excellent broth served in this establishment, before we walk to our house. Alice has been called to visit a woman she laid three days ago who has become unwell, but she expects to be home by the time we arrive.'

At last in the warmth of the Wallis's townhouse, Lucie enjoyed becoming acquainted with Alice's four children. The boisterous but well-mannered group were being supervised by Alice's servant, Betsy, while their mother was out. Lucie had not been in her home many minutes when Alice came through the door in a blast of cold air. She rushed to hug Lucie, even before removing her cloak and pattens.

'Oh Alice,' breathed Lucie. 'It does my heart good to see you.' She stepped back to take her in. 'And another child on the way? Make sure you don't work too hard now you are big-bellied.'

'No need for concern, Widow Smith, I am quite well. I admit I am a little more weary than I remember being when I was carrying my firstborn, but that was ten years ago, and I'm nearer forty than thirty, so it is to be expected.'

Later that evening, once the children were in bed and the servants retired, Mister Wallis retreated to his study to allow the two old friends to talk undisturbed.

'It is a pity Simon decided to sleep at the Lion, and not here,' Alice said.

'He wishes to make an early start back to Tupingham on the morrow, Alice. He will rise by candlelight at six, he said, and be on his way by half past at the latest. Then he'll be home in time to open the Three Doves for an hour or two while it is daylight.'

'How does Simon go, though, Widow Smith? It was a terrible business what happened to him on his last trip here,' Alice poured more beer into their cups from the jug on the table.

'Yes, you mean the attempted robbery? He had a sore bruised eye to show for it, but I treated it and it healed well enough.'

'Robbery? Please don't tell me he was robbed as well. The injuries he received from Lord Calstone were bad enough. Oh this is awful,' Alice appeared greatly distressed.

'Pardon me?' Lucie frowned, puzzlement tightening her face. 'How does Lord Calstone fit into this story? Pray tell me all and leave nothing out. It seems my son has been less than frank with me.'

Simon had been taking supper with Mister Wallis, Alice explained, when Lord Calstone had entered the tavern they dined in. His Lordship had been outraged that the private dining room it was his custom to take was already in use and his choler had been raised even higher when he saw one of those present was Simon Smith. Calstone had shouted that Simon was to get out and not return to Grantby if he knew what was good for him.

'My husband told me that Simon made a mild response about it being his Lordship who should keep away, not he,' Alice said. 'His Lordship's rage deepened, and he knocked Simon clean to the ground.'

Lucie struggled to catch a breath. 'There is more, I'm afraid,' said Alice, 'but perhaps Simon should be the one to tell you.'

'No, please continue,' Lucie worked on steadying her breathing.

'His Lordship drew his sword.'

Lucie gasped. 'No!'

'My husband and the steward from the Manor restrained his Lordship.' Alice took Lucie's hand and held it firmly.

'Pray tell me how the matter ended, Alice,' Lucie heard the tremor in her own voice.

'Let me get you a measure of brandy first, for your nerves.' While Alice slipped out of her seat, Lucie rested her head in her hands.

'I should never have told you this, Widow Smith,' Alice placed a small glass with brandy and sugar in it in front of her. She raised her head and took a shuddering breath before sipping at the restorative.

'If Simon had wanted his mother to know of this, wife, he would have told her the truth instead of concocting a story about being robbed,' Alice's husband Michael had walked into the kitchen where the two women sat.

Lucie heard his words, and opened her mouth, but nothing came out. Her hands shook and the brandy was in danger of landing in her lap.

'Try not to fret, Widow Smith. From what I hear we have a reprieve from the antics of his Lordship for the next twelve months,' Mister Wallis took the glass from Lucie's hand and placed it on the table. 'Word has reached me that Calstone has been ordered to the Caribbean in some minor government capacity.'

Lucie closed her eyes and offered up a silent prayer for that small mercy.

'Come Widow Smith, let's get you to bed,' Alice's mouth curved down at the corners. 'I'm so very sorry for upsetting you.'

Lucie was up with the servants the next day. As they went about their work, she sat at the kitchen table quietly sipping from a cup of beer. She'd tossed and turned all night, and been fearful she would wake her bedmate Mary, Alice's ten-year-old daughter. Round and round her thoughts went. Suddenly she jumped up from the table and pulled her cloak from the wooden hook on the back of Alice's kitchen door. She did not pause to put on her pattens, but went out into the dark frozen morning in her boots.

Simon's face showed his astonishment at his mother's appearance in the stables. He had just checked both horses and was about to set out for home.

'Why ever did you not tell me about your dispute with Lord Calstone, son?' Lucie asked in a quiet voice. She felt like a woman with the weight of the world on her weary shoulders.

‘I did not wish to worry you, Mother, since I had but a bruised eye to show for it.’ Simon rested his hand on his horse’s neck. ‘His man and Friswell pulled him off me, and Michael Wallis helped me to Dapple and rode with me the first league of the way home to ensure I was safely out of the city in case Lord Calstone should pursue me.’

‘Simon, tell me truly. Why did his Lordship behave so terribly to you?’

Simon looked down. ‘Calstone and his man Friswell suspect we know the truth about what happened to Prudence Potton and hate us for it, I’ll warrant. Though he claims he disapproves of his son being close friends with a tradesman’s son.’ Lucie sensed her son could not meet her eye from shame. It broke her heart that he should feel thus about his perfectly respectable status in life.

‘The Calstone name was founded in wine selling. That is a trade and one that does less for the common good than your father’s,’ she snapped.

‘Friswell made a few barbs in summer that I was profiting from my friendship to Sir Robert, that I was after their money.’

‘That makes sense. Lord Calstone is very concerned to show off his wealth! But Simon, every penny his son spent on your father’s funeral was repaid by us immediately. You have accepted nothing from him, have you?’

‘Just some handed down suits and the like, and he once made me a gift of a writing tablet,’ Simon smiled slightly. ‘I’d not get rich off that. No, Sir Robert and I share an affinity to the playhouses and other such pursuits. I did not befriend him for his money. Indeed, I’d no notion who he was for months. He was just my friend Robbie.’

‘I see. You understand, I had to speak with you personally after your lack of candour about your injury. I’d thank you not to deceive me like that again.’ She watched as he mounted and kicked the blacksmith’s horse with his heels, urging the animal to set off. She watched a little while longer to see Dapple keep the pace to Simon’s left on the lead rein.

Chapter Twenty-eight

Lucie trudged back to the Wallis house through the foggy morning haze and let herself in, just as the family were beginning to rise. The smells of a family breakfast transported Lucie back to her own days with young ones. The children tucked into pottage and beer, with the littlest one having a cup of warm ass's milk. Michael ate heartily from a plate of fried bacon.

'Goodness, Widow Smith, you are up and about early,' Alice said. 'Have you broken your fast?'

Lucie shook her head.

'Let me get you some food. There is some bacon left in the pan. It's not good for people with weak stomachs, but you are welcome to it. Or some pottage? Some bread? I can toast some if you'd like?'

'A bowl of pottage and a cup of small beer will do me nicely, please Alice. I wanted a word with my son before he left for home, and I was fortunate to catch up with him at the stables.'

Alice exchanged a worried glance with her husband. 'He is well?' Michael asked.

'Quite well, thank you,' Lucie lifted a spoonful of steaming pottage towards her mouth. She was mindful that the children were at the table and didn't want to discourse in front of them.

'Would you care to visit one of my newly lain women with me? Nany Gibson had an easy delivery but has since succumbed to a fever. I left her some medicaments last evening but said I would call in this morning.'

'I should like that,' Lucie replied. She gave each of the older three children a penny as they set out for the small school a few doors up. The youngest was on the floor diverted with a spinning top, which he'd play with under Betsy's watchful eye until his mother's return.

'I will pop Mark's penny on your mantel shelf, Alice,' she said as she walked over to take her cloak down from the peg.

The house Mistress Wallis led Lucie to was of a similar style to the Wallis's own. Mistress Gibson was a gentlewoman of some standing in Grantby, aged twenty-nine, and had been delivered five days ago. She was sitting up in bed, pale-faced, with roses on her cheeks from her fever. Alice had given her a decoction of hartshorn with lemon juice, rosewater, and sugar, which she'd had mixed by her local apothecary. Mistress Gibson had drunk all three pints. She had reported that the solution had an unpleasant sharpness, though she'd not objected to its taste. As they were discussing how best to continue her care, Dr Somerton walked into the chamber with Nany Gibson's husband.

'How do you do, Mistress Gibson?' Herbert Somerton took the woman's wrist to feel for her pulse without awaiting an answer. 'Mistress Wallis, you are well? Please tell me how you have been treating your patient up to now, that I might assess the best way to proceed.'

It seemed to Lucie that Dr Somerton hadn't noticed her in the shadows of the chamber, and also that he was talking in a less dismissive way to the company than he did to her. How interesting. She determined that it was in her best interests to remain where she was for the moment. Alice described Nany's ordinary delivery and the uneventful first days of her recovery, then explained how she had succumbed to a fever a few days later. She described the treatment regime she had instigated. The physician was satisfied with what he heard and with the rate of Nany's pulse. He let her arm drop back onto the coverlet.

'And Widow Smith, how would you suggest proceeding?' he turned his gaze directly on to Lucie.

'I did not wish to interrupt, Dr Somerton. Mistress Wallis has been exemplary in her care for this woman. In my opinion her patient is like to make a full recovery in a day or two,' Lucie turned to smile reassuringly at Nany. She was in a maze at Dr Somerton's reaction to seeing her; either he was a good actor, or more likely he'd already known she was in Grantby. But more intriguing was why he spoke in an entirely different tone in the city to that he used in the country town.

'Hmmm, well we'll see. Immediately increase the dose of hartshorn in the decoction to three drams in a half pint of rainwater, morning and night, if you please Mistress Wallis.' He then turned on his heel and stalked towards the door. Mister Gibson followed him, assuring the physician that he would personally visit the apothecary shop to have the new prescription filled. As Dr Somerton reached the chamber door he called out to Lucie, 'A moment of your time, Widow Smith.'

He ushered Lucie into Mister Gibson's study.

'I should prefer it if you would forget the conversation we had in thy chamber at Christmastide, Widow Smith,' he said. 'In case it is not clear, I am withdrawing any offer of matrimony I may have made.' His usual bombast was absent, but the condescension was clear.

'That accords with my wish too. But pray, why do you not make your usual monthly visits to the town? I had understood from you that you were in negotiations to take the lease of Chestnut House from the Hills, in addition. Was this information false?' Lucie asked.

'It is true I had made some enquiries about that house, a fine one it is too, and fitting for a gentleman physician, but I have decided to return to Birmingham and sever my connections with Grantby and its environs.' He explained that the roads to Tupingham were unsafe in the winter months, and he had insufficient incentive to visit the town where the residents appeared satisfied enough with the services of their chirurgeon and their she-apothecary. He added that many residents also could not easily afford the services of a physician.

'I am surprised to hear this, Dr Somerton. It was my belief that you wrote a good number of prescriptions each month.' Lucie should know, as she had had the task of filling them, which had often meant sending to Grantby for the more exotic ingredients the physician ordered. The sorts of items her Jasper had eschewed on the whole.

Dr Somerton took a huffing breath. 'I confess that I have dined with my Lord Calstone on a number of occasions recently. It seems he has a low opinion of thy family, Widow Smith. I am relieved I did not have to appraise him of the hasty offer I lately made.' His tone turned colder. 'I know midwives in general are an interfering and prying tribe, but it seems you are of a different order, inviting thyself to Calstone Manor and treating his Lordship's heir. And then there is thy son looking to profit from his acquaintance with Sir Robert.'

Lucie felt her eyes flashing. 'What you call *prying* with women's private affairs is part of the midwife's oath, as I am sure you know, Dr Somerton.' She was aware of spots of anger burning on her cheeks. She rose to her full height and puffed out her chest. 'How fortunate am I that I did *not* accept your hand, doctor. I know you consider that of no relevance, but I did not nor ever would have agreed to be your wife.' She turned and walked towards the door of the study. 'And one thing more. My son does not abuse his friendship. He's a hardworking master printer.'

In the corridor, she couldn't breathe, but did not want to give the odious man the satisfaction of seeing her further distress, so she turned on her heel and walked away, using a hand on the wall to steady herself. She did not wait for Alice but carried on walking, right out of the house. At the market square she bought a cup of beer from a stall holder to cool her passions. The air around her felt thick, and the noises of the market sounded like they were coming from underwater. Realising she was likely to swoon, Lucie sat down on the edge of the stone fountain in the middle of the square and put her head in her hands. *Blast that arrogant physician.*

'Widow Smith, there you are! I have been looking all over the city. I was worried. Why did you leave the Gibson house so abruptly?'

'Alice, I am so sorry,' Lucie flushed with embarrassment. 'Please sit and take some food with me. I have a dish of sausages and fritters coming and shall call the serving maid over and order a second one for you.'

She had taken herself to the Silver Lion after her breathing had settled. While they awaited their hot food, Lucie narrated the conversation she'd had with the physician. She told her too of her illness, and of the two marriage proposals she had received while she was in her sick bed. Alice's mouth fell open.

They both recovered somewhat from the shock as their food was placed on the table between them. The sausages and fritters were in two separate dishes. The serving maid put two plates down in front of the women and left them to help themselves. Lucie took her knife from her pocket and speared one of the sausages. The women ate in silence for a few minutes.

'Simon told me your husband rode out with him when he last left here to set off for Tupingham. Please give him my thanks for that kindness.'

'It was his pleasure. Don't pay too much mind to the spat between Lord Calstone and Simon. Michael tells me his Lordship was so far in his cups, he'll likely remember nothing about it. My Lord's reputation goes ill in this city. He has but few friends. I am in a maze to learn that Dr Somerton has found his company bearable.'

Lucie's lips pursed as she let out a long sigh. She suspected she knew all too well. The gall of the man repeating unfounded accusations that Simon was seeking to profit from his friendship with the Calstone family.

Chapter Twenty-nine

The cathedral's sanctuary calmed and soothed Lucie's ragged nerves as she'd hoped it might. The scale of the five-hundred-year-old church inspired her awe as it had on previous visits. She found the tall multi-coloured lights mesmerising, and after a few busy days at Alice's, she could have spent her whole afternoon picking out the biblical scenes and allegories. Except for the stiffness creeping into her joints. Reluctantly she got up and headed into the street.

'Have a care,' she snapped at a butcher's boy, who had just attempted to tip his pail of ruddy water into the street's gully without looking to see if the road was clear or not.

'Sorry, missus,' the lad said, looking anything but.

'No harm done, this time. But pray tell me what is the attraction that brings all the folk yonder to the town square?'

The boy shrugged and walked back inside the shop, swinging his bucket. Lucie's curiosity got the better of her and she walked on, taking care to avoid the puddle and entrails the boy had thrown down. Before she could see the reason for the crowd, she heard a cry accompanied by a drumbeat:

'See! Sirs, see here!
A doctor most rare,
Who Travels much at Home!
Here, take my Bills,
I cure all Ills,
Past, present and to come;

The Cramp, the Stitch,
The Squirt, the Itch,
The Gout, the Stone, the Pox,
The Mulligrubs,
The Bonny Scrubs,
And all Pandora's Box.'

Her heart sank. A mountebank and his band of rogues. She felt her face flush with anger. If one pill could cure all ailments from cramp to itches and all besides, then there would be no occasion for men like Jasper to undergo a six-year apprenticeship to learn the healing art of chemistry.

'Let me see, please,' Lucie grabbed one of the handbills being given out to the gathered citizens. She pushed her way through the crowd. In the centre of the town square the quack stood on a stage made from the back of a cart. He was dressed to attract attention with a red hooded cape, a large floppy hat, with a ruff in the old-style around his neck. Around his waist was a belt with a leash upon the end of which stood a monkey, sporting a waistcoat and hat which matched his master's. An accomplice at his side had banged the drum to mark the beat of the mountebank's speech. At the back of the stage sat an elderly man with a gouty looking foot resting upon a stool. Lucie could not tell if he was the next mark or one of the charlatans themselves who would doubtless stand and dance a jig, declaring himself cured after a single dose.

'What, pray, is the composition of your miraculous pill, sirrah?' Lucie shouted, waving the bill, her features set hard.

'Madam, madam, do not let such matters trouble your head. My pills contain only the best, most efficacious ingredients. Why I could supply a list of folks as long as my arm who'd willingly swear they'd been cured of the most unspeakable diseases after their doctors, or should I perhaps say *doctoresses*, had lost hope,' he winked theatrically to the crowd and raised a ripple of laughter.

'Come, tell my assistant here what ails you and he will supply you a cure presently. Free of all charge!' he turned to the crowd with a flourish of his arm.

The crowd was captivated, hanging on the speaker's every word. Some were laughing in Lucie's face for challenging the mountebank. A carnival atmosphere was growing.

'Some things are beyond the ordinary. Stay your tongue Madam and watch closely. You will receive indisputable proof of my unique abilities.'

'I want no part of this charade,' Lucie said, turning to walk away. Before she could move, a man in an alarming particoloured doublet and hose came towards her. He smiled and bowed for the benefit of the crowd, who moved aside to afford him room, while at the same time grabbing Lucie's arm. He twisted it to force her to move along with him.

'We insist you stay. You must be our honoured guest for the next part of our oration.' He spoke through gritted teeth.

Lucie couldn't easily break away from the strangely dressed man's strong grip. She felt her guts twist with fear.

'See here, gather closer,' the mountebank beckoned to the crowd. 'Look as I show proof of my talents. Madam, you read?' Lucie nodded. 'Pray tell the good people what the word on this paper is?'

The mountebank flourished a scrap of paper with the word 'Christall' written on it. Lucie mouthed the word with the driest of tongues. She shrank back as the mountebank's little monkey, dressed in a scarlet waistcoat, grabbed at the paper.

'Christall, that is I. The old woman speaks it true. Now watch closely as the letters appear on my hand before your very eyes.'

He showed his bare hand to the crowd all around the stage that all might see there was nothing visible before he started.

'My taper, if you please,' he called to a young female assistant, then held the paper with his name written on it to the taper until it burned almost through. Next, he clapped the ashes upon the back of his hand and rubbed. With a triumphant look, he held up his hand as the same letters as were on the paper appeared right before the onlookers' eyes. The crowd gasped, then a ripple of applause grew into loud cheering and stamping. Most of them would have no idea what the letters spelled out, but they were sufficiently enthralled by the charlatan crew to accept what they were told. Lucie had to admire the way this chancer worked the crowd; they would now happily eat out of the palm of his hand.

The man holding Lucie's arm hissed, 'Seen enough? On your way, you old crone. You'll cause no further disruption, if you know what's good for you.'

Lucie needed no further bidding. She pushed back through the crowd. As she went she heard the mountebank continue with his patter, 'There she goes, we're the best of friends now, see good townspeople. My man will make sure the old woman has all she needs. Now gather back around. Come, come, closer still. This is my promise to you: read my bill, judge the medication for yourself, and try it out.'

Christall grabbed the small drum and beat out the rhythm as he repeated his offer:

'Read, Judge, and Try,

And if you Die,

Never believe me more!'

Lucie stopped to watch from a safe distance, and shook her head. The crowd had evidently been persuaded, despite the ridiculousness of the message. The mountebank's assistant was rushed off her feet handing out tiny paper twists with the mountebank's secret pills inside. She gathered the pennies the gullible citizens were handing over in exchange. Christall and his monkey left the stage and went into a small tent at the side of the wagon.

Lucie walked back to the Wallis house, shaking. She needed a cup of warm wine to sooth her nerves. Waiting for her there she found a letter from Simon. With her back to Alice, she composed herself.

'This is unexpected, but I suppose I have been away from Tupingham a little longer than we planned.' She ripped open the seal on the letter.

'I am just pleased I persuaded you to stay here and let Simon deal with packing up the Three Doves, Widow Smith. It's done my heart good to have you here,' Alice spoke warmly, but Lucie noticed how she rubbed her back.

Lucie frowned. 'I hope I haven't made extra work for you with my stay,' She rummaged under her apron, searching her pocket for her spectacles.

'No, of course not,' Alice straightened. 'Now what news does Simon send?'

Lucie moved over to the window where the light was better. She read the letter aloud.

> *Dearest Mother,*
>
> *I hope God keeps you well. I write to send you news of your building which grows each day. It will be a fine dwelling, and you may be assured that I am keeping a close eye on the builders. All your women are asking after you. I am afraid I make a poor substitute as a chemist. I can never find anything customers ask for.*
>
> *You may imagine my surprise and delight therefore when Ned Brocke reappeared at the Three Doves the day before yesterday. What a happy day that was for me. He has agreed to work as the apothecary for the townsfolk until your return. I fear he has not been entirely frank about the occasion of his return, but you know Ned better than I do, and I am sure he will reveal his truth to you upon your homecoming.*
>
> *The other news I have is that the council have determined to tear down our side of the High Street. Can you believe it? There was a public meeting under the new Town Hall yesterday, called with just a few hours' notice. It was not to solicit opinion, for their course of action is already set. The old*

buildings, they say, are not in keeping with an ambitious market town and the fine Town Hall.
We need to remove all our belongings to the rectory by Lady Day, but as we were due to quit that day in any case, we're not as badly effected as our neighbours. I am making the necessary arrangements. They are starting the demolition with Henry's house next to the Three Doves, as it has stood empty since his passing last year.

Mister Collins spoke up at the meeting but was shouted down by Alderman Robbins, who said the council have torn up his lease and he will not be able to remove to the Three Doves as he planned. Nor will he be compensated for his inconvenience. Hard words were said on both sides, with Mister Collins becoming quite choleric. He and I had a long evening in the Bull after the day's excitement. We discoursed at length on this outrage and find that we're of one mind on this matter. The council's reasons for keeping Henry's house empty when it might have provided a home to some of our new residents makes sense now. Mister Collins asked that I send you his kind regards.

Martha bids me tell you she has lain Goodwife Hales of a lusty son. Mother and child do well, as do all the Higgs.

Your affectionate son,
Sim. Smith

Lucie's eyebrows had shot up at the news of Ned's return. Back up they went again at the news of the demolition of the Three Doves. With a sigh she folded the letter and tucked it into her pocket.

'My ties to the High Street are to be truly sundered, it seems.' She felt rooted to the spot, but nevertheless reached out to hold onto the windowsill. Alice strode over and threw her arms around Lucie, quietly holding her in a tight embrace.

'How are you finding Mister Culpeper's treatise, Widow Smith? Is it to your liking?'

'It was a welcome gift Mister Wallis. I thank you for it again, but I fear young Culpeper revealed how much knowledge he lacked in writing about the art of midwifery.'

'How so?' Alice looked up with a raised eyebrow.

'For a start, it is abundantly clear he had never attended a birthing.'

'I wonder at him publishing *A Directory for Midwives* in that case. May I?' Michael reached over and took the book from Lucie.

'My late husband knew him a little as a fellow apothecary. He was much younger than Jasper, of course. He had made a name for himself as a translator of medical books, and Jasper held his *Complete Herbal* in high esteem. We have it on the shelf at the Three Doves.'

Mister Wallis had found a second-hand copy of the *Directory* in the booksellers, and said he'd bought it as a diversion for Lucie while she stayed with them. 'It states it was printed in 1662. I wonder if the Cole publishing house survived the fire. We'll have to ask Simon.'

'I know not. But Mister Culpeper was long dead by then. I can't recall precisely but have a notion he died early in the days of the Commonwealth. This must be a posthumous reprint.'

Alice's head jerked up from the sock she was darning as Michael asked, 'Have you given any more thought to publishing a collection of your case notes, Widow Smith?'

Lucie frowned, feeling a tingle of annoyance at the question. Michael surely knew Jasper had forbidden any talk of the project.

'Don't be cross, Widow Smith,' Mister Wallis passed back the book. 'I confess Simon mentioned he still had hopes you might change your mind about allowing him to publish a memoir of your years practising your art, for the betterment of young midwives.'

Lucie felt her face soften. Simon had made no such comment to her, and she was grateful for it.

'I'd have said nothing, but for how you've found Culpeper's book so troubling. And there is no doubt having a work from you to bring to the presses would be an ideal way for Simon to launch his new printing house in due course.' He took a swig of ale and looked away. Lucie thought she saw a blush on the merchant's face.

'Did you and Simon cook this up between you?' Lucie bit her lip to suppress a smile. She was unexpectedly amused by the audacity of this plot.

'Husband. Surely not.' Alice sounded shocked, but Lucie couldn't miss the crinkle in the corner of her friend's eyes.

'It is true, I confess. But I told no lies, I did come across the book and mentioned it to Simon. He was adamant that it was high time an English midwife took up her pen. His mother, in fact. Forgive us, ladies.' Michael held open his palms. 'Simon does genuinely believe there is a need for such a book, and I rather thought such an undertaking might be a pleasant diversion for you to take your mind off your forthcoming removal, Widow Smith. My wife often mentions the hours you were accustomed to spending writing up your cases.'

Lucie caught Alice's eye and found she could hold in her laughter no longer. Alice smiled nervously; evidently unsure of what Lucie's reaction signified.

'Rogues, the pair of you men.' Lucie spluttered with a final outpouring of laughter. She wiped away a tear, shaking her head. This was one deception she'd not reproach Simon for. Most importantly it was meant with the best of intentions. Imagine going to all that trouble, she thought. But mayhap now she was in her widowed condition, she *would* give such a book some thought. After all, it was undeniable that a midwife would make a better fist of it than that apothecary, Culpeper.

Chapter Thirty

''Ere have you heard the news? It is true about Lord Calstone, Misses?'

Lucie looked around to see who was being addressed, but found she was the only one nearby. She walked across to the tavern where the alewife was resting on her broom.

'Were you calling to me?'

'Is it true he's blown himself sky high? That's what they were saying in here last night,' the alewife continued.

'His Lordship was killed in an accident onboard a ship in the Thames, yes. Along with three hundred other souls. But I have not heard anything to suggest it was other than a tragedy, not of his doing,' Lucie replied. Mister Wallis had imparted this shocking news to his household late last evening. The story went that the vessel upon which Lord Calstone was to voyage to the Caribbean was fully laden and prepared but had been destroyed by an explosion. The cause of this was not yet known. Lucie had tossed and turned all night, at first feeling horrified that she felt no benevolence for the man's soul and then worrying about the consequences of his death for her friend Lady Calstone and her little maids. Lastly, and as dawn broke, she felt concern about what this would mean for the rebuilding of Tupingham, which Calstone's patronage had been at the heart of.

'Pity,' spat the alewife. 'There's none who'll mourn *his* passing. I'll tell you this for nothing. Last year around the time of the assizes, he tried meddling with one of my wenches. Got my big leather pitcher round his head for his troubles, he did.'

Lucie grimaced. She could only too well imagine but did not wish to add to the tattle flying around Grantby that morning. Leaning on her broom, the alewife warmed to her topic.

'Like I always say, my girls might not be angels, but they don't deserve to be meddled with like that, his dirty great hand pushing up her petticoats. I'll not stand for it. He's not been over my threshold since, and now he never will again.'

The alewife turned back to her sweeping, appearing very much cheered at receiving confirmation of Lord Calstone's demise.

Mister Wallis had asked Lucie to meet him at the Silver Lion at eleven. One of his friends had offered to convey her to Tupingham in his chariot, far preferable to her making another long journey on horseback. She just hoped she'd be in time to be able to tell Simon about the Lord's demise herself. Simon would be bound to worry for his young friend, Sir Robert, now Lord of the Manor. But for now, she had a little time for some last-minute shopping. Calling in at a stationer's, she purchased two quires of paper and a packet of ink powder.

'Please have them taken to the Lion immediately, for my coach departs in a hour.'

'Going to be doing a lot of writing, are you Misses?' the shopkeeper asked as he packaged her goods.

'I rather think I am.' Lucie felt her eyes shining. Her back straightened as she took some coins from her pocket and handed them over. 'My son is establishing a new print house in Tupingham, so we'll have cause to make many more such purchases shortly, if your prices remain competitive.'

Next, she went to the ironmonger's and enquired after a pair of good quality scissors for Martha. No midwife could work without those, and Lucie did not want to relinquish her own pair permanently. The blacksmith had sharpened hers countless times over the years and they felt like part of herself, an extension of her hands. At the end of the row of stalls, Lucie spotted one packed with trinkets. She went over to browse. She was not given to fripperies and could not imagine who might wish to purchase a white posset dish painted to commemorate the coronation with 'CR II' and a likeness of the new king on it in blue. Ha, there won't be much of a market for that in these parts, she thought. Seems as though even his admirers are tiring of him and selling off such wares.

A twinkling goblet made of thick glass caught her eye. Lucie reached over and picked it up, twisting it before her eyes. She had glass bottles in the shop but never any glassware in her home, but wouldn't it be a fine thing to sup her wine out of something so pleasing in her own house? Before she could talk herself out of it, Lucie bargained with the stallholder and bought the second-hand goblet for a fair price. She had only a short time now until her coach would be ready at the inn. She thought to buy a custard pie to have in place of her dinner, as she would be on the road all through the afternoon.

The journey back to Tupingham was a pleasant one as the small chariot bounced along the county lanes without impediment. Lucie caught up on some lost sleep with a short snooze and as she awoke felt her excitement rise at the thought of being home and sleeping in her own bed this night. When she stepped down from the chariot on the cobbles outside the Three Doves, she looked in the shop window and was immediately transported back in time. There through the small panes, she saw Ned advising a customer, just as she had so often in the past. She gave him a little wave, and he came rushing out to carry her luggage inside.

'It is good to see you Widow Smith, and looking so well,' Ned said.

'And you too young man. Simon told me you were here, and I shall look forward to hearing your news when I have unpacked. I see you have kept the shop open much longer than was my custom, the townsfolk will have been glad of that I am sure.' She stepped forward and gave him a hug. Following him into the shop, she took in a deep breath of the familiar scent of frankincense and earthy herbs. But as she looked around her, she realised the counter and shelves were bare, barring a few odd gallipots. Ned evidently sensed her puzzlement.

'Very much changed isn't it, Widow Smith? It is our last day of trading today of course,' he said.

'Of course!' a tingle of shock went through her. In all the upheaval, she'd quite forgotten that tomorrow was Lady Day, the twenty-fifth of March, 1667. The exact date she was required to quit her home.

'Simon paid the lads from the smithy to load up their cart with your belongings. They have been back and forth to the rectory for the last few days. He says that there is a dry barn behind the rectory where your larger items have been placed. Dick Cobb has been helping too. He's barely left Simon's side.'

Lucie walked through to her kitchen. The fire was still ablaze and that felt right somehow. The table had gone, and Lucie was transported back to when she first saw the room as a young wife, before they had purchased the large oak table. She marvelled at the size of the room without it.

She climbed the stairs to her empty bed chamber, and as she stood there, Lucie felt a sensation similar to that she'd experienced last autumn when the Potton girls had been with her. Only now, instead of being cold, the tingling was warm, comforting.

'Sarah, can it be you?' she whispered. The figure of a young maid stood in the shadows near the partially shuttered window. The girl's apron and her glowing face were filthy. 'You've been playing abroad with Peter, I'll warrant.' Overcome with longing, Lucie opened her arms to receive her girl, but the figure didn't move. The still face continued smiling back at her but did not change expression at all.

'Ah,' air escaped Lucie's lungs. She lowered her arms, feeling weak. In this room she had borne all her children. She scanned every inch of it with her hungry gaze. And yes! There, sitting in the middle of the floor, was a young, redheaded boy. He held what looked like an inflated pig bladder between his knees as if he was preparing to play his beloved football soon.

'Peter, my firstborn, my love,' Lucie gasped. She moved to take a step forward but couldn't seem to get any closer to her son. 'I thought this would all be yours, one day, Son,' she spread her weak arms. 'You so loved to be in the shop with father, when you weren't organising football games in High Street.' The boy's smiling face gazed back at her, but in an oddly unresponsive manner. 'Where's Hannah? My baby?' Lucie pleaded softly. Her eyes darted again around the room, until there she was. The figure of a small girl with adorable rosebud lips and loose straight hair hanging past her shoulders. Hannah slowly manifested from behind the still figure of Sarah.

'Hannah, you've your doll with you! My mother, your grandame, sewed that for you,' Lucie's words caught in her throat. 'It's done my sore heart good to see you all.'

She rested her hand on the mantle shelf as she marvelled at the sight of them, warmed not by the empty grate but by her inner contentment. Her precious children, all smiling at her, no sign of the dreadful smallpox that had cut them down so very young. Automatically, her free hand went to her eyes to brush the tears she expected to find there, but her skin was dry. She felt calm, whole, and happy. As she moved her eyes, she fancied she could just discern a faint hint of another figure, just beyond her sight.

'Husband,' she whispered, and reached out a hand even though she knew he was not of the same world as her. 'I would that Simon were here to join us for this moment, that we all might be together.' Words spilled out of her, just as a creak on the stair caused her to look round. When she turned back the room was empty.

'I understand,' she said aloud. 'Thank you.' The old house had given her a parting gift. 'It is time for us all to move on, my precious ones, but wherever I go, you will be with me in my heart.' From the warmth she felt deep inside her, Lucie knew that she could now give thanks for the time she had had them, and no longer be tormented by her guilt at their passing.

She made her way back down the pair of stairs. It was only after she had taken the first half dozen steps that she realised she was walking, and not having to turn around and crawl. Simon was sitting on the flagstones in the kitchen when she got down, untying his boots which were an inch thick in mud.

'What on earth?' Lucie's mouth twitched with a smile at the real and solid sight of him.

'I was coming up the stairs to see you, then realised I would leave a trail of filth if I walked up in these, Mother,' he said.

'Yes, I heard the stair creak,' her smile widened. She had not felt so content in a long time.

'Ned said you were home. Who were you talking to?' He pushed his foot back into his boot.

'Just taking my leave of the house, and packing happy memories into my heart, Son.'

Simon put his head on one side, furrowing his brow, just for a second. Then he jumped up.

'Come, let me show you what I have been up to in your absence.'

He led Lucie out to the garden, where she found naught but a square of mud.

'Simon, what have you done? My herbs, my plants, my compost pile, the hens,' she clasped her hand to her mouth.

'So that is all the thanks I get for breaking my back this past sennight is it?' Simon laughed and placed an arm around his mother's shoulder. 'I had hoped to show you where they had been removed to and then show you this mess afterwards, but you arrived a little earlier than I anticipated. Come put your cloak back on and we shall walk to the new house. It'll do you good to stretch your legs after the coach ride.'

As they walked arm-in-arm along the cobbles, Lucie told Simon about Lord Calstone's death.

'There is not many who will mourn that man, I fear. He was exiled from Court in addition to all we now know about his disgraceful behaviour at home,' Simon said.

'I am not so sure. Alderman Robbins did well by him, didn't he? And he was still Sir Robert's and his four sisters' father.'

'Ah, yes. It will take some getting used to, thinking of Robbie as Lord Calstone,' Lucie could hear the affection in her son's voice.

'I wish you would refrain from calling him by such a familiar name. It isn't fitting. But no doubt your friend will be making his way back to London even as we speak.'

'He was in Southern France last time I heard from him. This news might not have reached him yet, and it'll take him a while to journey back, but I have no doubt he'll be before us resplendent in all the latest Continental fashions afore long,' Simon chuckled to himself. Lucie looked up into her son's face, relieved he'd not suggested racing off to escort his friend home. 'I know what you're thinking, Mother. No, I'll always hold his friendship dear, and I'm ashamed I took it so ill when he left for his tour in the manner he did. I see now that Calstone wished him away urgently.' The pair turned a corner and Lucie's house came into view. 'He lifted me up when my father died, and I did the like for him when he was wounded in the fire.'

'Woe to him that is alone when he falleth; for he hath not another to help him up,' Lucie muttered, squeezing her son's arm.

'Indeed. But I fear our lives will be lived very differently from here on. Perhaps in time he shall even be appointed to a role at Court.'

Lucie clapped her hands, excited as a child receiving a gift as she stood at the edge of her plot of land. Her house was almost built, much earlier than she had dared to hope for. There were just two men up on the roof laying tiles.

'There is much to be done on the inside, but the building is now almost watertight. Never mind that though, come and look to this side.' Simon slipped his hands over his mother's eyes and turned her around. He urged her forward a few steps, before letting his hands fall. Lucie's jaw dropped as she stood staring at her new garden.

'This is the best thing you could have done for me, son.' She stopped to gaze a moment, then walked over to her familiar plants, many looking a little limp due to having been transplanted. Some were already in leaf and fluttering in the light breeze of the late March day.

'Mother, Dick and I carried this out as if it were a military campaign. We took careful note of where the plant was situated in the garden of the Three Doves and then dug it up to be placed exactly as it was in relation to the others on the new site.' Simon pointed out the things which had been easier to dig out and the ones which had resisted his spade. 'So now you see why I am so muddy. My young friend may not be inclined to speak much but he is unafraid of hard work and he seems to have an instinct about plants and the land.'

'The hens?'

'Safely at Martha's. They seem well.' Simon's face opened in a smile that reminded her of him as a boy. It seemed fitting, as for a moment Lucie was taken back to the recent gift of seeing her other children. She felt warm inside all over again.

Mother and son walked back to the Three Doves with Simon stomping every few paces to dislodge mud from his soles. The light was starting to fade, and the temperature was dropping fast. Back in the shop Ned was waiting for them, having assembled the last of the apothecary stock on the counter. He was busily putting it all into a wooden box.

'Have you told my mother your news yet, Ned?' Simon asked.

'I've not had a moment, there were still customers in the shop when Widow Smith arrived.'

It seemed Ned's sister was prepared to finance him setting up in business as an apothecary now he was a journeyman. As young as he was, Mistress Scrawbrook was his only kin and through her marriage she had funds enough.

'I am not versed in matters to do with a business, keeping books and so on, so Simon suggested I speak to Mister Collins about a partnership. Him doing the bone sawing and me doing the plasters and pills. And by and by he can teach me the ropes,' Ned explained.

'I think it an excellent scheme,' Lucie said.

'I recall when I finished my own apprenticeship and felt I knew all, but I learned so much more when I was a journeyman printer,' said Simon. 'Mister Collins was very open to the notion, that is once he had got past his disappointment that his plans to remove here had come to nought.'

Simon had finished putting out the kitchen fire. Now the property could be safely left. Outside, the sky was becoming dark.

'Come now. It's time we set out for the rectory,' he said.

'I will walk with you part of the way,' said Ned, who was lodging at the Boar.

'That crate is the last of it?' Lucie asked.

'It is, but it is not so heavy. I'll carry it.' Simon hefted the box off the counter.

Ned cleared his throat. 'If I am to make a business in Tupingham, I shall need various items. I don't know how you would feel, Widow Smith, about allowing me to purchase some of my former master's tools of the trade?'

A new warmth flared in Lucie's chest. 'It is hard to credit you are the same unruly youth that left here sixteen months ago, Edward Brock. I am sure we can reach an accommodation about some items.'

Ned reached for the box, which Simon passed to him with a ceremonial bow. Lucie watched the two young men joking with one another with contentment. Simon gathered up Lucie's luggage and Grantby purchases and took the candle from the counter to guide them to the door. Lucie lifted the bunch of keys that hung behind Jasper's study door.

'The bolt is across the scullery door?' she asked.

Simon nodded. 'You don't want one last look around, Mother?'

Lucie shook her head. 'No indeed. Midwife Smith and the Three Doves said our goodbyes this afternoon. Come gentlemen, let's lock the door this last time.'

Epilogue

Late Summer, 1667

I could have sworn I'd seen a fox. It was hard to be certain because the glare from the stream babbling at the end of my garden was dazzling, even with my hand shielding my eyes. It had been a glorious morning, and now it was nearly midday the sun was strong in the sky. If there was a fox around, I'd better make sure the hen run was secure. I'd spent the morning pottering leisurely in my favourite place, my garden at Dove Cottage. The herbs and flowers Simon transplanted from the Three Doves were doing very well in their new situation, and even one or two of my old rose bushes were in full flower. I hadn't expected them to bloom in the first year. I took in the deepest of breaths, enjoying their heady scent. My old adversaries, the dandelions, old *pis-en-lits*, had come along too, of course, but I didn't mind a bit. Or maybe they had been here first and were not the ones from the Three Doves. Either way, I was happy to continue battling this stubborn herb, and thankful to have my health so that I was able to.

Baby Jasper propelled himself in his wheeled walker on the brick path that Simon and Dick had laid for me between the beds. That lad loved nothing more than being outside, and what a pleasure I found in listening to his babbled conversation with the butterflies that darted in and out of the blooms. Whenever one flew up in the air, Jasper screeched in delight, banging his little hands on the frame of his walker. Martha smiled across from where she was hanging linen garments on the line. Her belly was growing nicely, and young Jasper would have a new sibling before Christmas. Who'd have thought I'd have a house filled with a growing family again?

'Come, Master Higgs, let us go back inside and prepare dinner. It's close to noon and the family will all be home soon.' Martha moved to sweep up her son.

'You're a poet Martha,' I teased. I didn't want Jasper to go in yet, though. 'He'll be fine with me, Martha, if you want to get on with the work indoors. We'll follow you in a few minutes.'

The new house had already proved a wonderful home, one now gloriously full with my very favourite people. Martha and Anthony Higgs and their three children had moved in up the stairs. It was comforting to have Martha's company all day, and it made it easier for me to oversee the rest of her midwifery instruction. The kitchen pleased me, so filled with signs of family life: from Jasper's wooden animals, to dropped linen caps, discarded half-drunk cups of water, and hornbooks. Jemima's hoop was propped by the front door ready for her to take up the moment she arrived home from school each day. How she loved chasing that hoop!

Far from having two rooms to myself as I'd planned, I slept in what had meant to be my closet and Simon had my bedchamber, albeit temporarily. Dear Dick lived with us too. Joyce Cobb had succumbed to a sudden fever back in May. I did my best for her, but to no avail. Dick slept on a truckle bed in the kitchen. It helped me to know that even after Simon left there would be another soul on the ground floor with me while I slept. If anyone called for the midwife in the night, Dick knew to answer the door and run for Martha. As Martha's time approached, I'd have to take up my bag and chair once again. If you'd told me that a few months before, my guts would have been in agony at the thought, but I felt stronger than I had in a long time.

Some of my salad leaves were ready for cutting, so I popped them in the basket to add to our meal. The garden had looked after us well that summer.

Jasper's squealing ramped up just as I finished cutting the

leaves. I followed his gaze and saw he was looking at old Gyb, the cat that'd moved here with Martha. Its back arched and its tail fluffed out, the creature was evidently spooked. Then I saw what was amiss. The enormous daft wolfhound from the Boar had got in the garden, again, and was pissing up against my gatepost. Gyb hissed for all he was worth.

'Go off Lad,' I yelled. 'You don't live here. Dick, come get this animal, you'll need to return him to the Boar before Mister Bickle misses him.' Lad came to seek Dick out most days. Dick had come running and flung his arms around the hound.

'I don't suppose Bickle'll miss him if you tie him up outside the porch and have your dinner first though.' I shook my head at him, unable to stop myself from smiling.

The gate opened again before I could lift Jasper out of the walker. George and Jemima were home, they were always hungry after their morning at school. George plucked up his baby brother for me. I hoisted the baby onto my hip as I watched the older two race indoors to find Martha. They thought of her as their mother now, and I hoped one day they'd think of me as their grandame.

Inside, our meal was ready and waiting. Martha took the trug to give the leaves a quick rinse in the bucket before adding them to the table in a wooden dish. She'd prepared boiled chicken, pickles, and slices of thickly buttered bread. I was grateful, and not for the first time, that I'd decided to keep the large kitchen table when we left the Three Doves. It was too big for the new kitchen, but in the hall we all fit around it very nicely. I told the gathered family not to wait for the men and plated up some meat for Simon and Anthony. Dick's joy in food put me in mind of the apprentices we'd had in the Three Doves over the years. The boy paid his way by sweeping the floors and washing the dishes. He fetched water from the stream and emptied all the pots each morning.

'I forgot to tell you. Ned brought me a letter a few days ago from his sister,' I said to Martha. 'It contained a message from Prudence, which I was glad of. The maids are learning to use a pen, I understand, but are not up to writing letters yet of course. The message was written in Mistress Scrawbrook's hand.' I rose from the table to fetch it from the mantelpiece, and read a passage aloud.

> *Many have been the Tryals, Tribulations and Afflictions the which I have passed through, but the Lord hath delivered me out of them all; Glory be given to him, and blessed be his Name for ever, and evermore.*
>
> *The Lord has instructed me to tell of my deliverance and it is my intention to travel the country professing the Lord's Power and Mercy which He has wonderfully afforded me.*

'That's strange language for a young maid to use, Widow Smith, do you not think?' Martha said.

'She is become a Quaker like Mistress Scrawbrook, and this is how they speak. I admit I was in a maze to read that Prudence intends to travel abroad professing her beliefs, the girl barely said a word without her sister's prompting when I knew her. But it seems Prudence is content and has found her spiritual home. I shall worry about her though,' I was saying aloud what I had been thinking in the days since the letter arrived. 'You hear so many horrible tales of cruelty the authorities enact on Quakers. Remember that young mother I laid who had those awful scars on her back?'

'Oh goodness yes! That was around the time of the King's return, I think,' Martha answered.

'Yes, that's the one. I'll never forget her story of how she got 'em. She'd been preaching in Exeter and was arrested for a vagabond. Sent to prison. Do you recall?'

'I do indeed,' said Martha. 'She told such a dreadful tale.' Shaking her head, Martha sent the children out to play. 'A fine day like this is no time for children to be sitting indoors.' Jasper was suckling contentedly at her breast, about ready to be put down for his afternoon nap.

When the children had left, I shooed Dick out to take Lad back to the Boar. Jasper had nodded off, and Martha laid him down on a blanket atop the rush matting of the hall floor. He was too long now for the wicker cradle his father had fashioned for him as a baby.

'Do you remember her name? The Quaker mother?' I asked Martha when she rejoined me at the table. 'It will be in my case notes, of course, but the old ones are still packed in a crate.'

'I've an inkling she was called Isabel something. Does that sound right? I remember her telling us how she'd been in gaol but a day when the Sheriff came with a Beadle and took her off into a room where they whipt her till the blood ran down her back,' Martha shuddered.

'Oh yes. It was most strange how she said she rejoiced in her suffering, never startled at a blow, and how she'd sung loudly all through the beating which enraged her persecutors all the more, so they laid more stripes on her because she wouldn't cry.'

Martha finished sweeping the crumbs off the table into her hand and put them on an empty plate. We'd talked of that family for weeks after their stay in town. Thinking of incomers put me in mind of the Pooles. They had settled into Tupingham beautifully, and Adela sold their soaps at the market weekly. I saw her and baby Daisy from time to time.

'Another story I remember,' Martha said, 'is her telling us about when she went to Dublin, and the prison there. You remember? She had to lie in filthy straw and when it rained, the wet and filth of the house-of-office ran in under her back,' Martha grimaced. I felt queasy at the thought. 'Let's hope and pray that matters will not be so with Prudence Potton, the wench has suffered enough.'

'The Lord will not call her to more than she can endure, I am certain. Now where are your husband and my son? They are over half an hour late for their meal.'

I'd no sooner spoken than we heard the gate, and we both stood up to greet the men. Simon and Anthony walked up the path, each carrying a large piece of paper with printed squares upon them. Both were sporting silly grins on their faces.

'Look Mother, see here!' Simon came through the door waving his arm aloft. Martha hushed him, with a finger over her lips, pointing to the sleeping baby. I grabbed the proffered sheet. My jaw dropped and I could have sworn my heart was about to jump out of me, its beat was so fast and fierce. I was looking at a page of proof prints. Proofs of *my* book. Could it really be? I took the page to the window in order to see it more clearly. Simon was on pins waiting for my verdict. Slowly, I turned back to the men, working hard to keep my face calm.

'You got the press running I see,' I said with indifference. Then my mouth broke free of its restraints, spreading into the biggest smile.

'You forgive us for being late for our meal, Mother, Goodwife?' Simon said, looking from me to Martha. He was also smiling broadly.

'Oh I think so,' Martha answered. 'Provided you don't wake the young master.'

'What happens now?' I asked.

'Well, I want to eat, we've been at this since dawn. And you must read these sheets most carefully to check for errors in the setting. We have stopped the press now until they are checked, and we'll repeat this at each part, or gathering as we call it.'

We had only just got the house straight, when the lease on a small building in town came up which seemed suitable for Simon's work. It had been my suggestion that he ask Martha's husband to help him set up the machinery and tools he had bought in London. The dexterity of setting the threads on the loom turned out to have a lot in common with the work of setting letters on the printing press, Simon told me. He had been so impressed with the weaver's skills that he'd offered him a job, with full training. Anthony was already reading much more fluently too, due to his great determination.

'I trust we haven't made too many mistakes, Mother,' Simon called, his mouth full of chicken.

'I haven't seen one yet,' I answered. I could not stop smiling.

They weren't officially in business yet but were using my book as a test. I hadn't expected it to be ready for weeks. I might worry less about Simon's new endeavour after seeing these sheets, for he needed to start making money soon. He was paying Anthony from the remains of his inheritance, and it wouldn't last forever.

'I think I'll take these pages to my room, that I might give them my full attention.' In my chamber, the wainscotting was of light wood, and the whitewashed upper half of the walls had been painted with green vines and cream flowers. The painter I'd engaged had done splendid work. At the Three Doves there were shutters at all the windows, but for my new chamber I had chosen heavy green curtains tied to an iron rail. The like fabric formed my bed curtains too. It was a room that felt very much mine even though I had temporarily given up my bed to Simon. I stood and bent over my papers on the bed, as they were far too big for my small desk. At first all I did was gaze at the cover. I couldn't quite believe it was real.

Simon, I thought, would've been in equal parts amused and irritated to have witnessed my progress as I checked my proofs. But I got to the end eventually and rolled the sheets and tied them up. After all my hard work, I touched my face, pleased to discover my smile was still firmly in place.

As summer entered its dog days, and my work for the day was done, I pulled a shawl around my shoulders and set out for the barber-surgeon's shop. It made for a pleasant walk in the early evening, and Timothy Collins and I seemed to have settled into a comfortable routine where we took supper together once or twice a week. I had a special reason for making the trip that particular evening. The shop door was locked shut when I arrived, so I banged heartily on it with my fist. After a moment or two, I was shown in by the servant. My husband's former apprentice was waiting for me.

'Well, well. Edward Brock, I understand you have something to tell me.'

I was gratified to see Ned blush to his hair roots. I pressed my lips shut, having to work hard to suppress my smile.

'My good lady sister has written to you, Widow Smith? I am sorry I've not had time to tell you myself.'

'It's true then? You are formally betrothed to Hester Potton.' Ned looked at his feet as he nodded.

'Aye, on my last trip to Deptford,' he muttered.

'Come here my boy. I was but teasing you for not telling me in person. I am delighted for you. For both of you.' I stepped forward and drew this fine young man into a sincere embrace.

'We plan to wed in two years, Widow Smith, when I am established in my trade and can support a wife. My Hester wants to come back to this country to live. She is ever hopeful of a reconciliation between herself and her twin and their family.'

'May she be right,' I said. 'I pray that sorry business is resolved each evening when I retire and trust in the Lord's ability to move the hardened heart of Farmer Potton.'

When Mister Collins asked me if I would join them to eat, as I knew he would, I gladly accepted. We had been left a cold supper of partridge pie and chutney, and we washed it down with some Spanish sack, since it was a celebration.

Ned rose from the table. 'If you will excuse me, I think I'll take a walk.'

This meant, of course, that he was bound for the Bull for a tankard of ale. I watched him head towards the door.

'Leave him be Widow Smith. He is a grown man now, not a wayward lad. He takes his drink well. He works hard, and you will have seen for yourself how well he has organised the shop with the shelves of his wares. I often think how proud Apothecary Smith would have been at the man Ned Brock has become, and a betrothed one at that.'

I made a conscious effort to soften my expression. 'He is a little young for thoughts of marriage, but I had a notion right from the moment I saw him and Hester Potton blushing at one another in the kitchen of the Three Doves that their story would end like this. I am truly happy for them. It is natural enough that the Potton girl should want to move back this way. Although it is still a distance from her parents' new farm. Her sister Prudence is setting out on a different path, one of proselyting and travel.'

'Aye, the lad mentioned something about that. On another note, have you heard any news of the Calstone family recently?' Mister Collins took a long sip of his sack. He was godly enough but had little time for fanatics and considered everyone outside the ordinary church one such.

'Not a thing.' I realized I hadn't paid any mind to that family for a long time.

Mister Collins puffed out a cloud of smoke from his pipe. 'The only reason I say anything is that Ned went to Grantby the other day for supplies. He said the city was full of talk about that family.'

I jumped and quickly tried to disguise it by pulling my shawl tightly around myself.

'Did you catch a draught from the door, my dear?' More smoke puffed out of the chirurgeon's mouth.

'I must have done. Pray continue.' He looked at me quizzically for a second more than was comfortable.

'Seems like there were lots of irregularities in what his Lordship had done with Lady Eleanor's dowry. They are being investigated.'

That information didn't surprise me a bit.

'Ned said something about Calstone's widow being in legal disputes with the new Lord. That's why I wondered if you or Simon knew anything.'

I felt my shoulders relax and slowly lowered myself fully back into my chair. 'The concerns of that family will keep the tattlers of Grantby satisfied for a long time, it appears,' I took a sip of sack. I felt sad for my friend Lady Calstone. I put down the cup and made myself smile. 'Time for me to head home.'

As I knew he would, Timothy Collins walked me back to Dove Cottage.

'Look, see there,' we had reached the gate of my garden. 'What a pleasure it is to see these several glow-worms.'

'They are mighty pretty,' Mister Collins agreed, then he started shuffling his feet. Oh dear, my heart sank. Every few weeks my friend worked himself up to a version of the speech I knew was coming.

'You know marriage is not just for youngsters like Ned and his lass, Widow Smith. My offer to you was sincere. If you will do me the honour of becoming my wife, I should work to be equal to the trust you would place in me.'

'I know. You're a good man, Timothy, truly.' I reached over the gate to open the latch with one hand, taking his in the other.

'I meant what I said about your chattels, my dear. I would not ever take a penny of your inheritance from Apothecary Smith. You would be welcome to pass everything to your son before any contract was formalised between us.'

'You do me a great honour.' He was a good man, but clearly could not see that the solution he proposed was the exact reason I would not marry him. Or anyone. I missed my husband's counsel and company, but I had found a joy in being answerable to myself and myself alone.

'If the day comes when I am moved to alter my condition, I shall consider no man other than you. At present I am content in my widowed state, my dearest man, but you know I value your company. It is my sincere hope we shall enjoy a good many more agreeable evenings such as this one. Good night, Mister Collins, and thank you for seeing me home.'

I walked up the path somewhat disheartened that the glow-worms had disappeared from view.

'You two make a merry scene to come home to,' I said as I stepped into the main hall. Simon and Dick were sitting at the table drinking beer.

'What's in that package?' I untied my shawl. There was a parcel in front of them, on top of which was my fine glass goblet filled with wine. 'I could have done with that goblet at the chirurgeon's this evening for we took a cup of sweet Spanish sack. We were toasting Ned's betrothal.'

Simon's face lit up in a huge grin. 'Good man, our Ned. Betrothed.'

'Yes, may he be very contented, please God. So, what is the package, and what is the occasion that calls for wine? Twice in one evening.'

'Dick, would you kindly pass this to Widow Smith, please,' Simon said. 'Come, we are celebrating!'

I sat in my armchair and placed the full glass carefully on the arm. I was still no nearer finding out the contents of the mysterious package though. Simon brought it over as soon as I was settled, placing it in my lap.

It felt weighty. I unknotted the linen and oh my goodness. Six large, calf bound books. Could it be? I opened the top one as fast as I could, my heart pounding. It was my book. I clasped it to my chest, looking up at Simon through water-filled eyes.

'I wanted to surprise you, Mother,' Simon's gaze was as dewy as mine felt. 'These are all for you, I had them bound in Grantby and collected them today. I thought to get you a number since you will want to send Lady Calstone a copy, and will have homes for the rest, I'm sure.'

'You were in Grantby?' My body tensed. 'All is well there?' I tried to keep my voice light.

'What a strange question, Mother. I only went to the bookseller's and rode home. I didn't have occasion to discourse with anyone else. Too much to be getting on with at the print house.'

A strange noise jumped out of my throat, like a hiccough. 'Sorry, my wine must've gone down the wrong way.'

Simon looked at me sceptically, but thankfully said nothing.

'The bookseller in Grantby has agreed to take twenty as a start, and will sell them for 2 and 6d unbound,' Simon said. 'I'll be sending a catalogue of our new titles to London shortly and I am sure we will sell many copies there.'

'How much am I indebted to you for the cost of binding them, son?' I turned the pages, running my hand down the leaves. I needed to convince myself it was real. 'I cannot think your father would be angry about these works if he could see how well you have done them, Simon.'

Simon laughed. 'I cannot speak for my father, Mother.'

'No, indeed. He was set in his ways.' Tonight, I'll say an extra prayer for Jasper, I thought.

'We are none of us perfect, Mother.' My son sounded so wise suddenly. I smiled up at him as he continued. 'You are no debtor to me. Not a single penny. I negotiated with the bookseller in Grantby for a number of discounted copies of the unbound edition in exchange for these.'

I leaned back in my chair clasping the calf-bound book tight to my chest and closed my eyes. I offered up a prayer for my many blessings. The words of Titus came to mind. We elder women have a duty to teach the next generation. In my book, my truth gathered over many years, together with the knowledge I had learned from my own mother, were now set down for the benefit of my sister midwives and the women they assisted.

Note on the text

Like its predecessor *The Gossips' Choice*, this historical fiction is a mixture of facts taken from the historical record and things I've invented. For instance, the circumstances of the Great Fire of London in 1666 are well documented. For readers who are curious about my research for the novel, some of the incidents and birth stories dramatized are taken from a book by Percivall Willughby (1596 - 1685), who practised as a physician in Derby. He was educated at Oxford University, graduating with a BA. In 1640 he was examined and admitted an Extra-Licentiate of the College of Physicians, which meant he was licensed to work as a physician despite not holding a medical degree. In the nineteenth century, his manuscript was published as *Observations in Midwifery: as also The Country Midwifes Opusculum or Vade Mecum* (1863). In it Willughby laments the failings of unskilled midwives and repeatedly claims that having no midwife is better than a bad one. The comments Dr Somerton makes about Dame Nature being all the midwife most women needed are adapted from Willughby's own views. The extraordinary tale of the woman who performed her own hysterectomy appears in Willughby's manuscript too. Willughby attempted to stitch the woman's wound, but the stitches rotted and the problem of her lack of urinary control remained until her death some years later.

As with *The Gossips' Choice*, some of my inspiration was taken from Sarah Stone's *Complete Practice of Midwifery* (1737). Stone was originally from Somerset where she trained under her own mother, a well-reputed midwife, Mistress Holmes, during a six-year apprenticeship. Sarah Holmes married apothecary Samuel Stone on 29 November 1700 in Bridgewater. Some of the procedures and cures Lucie uses are adapted from Jane Sharp's *The Midwife's Book* (1671).

As remarkable as some of them are, no cures are made up but have been taken from a wide variety of medical texts published at the time this novel is set. All were logical remedies in a culture in which the body was envisaged as a humoral one. A world which believed that a healthy body was one where all four main bodily fluids (blood, bile, melancholy and phlegm) were to be kept in balance.

The Quaker woman who describes her harsh punishments is taken from an account of her travels by Quaker Barbara Blaugdone, *An Account of the Travels, Sufferings and Persecutions of Barbara Blaugdone Given Forth as a Testimony to the Lord's Power, and for the Encouragement of Friends* (1691).

The ancestor that Kate, the Millers' London servant, claims for herself is based on a historical figure called John Blanke, who was a trumpeter, and served as musician at the courts of both Henry VII and Henry VIII. The National Archives note that 'There are several payments recorded to a John Blanke, the blacke trumpeter. This trumpeter was paid 8d a day, first by Henry VII and then from 1509 by Henry VIII.' His likeness has been preserved on a 60ft-long Westminster Tournament Roll, which recorded one of Henry VIII's famous festivals.

The Company of Royal Adventurers Trading with Africa was founded in 1660 by the Stuart monarchy. Set up to find gold in the west coast of Africa, a new charter in 1663 expanded the operation to trade in enslaved people. The company was swamped with debts incurred by the Second Anglo-Dutch wars of 1667 and was re-founded as the notorious Royal Africa Company in 1672.

The lyrics chanted by the mountebank Christall are taken from 'The Infallible MOUNTABANK, or, QUACK DOCTOR' published in *The Harangues or Speeches of Several Famous Mountebanks in Town and Country* published anonymously in London in 1700. The trick Christall performed is described in Richard Amyas's *An Antidote Against Melancholy; or a Treasury of 53 Rare Secrets & Arts*

Discovered, by an Expert Artist (1659). It explained that you should write letters on the back of your hand in urine, then apply the burned paper to the same place and rub it which will make the letters visible.

The loss of the ship with Lord Calstone on board in March 1667 is very loosely based on an incident which happened two years earlier when a ship by the same name was accidentally blown up in the Thames Estuary on 7 March 1665. *The London* was a fully rigged ship with 450 men and 76 guns on board. Gunpower stowed on board was accidentally ignited which some claimed was the result of unstable cheap gunpowder being used. Over three hundred of those aboard died instantly, while twenty-five were blown clear and survived.

Acknowledgements

I had the privilege of reading Jennifer Evans's work on the subject of men's sexual health in early modern England in an early draft, and the story of the butcher with the swollen and torn scrotum and the child with the stone which needed sucking out are adapted from cases in her fascinating research.

My thanks are due to Catie Gill for pointing me to the text on Barbara Blaugdone. I am grateful to Lynne Tuplin and Kelly Read for their help in spotting errors in early drafts, and to Elaine Hobby and Heather Shepherd for running careful eyes over later ones. I've had some stimulating discussions about historical fiction with my Creative Writing and the Writing Industry Master's students at Loughborough University over the last couple of years, and I am grateful to them for their thoughts.

As always, my thanks are due to Tracey Scott-Townsend at Wild Pressed Books for her tireless work on my manuscript, and at each stage of its journey to press, and for the wonderful cover design. Thanks go to Phil Scott-Townsend too for his careful typesetting.

Above all, I am grateful for the encouraging and enthusiastic response *The Gossips' Choice* received, and for those asking to read more of Lucie's story. I hope you are as happy as me to see her come through this tumultuous time contented and ready to face whatever life brings next.

About the author

Sara Read is an academic who specialises in the cultural and literary representations of women, reproduction and medicine in the seventeenth century. She is a senior lecturer in English at Loughborough University. She has published two academic books: *Menstruation and the Female Body in Early Modern England* (2013) published by Palgrave Macmillan and *Flesh and Spirit: An Anthology of Seventeenth-century Women's Writing* published by Manchester University Press (2014). She has written a popular history of women's lives, *Maids, Wives, Widows: Exploring Early Modern Women's Lives, 1540-1740* (2015) and co-authored *Maladies and Medicine: Exploring Health and Healing, 1540-1740* (2017) published by Pen and Sword.

In addition to her academic articles on the subject of matters relating to reproduction in this era, Sara regularly writes for magazines and periodicals.

The Midwife's Truth is her second novel and follows on the story of Lucie Smith which began in her debut novel *The Gossips' Choice* also published by Wild Pressed Books. See more on sararead.co.uk or follow Sara on Twitter @saralread.

Printed in Great Britain
by Amazon